"I can't do this."

Sara was strong enough to control her body and its desires. She'd had a lot of practice. She didn't need to understand the darkness lurking inside—whatever it was—to know that she didn't want to have anything to do with it.

"Damn it, Sara." A thread of desperation rang in Rem's voice. "Let go for once in your life."

"No. I did that once. With you. Remember? And I ended up pregnant. You walked out on us. I've raised a great kid. All by myself. I don't need you."

"I'm not talking about need. I'm talking about love. We belong together. We always have. We're connected."

Sara shook her head sadly. "We might have been at one time. But everything has changed."

Dear Reader,

Remington Caldwell begged for his own story. He first appeared in *Beyond Ordinary*, as the hero, Timm Franck's, best friend. The idea of writing about the gorgeous bad boy who had worked hard to reform appealed to me. Where would his life go after redemption? And why couldn't he forget Timm's sister, Sara, a gray wren who was hard to ignore?

They'd traveled a rocky road because of one incident that changed their lives forever, that wreaked havoc with their best intentions and with their futures. Sara started as Rem's little buddy, though. So the only way this story could go, despite having difficulties to resolve, was for them to end as friends.

I wanted to explore the idea that, although every friend we make in life counts, sometimes it's those old friends who call to us and make us feel like we're coming home. Throughout our lives, those friends act as landmarks that ground us, that remind us about the best parts of ourselves.

When Sara finally comes home, she steps straight into Rem's arms.

Happy reading!

Mary Sullivan

These Ties That Bind
Mary Sullivan

TORONTO NEW YORK LONDON
AMSTERDAM PARIS SYDNEY HAMBURG
STOCKHOLM ATHENS TOKYO MILAN MADRID
PRAGUE WARSAW BUDAPEST AUCKLAND

Recycling programs
for this product may
not exist in your area.

ISBN-13: 978-0-373-71743-9

THESE TIES THAT BIND

ABOUT THE AUTHOR

Mary Sullivan recently moved back into her old neighborhood and is getting in touch with old friends. The joy of renewing these friendships enriches her life these days. Funny how easy it is to slip into those relationships as though time never passed, as though we are still those young children with our lives ahead of us. As much as she loves her old friends, Mary also enjoys making new ones and hearing from readers. You can reach her at www.marysullivanbooks.com.

Books by Mary Sullivan

HARLEQUIN SUPERROMANCE

Thank you, Megan,
for making this a better book.

CHAPTER ONE

SARA FRANCK HAD NEVER considered herself a coward, but walking into Chester's Bar and Grill this evening was about to be the hardest thing she'd ever done. She hesitated on the doorstep.

Earlier today, Remington Caldwell had sent her a note.

Tonight. Seven o'clock. Chester's. Far corner, back booth. Just you and me, babe. Time for a reckoning.
Rem

To a woman who prided herself on her common sense, the butterflies in her stomach were disconcerting, but she'd been off balance since June—the last time she'd seen Rem.

He'd asked her to marry him...

"Sara?" Her brother, Timm, held the front door open for her. "You coming?"

The scents of beer and grilled meats, and the welcoming warmth of the place enveloped her.

Drawing on the determination that had pulled her through every hardship she'd ever faced, Sara followed Timm in out of the frosty December night, to Christmas carols filling the air and candles winking on every table. Silver garlands hung from the rafters. Fresh cedar swags gathered with red velvet bows covered the walls. A decorated Christmas tree took pride of place on a small stage.

Chester and his wife, Missy, had invited all of Ordinary,

Montana, to their first annual Christmas party and it looked as if the whole town had shown up. The sounds of conversation and merriment saturated the big room, but Sara heard little. Rem was here.

Timm went straight to the bar, to visit with his new wife, Angel, who was helping out for the night as bartender and waitress. No surprise. After all, Missy was her mom and Chester her stepfather.

Sara stepped farther into the room and, as though her heart were a compass, spotted Rem in the far corner. Ha. Some compass. It had been slipping since the summer, careening off center, along with her ability to keep focus on the direction her life had always taken and should continue to take, and all of it Rem's fault.

She started toward him with her tender feelings locked down. She didn't want or need to be vulnerable to this man.

Someone called out a greeting. She answered in kind, but had no idea to whom.

Rem watched her as she crossed the busy restaurant, the hot blue of his eyes a guiding light.

Don't look at me like that.

He raised a glass of clear liquid to his lips. So, he was still drinking. What was in that glass? Gin? Vodka?

Sara, I'm a changed man, he'd said in June. *I want you to see the new me.*

Sitting here in the bar amid the hubbub of a happy crowd, the new Rem didn't look much different from the old and it proved that she'd made the right decision when she'd turned him down. He'd lied about changing.

He drained the last of his drink. Her gaze followed. With that mouth, how could it not? He'd kissed her that day in June, just before proposing.

Why did that kiss still haunt her? Because it had been sweet and tempting and seductive. But he'd been sweet and tempting before, when he was a teenager, and things hadn't worked out then. Why would anything work now?

She slid into the booth across from him.

He kept his eyes on her, but didn't say anything.

Angel showed up beside them. "What can I get you, Sara?"

"We'll have a couple of club sodas on ice," Rem answered before Sara could.

Angel nodded and walked away, taking Rem's empty glass with her.

"When you get a minute, Angel," someone shouted. "We need another round here."

"I'm on it, folks," Angel called.

Sara ignored all of it, her focus on the man who had the power to shift her world's axis. "I'm a big girl, Rem. I could have ordered my own drink."

"I know."

"So, you're not drinking?"

"Not a drop."

The scent of French fries wafted from the table beside them. Sara knew she should eat, but couldn't. Her stomach rejected the thought, at least until she'd finished her business with Rem—whatever this business was.

"Since when have you not been drinking, Rem?"

"Since I got stabbed in the summer."

Sara didn't want to think about the stabbing. Instead, she concentrated on the drinking issue. "How long will it last this time?"

"Forever. Those two months last summer were an aberration, Sara, because you turned me down. I was hurting. That was the first alcohol I'd had in six years. I'm over the drinking and the disappointment."

"Why am I here?" she asked. "You proposed. I said no. What's left to discuss?"

Rem got out of the booth and she wondered where he was going. Before she could stop him, he sat beside her.

"What—?"

He forced her into the corner, facing him with her back against the wall, and laid his warm hands on her thighs. She knew she should protest, should push him out of the booth because he was too big and too close, but her body craved him even as her mind rallied against him.

"Damn it, Rem."

He turned toward her.

"I—" Whatever she was going to say died on her lips, the festive crowd faded away and they might as well have been alone in the room. Rem stared at her with brilliant blue eyes framed by dark lashes, reflections of the white lights hanging from the ceiling shining in his pupils.

Black hair fell across his forehead and she almost reached out to push it back, managing to stop before making a fool of herself.

He smelled like cedar and pine. Maybe he'd helped Chester decorate today.

Amy Grant sang about having a merry little Christmas. *Let your heart be light.* But Sara's wasn't. It was dark and scared and off-kilter. She wanted her sanity back, her old life before Rem had proposed.

"Why?" she asked, as though he could know her thoughts. "Why couldn't you have left well enough alone?"

"I wanted to make things right."

"They already were right. My life was perfect."

"Nothing was right between us, Sara." He ran a finger down her cheek and she jerked away.

"Keep your hands to yourself."

He let his hand fall to the table. "Nothing's been right since that night in the hospital after Finn was born. I rejected you both. I was scared and immature and dead wrong. I should have married you then."

"For Finn. Because I got pregnant." It wasn't a question. "So, more than eleven years later you proposed out of guilt?"

"No!" Rem slapped his palm on the table. "Are you blind? I love you." He hauled her close and wrapped his fingers around her nape. Before she could protest, his lips were on hers and there was nothing sweet or seductive about this kiss.

It was carnal. Heat-drenched. Laden with so much anger and frustration, Sara could taste it. She felt the same things herself.

Her body begged her to give in to the kiss, but she wouldn't, because that darkness inside her that she'd felt toward Rem for years had grown bigger in the past six months. Since June. Since that devastating marriage proposal. She didn't know where the darkness came from or what it was, but it was profound and terrified her to her toes. Something that had been hidden for a long time had worked its way too close to the surface. A flood of emotion threatened to pour out of her and all she could do was stick her finger in the hole, resist the pressure and hang on for dear life.

She thought she heard someone whisper, "Wow, it's about time."

Sara took one last taste of Rem's tongue and lips, because it would be their last kiss—ever—then forced herself to pull away. His moisture cooled on her lips and his breath feathered bits of hair around her face.

"I can't do this." She was strong enough to control her body and its desires. She'd had a lot of practice.

She didn't need to understand the darkness lurking inside—whatever it was—to know that she didn't want to have anything to do with it. She and Finn had a good life. Things would stay the way they were.

"Damn it, Sara." A thread of desperation rang in Rem's voice. "Let go for once in your life."

"No. I did that once. With you. Remember? And I ended up pregnant. I wouldn't give up Finn for the world, but it's been anything but easy. You walked out on us. You decided you didn't want to be a father. I've raised a great kid. All by myself. I don't need you."

"I'm not talking about need. I'm talking about love and companionship. We belong together. We always have. We're connected." He leaned forward. "If we don't belong together, why did you sleep with me that night last summer?"

"That was a mistake." She traced a scar on the tabletop with her nail. "Do you think your mom knew I stayed late that night? Do you think she heard me when I ran out?"

"I don't know. It doesn't matter. We aren't kids anymore." He lifted her chin with his finger, forcing her to look into his intense blue eyes. "Answer my question. *Why* did you make love to me that night?"

"You'd been stabbed. You almost died."

"And it scared you because we're connected. Because if I died, part of you would die, too."

She shook her head sadly. "We might have been at one time, before you burned Timm. But that changed everything."

Rem cursed and bracketed her face with his hands. He rested his forehead on hers, breathing hard. "That was an accident. I was a kid. You know that. Timm's forgiven me. Why can't you?"

She wanted to touch him so she curled her hands into fists in her lap. She had to protect herself and her son.

"What about all of that stuff when you were a teenager? The drinking? The girls? The street racing?"

"There's a difference between what I did as a teenager and what I did last summer. When I was a kid, drinking and partying were a pattern in my life. I'd burned my best friend. I didn't think I deserved better for myself. Last summer's drinking was an aberration after six years of sobriety. Can't you see they aren't the same?"

He backed away and the bar came into focus again. People talked, laughed, sang along with the Christmas carol tinting the air with nostalgia.

Two glasses filled with clear soda and ice sat side by side on the table. Angel must have brought them while they were kissing.

Heat crawled up Sara's neck.

Rem picked up one of the glasses. "Club soda. No alcohol. I haven't had a drop since the stabbing. I've changed, Sara. You need to accept that."

He slammed the glass down and soda splashed onto the table.

"But I haven't *seen* any change," she said. "You drank in the summer. You sure looked like the old Rem."

"That was temporary. I was upset after you turned me down."

"Okay, so you haven't had a drink since then. But you could again at any time. It shouldn't have happened in the summer."

"It happened because I'm human. No one is perfect. Not even you." He rammed his fingers through his hair, his frustration a palpable thing beating between them. "There are things you don't know."

"What are you talking about? What things?"

He got out of the booth and his absence sucked all of the warmth out of the room. He reclaimed the bench on the other side and she felt a loss whose source she couldn't identify.

"Nothing," he said. "Forget I said anything." He took a deep breath and then let it out slowly. "Okay, listen. You haven't seen the changes in me because you were away too many years at school and then working. Your visits have been short. A week here. A week there. Just like now."

He took a long swallow of soda. "Dad died seven years ago. His death scared me straight. I knew I had to save myself. Ma needed me to grow up and take responsibility. I did, Sara. I went to school for six years. I didn't drink. Didn't party. I'm a veterinarian now. I take care of the ranch. I take care of Ma."

He reached across the table and took her hands in his. His gaze shot to her face. "Your fingers are icicles."

"I know." This year she felt winter's chill so deeply. She didn't know why she couldn't get warm.

You were warm a minute ago, in this man's arms. She ignored that sentiment.

"Before last summer," Rem went on, "I'd been sober for six and a half years. That's a long time."

"Yes, it is, but you *did* drink again last summer."

"And I don't now. We're going around in circles, Sara."

She didn't respond. What ruled her decisions about Rem were the times when he lost control, because those times destroyed her, devastated her, starting with her brother's eleventh birthday party. Rem had sprayed Timm with foam streamers and the birthday candles had set the foam—and Timm—on fire. Rem's questionable choices were terrifying.

"What about the car you crashed when you were sixteen? You were lucky to survive."

He tapped one fist against his forehead. "I'm thirty-two years old. Why are you dwelling on ancient history?"

"Because it will always be there between us."

"It doesn't have to be. Life changes. Only your memories stay the same."

"That's true. My memories don't change."

As much as it hurt her to do so, she took her fingers out of his grasp.

"Nothing is going to happen between us, Rem. That's final." She moved to slide out of the booth, but he stopped her with a hand on her arm.

"If you leave now, it *will* be final. For me, too. I'm done with you, Sara."

Rem sounded so strong, so determined, that Sara hesitated. He had hovered on the edges of her life for so many years. Had always been there, a constant, undeniable shadow. A man who'd loved her unceasingly. As of this moment, that all ended.

"I understand," she said, and left the booth.

It was over. This time, for good.

She walked away, through the warm and festive restaurant and straight out the door into the quiet night, where falling snow coated the ground like a feather duvet, cloaking the world in a reverent hush. And all Sara felt as she trudged to her mother's home was hollowness in the pit of her stomach and a bone-deep chill.

CHAPTER TWO

THE MOMENT HE HEARD THE CRASH, Rem shot out of his sweat-soaked bed and ran to the open window. Light-headed, he grasped the sill for support.

The June sun was too bright, already too high. Must be eight-thirty or nine o'clock. He'd slept in.

He'd been dreaming of Sara Franck again. And fire.

On the small highway that ran along his land, a patch of orange glimmered, so pretty it looked almost harmless. Was that actually fire or a remnant of his heat-wrought imagination?

He scrubbed his eyes and peered out the window to see a car nose-deep in the ancient oak beside his front gate.

The glow of orange grew.

Fire! Real, not dream-induced.

Lord, was there someone in that car?

With no time for a shirt, he scrambled into his jeans, almost falling when he hit the stairs.

His cell phone sat on the hall table where he'd left it beside his car keys.

As he ran out of the house, he tried to see whether any-one was up and walking around the car in the distance. Nothing moved.

Rem dove into his old SUV and sped down his long driveway toward the road that led to Ordinary, Montana.

He needed the fire department. Fast.

His hands shook and he dropped his phone.

Damn!

He wiped his eyes to clear them of sleep.

Wake up, already.

A too-long moment later, he pulled to a screeching stop at the end of the drive, scrabbled around under his seat for the phone and dialed 9-1-1.

"It's Rem Caldwell. There's been a car crash. Looks bad. I need the fire department and an ambulance." He rattled off his address and jumped out of his vehicle.

Thick smoke obscured the compact car that had torn a gash into the oak, making it impossible to tell whether anyone was trapped inside.

Fire crackled in the front of the vehicle.

His heart in his throat, he rounded the car. A woman sat on the road holding her head and looking bewildered.

Thank God she'd gotten out.

"There's a woman on the road," he shouted to the emergency operator. "Alive, but hurt." He shoved the phone into his pocket.

At least she wasn't burning in that twisted wreckage, her flesh on fire and smelling of roasting meat.

Rem shook his head to rid his mind of old images.

"I'm coming!" he called to the woman. She didn't react. Blood matted her hair and the asphalt around her.

On the far side of the road, in another pool of blood, lay a large stag. If he wasn't dead already, then soon. The impact with the animal had crushed the front of the car right to the steering wheel.

The driver was lucky to be alive.

He squatted beside her. "Where are you hurt besides your head?" Judging by the way she held her ribs, she'd cracked or broken at least one. He guessed her arm was broken, too.

"What happened?" she whispered, the words slurred. Concussion, maybe?

"You hit a stag."

She rubbed her ear, then turned to her side and vomited.

He supported her until she was finished.

"What happened?" she asked again and, with that evidence of confusion, he knew she had a concussion.

A high-pitched scream burst from the wreckage and the hair on Rem's arms stood on end.

Dear God.

Someone was inside that burning metal box.

"Who else was in the car with you?" Rem yelled over his shoulder as he ran toward the vehicle.

The driver didn't respond.

He scanned the car. Too much fire. "Who's in there?"

A young voice inside the car screamed, "Mom, help me!"

SARA FRANCK GLANCED at the cast on her son's broken wrist, disappointed that Finn had been so foolish. He sat in the passenger seat staring out his window and avoiding talking to her, as was usual lately. If he was this moody at eleven, she dreaded his teen years.

She gripped the steering wheel. She'd hoped that moving back to Ordinary would settle him down.

"Are you sure you're okay for your horseback riding lesson today?"

Finn shook his hair out of his eyes and mumbled, "Yeah."

She pointed to his cast. "You won't be able to attend the lifeguard lessons I signed you up for. You can't go in a pool with that on your arm."

"Why do I have to do so much stuff every day? It's summer. Why can't I just hang out like other kids?"

"To keep you busy. To keep you out of trouble."

"Mo-om, how many times do I hafta tell you? I'm not going to get into trouble."

And yet, he'd broken his wrist yesterday.

"I have four words for you, Finn. Those boys in Bozeman."

"Well, I'm not there anymore. I can't hang out with them again, can I?"

Determined to check out the scene of his accident, Sara turned off Main and drove by the parking lot where his wrist had done battle with asphalt and had lost.

Her foot hit the brakes. Makeshift skateboarding ramps littered the asphalt. Obviously, kids had cobbled together whatever materials they could find. Oh, dear Lord, one of the ramps looked like an old rec room door. Finn could have killed himself.

"*That's* where you were skateboarding?" Fear sharpened her tone. "Oh, Finn, you're lucky you didn't die."

"God, Mom, don't exaggerate." Finn crossed his arms and curled his shoulders in on himself, his lower lip jutting even more than normal these days.

"I'm happy to see you out doing something other than lying around listening to music and doodling in your sketchbook," she said. "Skateboarding is fine, but doing it on wooden ramps over concrete is nuts. What were you thinking?"

"I was having fun," he shouted, then lapsed back into his "I'm too cool to care" attitude.

Foolish boy.

She shot out of town, driving faster than she should, but for Pete's sake, how was she supposed to survive motherhood?

"Thank goodness you were wearing your helmet."

"Of course I was. I'm not stupid, *Mom*." Why did the word sound like an insult when he used it?

Where have you gone, Finn? What have the aliens done with my sweet little boy and why did they leave this hostile stranger in his place?

He turned his back on her, as far as his seat belt would allow, and stared out the window.

Sara reached out to touch that bit of his neck peeking out from his too-long hair, but he flinched away from her. If she could, she'd encase him in bubble wrap for protection.

His twelfth birthday was less than two weeks away. His feet were getting big, almost man-size. That vulnerable neck, though? That was still little boy.

She'd thought she'd taught him how to be careful, but his streak of—of sheer *recklessness* worried her. What if he was like his father?

That left a bad taste in her mouth.

Adolescence barreled down on Finn, heedless and full of dangerous potential.

She glanced at his profile and saw his eyes widen.

"Mom, look," he shouted.

Farther down the road at the entrance to the Caldwell ranch, a car sent plumes of smoke into the air.

Rem's place!

Sara pushed the accelerator to the floor and the car surged forward.

"Wow, looks bad, Mom. Unbelievable! Check out all that smoke."

"Get my cell phone and dial 9-1-1. Tell them we need the fire department."

As she drew closer, she noticed two people in the road, one lying down.

"Tell them we need an ambulance, too."

The other person was running toward the burning car. Rem! What was he doing? Going *in?* Was he *nuts?*

She came to a gravel-spewing stop across from the accident, just shy of a large buck on the shoulder.

"Stay here," she ordered Finn, and jumped out of the car.

The first thing that struck her was the noise of the deer lowing pitifully, in pain, of the woman groaning, also in pain, and of the fire crackling, eating up the car that Rem was about to jump into.

She grabbed her first aid kit from the trunk and yelled, "Rem, what are you doing? Don't."

REM'S BODY HAD GONE COLD. Geez, there was a kid trapped in that inferno.

The driver's door stood ajar and he wrenched it open all the way.

Weirdly, he thought he heard Sara Franck's voice.

The child screamed again.

"Melody!" the woman lying in the road screamed, lucid and hysterical now.

Afraid she would run to the car, Rem whipped around to tell her to stay put.

Sara knelt beside the woman, restraining her. Where had she come from?

"Rem," she called, "don't be stupid! Don't go in there."

"Can't wait." He coughed on smoke. "She'll die."

Turning back to the smoke swathed car, he cried, "Where are you?" even while he leaned toward the burning passenger seat.

"Here." The terrified young voice came from the backseat. Thank God. He slammed the driver's seat forward into the steering wheel and climbed into the car, the heat intense.

The scent of burning skin and hair choked him. The fumes from melting fabric and metal stung his eyes. The child cried out again, her screams terrible.

Rem barely made out a small form huddled beside the window in the only corner of the car not engulfed in flames. She beat her fist against the glass.

Reaching blindly, he grasped a leg.

"Gotcha!" Rem pulled hard. A small body crashed into his chest sending him backward against the door.

With a jerk, he dragged her out with him. He batted at her burning hair with his bare hands, then checked her over. Fire had touched only her hair.

He blinked hard. His eyes watered from the smoke.

As he carried her away from the burning vehicle, putting distance between them in case it blew up, Rem stared into her wide eyes. "You were lucky you were in the only corner of the car that wasn't burning."

"Was on...other side," she gasped.

Hacking coughs wracked her thin body.

"When I woke up, there was fire everywhere. I undid my seat belt and moved over." She lifted her shaking hands to show him her burnt palms.

"I couldn't get Mom's seat out of the way." Her lower lip trembled. "I couldn't get out."

"Shh. You're safe now," Rem crooned, the same way he would to a balky horse. He wanted to rest his head on hers to soothe her, but he feared hurting her damaged scalp. Or maybe he wanted to soothe himself.

"Who are you? Where's my mom?" She should be crying more, he thought. Her scalp had to hurt like crazy. She was probably going into shock.

"I'm Rem. Your mom's okay. She got out of the car."

No sense mentioning her mother had been injured. Or that she'd stumbled out of the car on her own, likely forgetting about her daughter because of shock and a head injury.

Rem laid the girl on the grass, but hesitated to let her go. Maybe if he held on tightly enough, he could keep her safe.

The child looked older than her tiny body would indicate—about eight or nine, at a guess.

This close he could smell her burned skin and it gripped him with the talons of a familiar helplessness.

Sara was a nurse. She'd know what to do for the child. He searched for her.

"Sara?" She still knelt beside the injured woman wrapping her arm against her chest with gauze.

"Sara!" he barked. "Get over here. This girl's hurt."

Sara ran over.

"Fix her," he said.

Gingerly, she checked the girl. "I can't. They both need to get to the hospital."

"I'll take them."

"We shouldn't move the mother. The ambulance is on its way."

"Ambulance is probably still on the other side of Ordinary. How long will it take?"

"Twenty minutes."

"Each way. Too long." He gestured toward the injured woman. "She's already moved, sat up just as I got here. If one of those ribs punctured a lung, she'll get bad fast. We need to go."

He ran to the still-disoriented woman. "I'm going to lift her."

"Careful," Sara said.

Reaching under the woman's legs and with one arm across her back, Rem picked her up as if she were a porcelain doll, trying to keep her in the same position she was already in.

He was beyond gentle, but she cried out anyway. There was no way to do this without hurting her.

While they placed her into his Jeep, Sara supported her bloody head. Before resting the woman back onto the seat, Sara shimmied out of her sweater and balled it up to cushion her head.

"That sweater will be ruined," he said.

"Doesn't matter."

She'd never had a lick of vanity.

"We can't put her seat belt on," Sara said. "Drive carefully."

Yeah, right. While I speed like a demon. "I'll do my best."

"Do you keep a gun in the Jeep?"

"Yeah. A rifle. Why?"

"That stag's in pain. He can't be saved and he's dying too slowly."

"Let me get my kit and I'll give him an injection."

"We don't have time. Where's the gun?"

"I'll get it." Rem rushed to the back and reached in for his rifle.

When Sara tried to take it from him, he said, "Move."

"I can do it. Get those two to the hospital. Go. Now."

Here in full force was *über*capable Sara. She charged through life taking care of everyone and everything around her.

Rem and Sara had practically grown up together. He knew she loved animals as much as he did and he wanted to spare her this ugliness. But he also knew that look of determination. Fine. She could do it.

He shoved the rifle into her hands, then returned to the sobbing child, whispering inanities as he lifted her. A little bit of a thing, she whimpered against his chest like a kitten. So vulnerable. So helpless against life.

Rem cleared his throat of the fear blocking his breath. *She'll be fine. Have faith.*

He put her into the front passenger seat where he could keep an eye on her. Her chest seemed to be fine, so he buckled her in, ran around to the driver's side and pulled onto the highway.

As he sped off with his window open, he heard one rifle shot.

Sara had been a thorn in his side over the years, but he couldn't deny she had guts.

Sheriff Kavenagh's cruiser approached, barreling down the highway from the opposite direction, toward the cloud of dirty smoke the car threw into the air.

Easing to a stop, Rem rolled down his window. Cash did the same in the oncoming lane.

"I've got an injured woman and a burned child. I'm taking them to the hospital."

"I'll give you an escort."

The woman in the backseat moaned. Rem needed to get moving.

"Don't worry about it. You have a fire extinguisher in the trunk?" Rem asked.

"Sure," Cash answered. "I always keep a couple on hand. They won't put out a fire that size, though."

"Fire department isn't here yet. I'm worried about the brush on the side of the road. Last thing we need is a grass fire."

"No kidding. I'll see what I can do."

They separated and accelerated in their separate directions.

In his rearview mirror, he watched Sara pull a U-turn and speed down the highway after him.

Dark smoke still rose from the wreckage. With all the chemicals and plastics used in manufacturing these days, car fires burned hot and intense. That fire could spread to his fields and reach the house.

He couldn't think about that now.

Rem flew through town, blaring his horn for the length of Main Street. Sara caught up and stuck to his tail like contact cement, her horn blaring in unison with his.

Someone was sitting in Sara's passenger seat, someone as tall as she. Finn? Had he grown that much since Rem had seen him around town at Christmas?

The woman in his backseat had stopped moaning. Maybe she'd passed out.

The shops passed in a blur.

On the highway on the far side of town, an ambulance passed headed toward the accident scene. It would take too long to stop, wait for the ambulance to turn around and then transfer the patients over. Best to just keep going.

Rem got back on his cell and told 9-1-1 to cancel it and to hook him up to the local hospital in Haven.

While he waited to be patched through, he checked the girl. Her eyes were open, but unfocused. She'd started to shiver.

Shit!

She was getting worse.

He didn't have anything to cover her with.

Finally, the hospital came into view and he screeched into the emergency entrance, narrowly missing a car.

A few nurses he knew stood outside the doors with stretchers. Randy took the child from the front seat and placed her onto one of the gurneys.

"She's in shock," Rem said, jumping out and rounding the SUV.

"Got it," Randy responded, wheeling her into the hospital.

Kelly and Phil went to the back for her mother.

"Careful. She's got head injuries—concussion, for sure—and a broken arm and we're pretty sure some busted ribs."

"Park your car," Kelly told him, her voice calm but rushed. "Then get a nurse to help with your injuries,"

His injuries? What was she talking about? He was fine.

He parked the Jeep and ran back to the emergency doors. Just inside, white coats and nurses' scrubs swarmed the two stretchers. Nurses ripped plastic from IV needles and inserted them into the uninjured arms of the patients.

On her stretcher, the child glanced around, her eyes wide and scared. When her gaze settled on Rem, she seemed to settle. He gave her a thumbs-up.

Her tremulous smile tugged at something deep inside him, as though there were already a connection between them. What was that Asian proverb? If you save a life, you become responsible for that life? Forever after that, you were obligated to take care of them. Or was that just a myth? For whatever reason, Rem did feel responsible. He wanted to be able to fix her, to take away her pain and fear.

In a whirlwind of activity, the two patients were taken to examination rooms, followed by nurses and doctors. The gurneys disappeared behind closing doors and suddenly all was quiet.

In the vacuum, Rem bent over and struggled to breathe, air searing his throat as it passed through his windpipe. He hadn't realized he'd inhaled that much smoke. Didn't matter. He would live. He hoped like crazy those two would be okay.

When the adrenaline that had carried him this far gave

out, his knees buckled. He grasped the counter of the nurses' station.

If he'd slept through the crash...

Or what if he'd already been out working, taking care of animals on someone else's ranch...

Those two might be dead now, one on the road and the other burned to death in the backseat of their car. Sara would have helped them when she came along. Could she have climbed into a burning vehicle, though? He didn't know. Her shock after her brother had been burned had been profound. He just didn't know how much of that she'd got over.

Nausea rose into his throat along with memories he'd grown damn good at repressing, but here they were now, vivid and too real, brought on by the scent of roasted flesh—a ball of fire, Timm Franck's screams, the other children running away, parents scrambling to put out the fire. Sara frozen in place and staring at her injured brother.

The stinking horror of it rang in Rem's conscience— your fault. Your fault.

Those words—*your fault, Rem*—had dogged him for twenty years. Far too many years.

He'd put his worst memories behind him, but today's crash, that burning girl, played havoc with his equilibrium. Maybe he felt this connection to her because he'd saved her from getting burned as badly as Timm had.

Sara ran past him. On her way through the examination room doors, she said, "Sit down before you fall on your face."

Rem stumbled to a blue plastic chair, one of a row, and sagged into it.

That poor kid.

He slumped against the chair and his back burst into flame. Howling, he shot forward. What the hell? He stood and tried to see his reflection over his shoulder in the side of a chrome vending machine, but the finish was too dull.

"Where's your shirt?"

Rem turned. Finn Franck stood in front of the machine with a fistful of change, staring at Rem's back and his hands.

He'd combed masses of jet hair across his forehead like a modern-day Beatle look-alike. With silver-gray eyes he'd inherited from Sara, the kid promised to be a heartbreaker one day soon.

He'd grown a lot since the last time Rem had seen him. Must be taller than Sara by now.

He was turning twelve in a couple of weeks. Rem knew his birth date. He knew a lot about him.

"When I heard the car crash I jumped out of bed." Rem finally answered the boy's question. "Didn't have time to get fully dressed."

"There's a long scratch on your back. It's bleeding."

Must've happened when he pulled the girl out of the car.

Finn stared at him, unnerving him. "Does it hurt?"

"It didn't until a minute ago." Rem had driven all the way out here with his back against his car seat and, in those adrenaline-fueled moments, hadn't felt a thing.

"I saw you go into the burning car," the boy said. "That was cool. Really sick. You were great."

Finn's eyes gleamed with hero worship.

Lord no. Anything but that. Rem was no hero. Never had been. Never would be.

"Don't try it at home," he muttered. "Fire is dangerous business."

Rem slowly turned away from the boy and sat back down.

He couldn't handle this right now.

He'd just rescued a girl from a burning vehicle, but to have a conversation with his son scared the bejesus out of him. Over the years, during Sara's visits home from school, he'd seen Finn around town. He'd admired the fine job Sara was doing raising him, but Rem didn't know what to say, what to talk about, and that helplessness frustrated him.

He wanted to connect. To claim the boy. Badly.

Sara had finished her nursing degree a few years ago and had been working in Bozeman; but she'd returned to Ordinary with Finn last week, this time to stay for good.

Rem wanted to know why.

He stretched his neck to ease the tightness there, where his resentment of Sara had settled since last summer.

Finn poured coins into the pop machine. When a ginger ale fell into the bottom, he pulled it out and sat on a chair in the same row as Rem, holding the can level on his thigh.

Rem stared at the boy's smooth profile, at his straight nose and square jaw, as nonplussed as if Finn were a strange kind of animal Rem had never encountered before.

He wanted to touch the boy, to acknowledge him as his son. He was ready. Did Finn ever ask about his father?

With the utmost care, Finn popped the tab, then took a long gulp, all while Rem stared at Sara's reflection in his young face.

Rem pointed to the cast on Finn's left wrist. "What happened?"

"Skateboarding."

Rem nodded. "Shit happens."

Finn nodded, too. "Yeah, shit happens."

SARA STEPPED OUT OF THE emergency hallway and what she saw brought her up short. Rem sat beside her son. They were talking. *Get away from him,* she wanted to yell but didn't. She had more self-control than that. Instead, she brushed a quick hand down her torso to ease her panic.

When Rem bent toward Finn, motioning to his cast, Sara noticed what she'd spent most of the past eleven years ignoring—how her son often tilted his head the same way when he was curious about something, and how their lush dark hair curled in the same direction. If Finn didn't use product to keep his bangs straight across his forehead, they would flop forward like Rem's did.

It made Rem look like a rebel, like James Dean, but less sulky, more dangerous.

When Finn took a pencil out of his sketchbook and handed it to Rem to sign his cast, she called, "Remington Caldwell," too sharply.

Rem looked up at her and frowned at her tone, then deliberately took his time with his autograph. He knew what this was doing to her, how it unnerved her, but he did it anyway.

He's mine, not yours. Only mine.

Rem smiled at her son, stood and then walked toward her.

Sara didn't want to stare, but couldn't help it.

As a teenager, she'd worked hard to ignore Rem's charms. As a grown woman, she tried not to drool.

Why was it so hard to turn off her attraction to him?

He wasn't the only man on earth.

He's the only one who makes you feel alive.

That had been brought home to her too clearly with the recent situation with Peter, yet another man who couldn't measure up to Rem. She'd broken up with Peter simply because he wasn't Rem, and wasn't that ridiculous considering how unsentimental she was supposed to be. Nononsense, dependable Sara.

Wasn't it serendipitous that shortly after, she'd moved home with Finn to get him away from that gang's influence? She no longer had to see Peter at the hospital every day and be reminded of her own foolishness. She didn't have to see that bewildered look on his face whenever they met. He had no clue why she'd ended their relationship after his proposal. She hadn't been able to explain fully to either him or herself exactly what her problems were.

She continued to stare. Rem was the handsomest man in Ordinary, Montana, and she was only human. Usually, she coped. It was just that she hadn't seen him since Christmas and now without a shirt. That was all.

Her stomach rebelled when she noticed the scar on his abdomen and remembered the terror of the night last summer when he'd been stabbed in a bar, and her own helplessness, of how little she'd been able to do for him while they'd waited for the ambulance.

She'd almost lost him that night. He'd been drinking in Chester's when it was still the Roadhouse and a biker had hassled one of the waitresses. When Rem stepped in to protect her, the biker stabbed him in the stomach. Foolish, courageous Rem who never thought of the danger to himself.

It didn't matter that it really hadn't been his fault. Trouble stalked Rem and that scared her.

The strawberry birthmark above his left nipple had faded over the years. The last time she'd seen it in daylight, they'd gone swimming with Timm. Her brother and Rem had been only ten and she nine.

Time had changed them all.

Rem's arms and chest had been scrawny back then, but weren't now.

When he lifted his hands to his hair to tidy it, his biceps flexed. Those unruly locks fell back onto his forehead.

He winced. He'd hurt his hands.

The small scar that bisected his upper lip—from a minor childhood mishap she no longer remembered—served to accentuate how full it was. The things that would be flaws on regular people looked like heaven on Rem.

To a plain woman like Sara, it smacked of unfairness.

He was still the best bad boy Ordinary had ever produced and Sara hated that she was so aware of him.

"Follow me," she said.

"What do you want?" he asked, belligerent as hell.

"I'll take care of your back."

"Someone else can do it." His lips barely moved. He was being rude.

"Little pitchers have big ears," she said.

"What?"

She motioned with her head toward Finn. "Mind your manners."

He blushed, obviously only now remembering that Finn would hear every word they said.

"There is no one else to do it," Sara said. "They're busy with the accident victims."

He approached and said under his breath, "You live to make my life miserable, don't you?"

"I do my best."

She led him to an examination cubicle, all the while too aware of how close he was.

"You look like you're chewing on a mouthful of finishing nails," Rem observed.

He wasn't far off. She felt that tense. With a flick of her wrist, she pulled the privacy curtain across the opening of the cubicle, closing them into a space too small for Sara's comfort.

"What did I do wrong?" Rem muttered.

"Shut up and sit." She pushed him onto the bed.

"Nice talk, Sara." Rem sat gingerly on the edge of the mattress. "Great bedside manner."

She ignored his sarcasm and examined his back. Despite her feelings, she made sure to keep her touch gentle. She checked out the burns on his hands.

"Ouch," he said. "I didn't even realize those were there."

"They must hurt." Sara sterilized the wounds.

"They do now. That poor little girl has worse burns on her hands and the top of her head."

Although she was being careful, he flinched. Burns were tricky to clean without hurting the patient.

"Have you heard how the girl is?" he asked.

Sara's tension eased a bit. Rem had a soft spot a mile wide for children. And animals. "No. If I hear anything I'll let you know."

Rem stared at her clothes. "Why aren't you in scrubs?"

"I'm not scheduled to work today." She glared at him. "That was a stupid stunt."

"Excuse me? What *stunt?*"

"Climbing into a burning car." Sara tore open packages of gauze so hard she nearly ripped the bags in half. When she started to clean the cut on his back, he hissed, and she struggled to relax, to ease her pressure on his cut. He'd terrified her when he'd climbed into that car.

"Do you think you're invincible?" She knew full well how vulnerable people were, how easily they could be hurt, and how hard it was to come back from some injuries. Like burns.

She'd spent her teenage years helping her brother recover from his burns.

"Saving someone is wrong?" Rem asked. She watched him grit his teeth, but she couldn't be any more careful than she already was and still do the cleaning and patching that needed to be done.

She secured his injury with gauze then handed him a scrub top to wear. He shrugged into it.

"Saving someone isn't wrong, but why couldn't you have waited until the firefighters got there? They wear protective gear." She refused to look at him, didn't want him to see her fear, didn't want him to think she still cared for him. "They don't reach into burning cars half dressed. After all these years you're still reckless."

"Sara, you're being unreasonable. On the way to the hospital, did we pass any fire trucks?"

"No, but—"

"There is no *but*. That girl needed to be rescued."

"And *you* just have to be the hero, don't you?" she said.

"It wasn't about me!" he shouted. "You're being unfair."

He was right. She needed to bring her irrational anger under control. She usually didn't have this much trouble, but then she'd spent years away from Ordinary so she wouldn't have to deal with Rem.

"Honest to God, Sara, I really don't need to be a hero." He touched her chin and forced her to look at him.

"We both know there's nothing heroic about me," he said. "But sometimes there isn't time to wait for someone else to show up."

But he was a hero. He'd just proven it and it went so far toward redeeming him, toward paying for all of the faults he'd shown when he was a teenager, that she had trouble keeping up. She'd thought badly of him for so many years. But he'd apparently been able to give up drinking and women and any number of destructive habits. Apparently, he was a responsible man now. And he'd just saved a child's life in a way that was pretty hard to beat. Sara didn't want to be impressed, but she was.

When he'd climbed into that burning vehicle, she'd thought she would lose him. She needed to be honest with him. "I know you couldn't wait, but I was scared. It was hard to watch. I remembered Timm." Her voice fell quiet, to barely above a whisper.

"I didn't have time to think. I just did."

"But that's exactly it, Rem. You never think. You haven't changed." Memories of the day that altered their lives burned her eyes and sizzled between them.

"Sara, I'm not the kid I used to be. You *know* that."

Yes, but why was it so hard for her to accept? Sara tossed bloody gauze into a wastebasket. "Half an hour ago, you sure looked like the same crazy kid."

He captured her hands and she could feel his warmth through her gloves. "Sara, stop and think. Today brought back memories of Timm being burned, yes, but you know I had to go in to get that girl."

She pulled her fingers out of his grasp and dropped a package of gauze. When she bent over to pick it up, her hands shook. "Yes."

"There's a difference between recklessness and courage. I wasn't being reckless this morning. I was doing what had to be done."

"I know," she whispered. "I get your point."

She reached for a bottle of ointment and the panic she'd felt when Rem had climbed into that car, and the bleakness at the thought of losing him forever, surfaced. "The car could have exploded while you were in it. Then both of you would be dead."

She picked up one of his hands to apply ointment, but he wrapped his fingers around hers and held them captive in his callused palm.

"Nice to see you care." For once, he didn't sound sarcastic. "You tie me in knots so often, can be so critical, I'm never sure if we're still friends."

She'd been careful to look only at his injuries, but now she met his gaze and couldn't hide what she felt, as impossible and self-defeating as it was.

CHAPTER THREE

REM COULDN'T BELIEVE the longing he saw on Sara's face. He understood the emotion, had felt it too often for her, but they could have been acting on it for the past year. They could have been married and loving each other every day and night.

Her longing angered him. "Uh-uh, Sara. You don't get to look at me like that."

"Like what?"

"As though you want me. Nothing's going to happen between us. That ship has sailed, sweetheart, and it ain't ever coming back."

Her fingers flinched within his grasp.

"Why are you back in Ordinary?" he asked. "Why didn't you stay in Bozeman? You had a good job there."

"Mama's here. Timm and Angel are here and soon their new baby. I wanted to be with my family."

Hmm. Maybe. "What aren't you telling me?"

She pressed her lips together as though she wouldn't answer but finally did. "Finn was hanging out with kids I didn't like and getting wild. They got into trouble with the police. It scared me. I thought it would be good for him to be with family."

It sounded plausible enough, but still not like the full story. He'd leave it for now. He had more important fish to fry. "*I'm* Finn's family."

She jerked to attention, the longing gone like last Sunday's dinner, and tugged her hands out of his grasp. She opened his fists to tend to his palms in her usual no-nonsense way, the vulnerable woman vanishing behind her professional facade.

Damn your self-control to hell, Sara.

Time to hit her with the decision he'd made.

He'd spent the past seven years turning his life around, righting so many of the wrongs he'd committed before his father's death had given him a rude wake-up call. Rem had made the decision to straighten out, but he wasn't finished making amends yet. His father had been a great role model. It was time for Rem to be the same for his son. He'd hurt people. He wanted that to stop. Here. Now. Today. Starting with the most important people in his life.

"I want to get to know him."

"Who?" Sara asked, turning away so he couldn't see her expression.

"Santa Claus," he snapped. "Who do you think? Finn."

She spun back to him. "No. We had an agreement."

"That agreement is almost twelve years old. I've paid my dues since then."

"I don't care. We agreed. You promised you'd never go back on your decision."

"It was the wrong decision. I'm old enough and strong enough to see that now."

"I don't care."

"Does he ever ask about his father?"

Sara flinched. Bingo.

He changed his tactic, knew what would work in convincing her.

"Ma had another stroke." A week ago. It was her third stroke in a year and a half and the worst yet. How much longer would he have her around? He needed to set so many things right.

"I know," Sara answered. "I've been visiting her."

Of course she had, because underneath all of her stubborn grittiness Sara was a caring person.

"So why shouldn't she get to know her grandson before she dies? What if the next stroke kills her?" His voice rose. "Finn's my son."

"Be quiet," Sara warned. "We're not private here."

"So what? It wouldn't kill either of us if people found out."

She leaned close and pointed a finger in his face. "*You* were the one who decided not to be in his life, that you weren't father material. The fact that you wanted out so quickly proved you were right. You'd make a terrible father."

"I was young and stupid. I was scared. I thought Finn would be better off without me." He stood, loomed over her and lowered his voice, infusing it with a dark intensity because she had to understand how serious he was. "That's no longer true. I think I'd be a good father now. That boy needs one. And I need my son."

She refused to make eye contact even though he stood mere inches from her. Instead, she stared at his collarbone.

"You agreed to the deal pretty damn quickly," he accused. "You didn't want me to acknowledge Finn, either."

Her chest rose and fell too rapidly. He knew Sara through and through and, although she looked calm, he could tell she was scared. He didn't blame her. This was new territory for him, too.

"I've come to terms with who I am, with the mistake I made burning Timm, with all of the mistakes I made in my crazy adolescence. I can't take back what I've done, Sara, but I'm moving on. I've proven that I'm a responsible man."

She hadn't been around to witness his change, but he *had* changed, and she was going to have to trust him.

She still wouldn't look at him, but said, "Fine, so you've come to terms with your guilt."

Guilt. Of course she would use a word that loaded.

"It was a child's mistake, Sara. I've finally accepted it. Someday, you're going to have to let it go, too."

"I know you were a child and I've tried to come to terms with it, Rem. I truly have. But it was a *huge* mistake with consequences that still affect us to this day."

"Yes. I know. But it's done. Nothing can be taken back."

Finally, she looked at him, uncertainty in those steel-gray eyes. "If something goes wrong again, how do you know you won't end up bingeing like last summer?"

"I don't, but I do know that I spend ninety percent of my days being a good person. If I slip, I slip. Big deal. I'm human."

He wanted to tell her how human she was, too; but that truth was one she had to come to on her own.

"If I slipped up," he continued, "Finn could handle it."

"He could handle it only because I raised him well." She tried to push him away, but he was too strong.

Rem watched Sara control the heat that flared between them.

He stepped back.

"You've done a fine job of raising Finn. He's a great kid." Rem was ready to stop thinking of Finn as Sara's son and to start accepting him as his own.

"Get used to this, Sara, 'cause I'm not backing down. You're not going to win this fight."

Something more flared in her eyes, something beneath the anger she wore like a badge. He thought it might be fear. He wracked his brain for a way to convince her that he was serious about changing, about becoming stronger, and that everything would work out fine, and he hit on one thing.

"Since the day Finn was born, I've been helping to support him, starting with your hospital bills when he was born. Every month without fail, I've sent you money for him. In twelve years, I didn't miss once. I've been responsible. I've proven that I have staying power. Right?"

"You never missed a payment," she acknowledged.

"I won't relapse, Sara."

She wouldn't look at him.

"Fine, if you can't do this for me, do it for Ma. She has a right to know Finn. I'm going to tell her."

"Don't," Sara rasped. "Just don't."

"It's no longer your choice to make."

Beneath the defiance and fear on her face, he saw devastation. Her world was about to change.

Too bad. Rem needed everyone to know that he was Finn's father.

He stalked out of the emergency room.

It was long past time to *be* a father.

SARA PRESSED A HAND AGAINST her stomach.

The controlled, defined, *safe* world she'd struggled to build since her son's birth was about to crumble. She'd worked so hard and Rem could rip it all apart with a few words.

Don't hurt my baby.

Rem was a master at finding chinks in her armor.

He didn't understand the chance he took. His decision didn't affect only her. Didn't he know how hurt Finn could be if Rem let him down, if he couldn't carry through as a father? Once he started, there was no turning back.

She listened to the familiar sounds of the hospital, her home away from home, but saw only the small recovery room she'd been in after Finn's birth. She'd thought things were going to work out for her. She'd been so wrong.

It hurt to remember how excited she'd been and then how devastated after Rem had rejected both of them.

After she'd buried her emotions and thought things through rationally, she'd realized that she and Finn could survive just fine without Rem. And they had.

That day, she'd decided that she'd work her butt off for independence, to support herself and Finn, and the hell with Rem. She didn't need him. She and Finn were on their own and that's how they would stay.

Sara and her son had been a team—until lately, at any rate.

Now Rem was changing his mind and he expected her to fall into line.

That wasn't going to happen.

Sara still stood in the small, curtained emergency room with the familiar equipment that could mend broken bodies, that could take blood and mess and dirt and transform the chaos into the order she craved.

She brushed off the past.

She would get through this. She always did.

Taking an antiseptic wipe from a container, she ran it across the small counter and into every corner and cranny.

She replaced the sheet of protective paper on the bed.

Rem had disappointed her before and there wasn't a speck of doubt in her mind that he would do so again. She just didn't want him pulling his old tricks on Finn.

No matter what it took, she'd make sure Finn didn't get hurt. She'd bet her last dollar that Rem had gone up to visit Nell. She was going to march up there right now to lay down a few parameters, rules that Rem had to follow.

She would see Nell then, too. Rem had hit a nerve when

he'd talked about his mom—a problem she'd been aware of since Finn's birth.

Sara had loved Nell ever since she was a child and running everywhere with Timm and Rem. Nell had treated her as her own daughter. Over the years, Sara had worried about keeping Finn away from Nell, about how it would affect Nell if she ever found out. Nell didn't know she was a grandmother and the guilt ate away at Sara.

Nell had had three strokes and now Rem was talking about the very real possibility of her death. It was hard to think of Nell dying without ever learning the truth. Rem was right.

Fine, Nell could get to know her grandson, but Sara would have to make sure she understood that Finn wasn't to know whose mother she was. No way would Sara let Finn find out that Rem was his father.

Sara would keep as much control of the situation as she could.

Finished with her straightening of the room, Sara stopped and gripped the counter, overwhelmed by Rem's threat. She squeezed her eyes shut, but still saw his face and that body she wanted to hold despite his past betrayals.

She snapped her eyes open.

Mixed in with all of that desire was a backwash of emotion too toxic for her to sort out—guilt, anger, tenderness and even love. And that terrible and unrelenting darkness.

Her head had to rule. Experience had taught her that Rem could cost her pieces of herself that she didn't want to give. But she was faced with the same old struggle between desire and reality.

Over the years, she'd grown so good at quashing her dreams of Rem, of suppressing memories and desires. But today, at this moment, Sara Franck still wanted Remington Caldwell.

You poor unfortunate fool.

REM TOOK THE ELEVATOR to Ma's floor, to make sure she was all right and to let her know he'd made the arrangements for her homecoming.

At least he'd had the chance to tell Sara what he wanted with Finn. She was dead set against him getting to know his son. Surprise, surprise.

Calming himself before entering Ma's room, he put aside all thoughts of Sara.

When he approached the bed, Ma's eyes followed him, but her head remained still. This latest stroke had immobilized her so much and it hurt to see her like this.

"What?" she asked, glancing at his bandaged hands. Her speech had been affected and her words clipped short. "What happen?"

He raised his hands so she could see them better. "It isn't as bad as it looks. I pulled a girl out of a car fire."

"Fire?" He didn't miss the flicker of fear in her eyes. "You okay?"

"Yeah, Ma, I'm good." Blinking rapidly, he kissed her forehead, unsure whether she could even feel it.

Get your shit together. Get over all of this stupid emotion.

"She okay?"

"I don't know how she's doing. She had burns on her head, but I haven't seen her since we got here. I hope so."

"How old?"

"I think maybe nine."

"Poor girl."

With her good hand, she pointed at the scrub shirt he wore. "Where's...own...shirt?"

"The accident was at the end of our lane. It woke me up and I rushed out to see if everyone was all right. Only got as far as pulling on my pants 'cause the car was on fire."

Ma smiled but it looked bizarre with that one side drooping.

Ma's eyes flickered to the doorway and her expression softened. Rem turned to see who had entered.

Sara.

His gaze flickered to check out her conservative shirt and blue jeans. He remembered her tight body as though it were tattooed on his eyelids.

Sara approached the bed and gave Ma the kind of warm smile he hadn't seen from her in years.

He'd always wanted a piece of that, of the soft, affectionate side of Sara's character she reserved for everyone but him.

"How are you feeling?" Sara asked.

"Good."

"When are you going to the convalescent home?"

Nell glanced at Rem.

"She leaves here tomorrow," he said. "I've already arranged everything. She's coming home with me."

She turned to him with a frown. "May I talk to you out in the hall?"

He didn't like the seriousness of her expression, but followed her out. Was she going to argue more about Finn? He wouldn't allow it.

Once away from the door, Sara crossed her arms. "Why are you taking Nell home instead of putting her into Tender Loving Care? She needs full-time attention."

That took him aback. She wanted to talk about Ma, not Finn. "She wants to come home."

"It doesn't matter what the patient *wants*. What does matter is that she gets the care she *needs*."

"She's my mother—I care what she wants. I'm not putting her in a place run by a bunch of strangers. I won't know how well she's being taken care of, or if they'll give her enough attention. I've heard horror stories about old folks being neglected."

"TLC has an excellent reputation. She would receive everything she needs."

Rem chewed on his lip. "I can't." He'd neglected his parents for too many years. His wild ways had kept him isolated from everyone. When his father died, Rem realized just how much of his life he'd been throwing away. How much he was hurting those around him.

No way was he letting Ma go to an institution.

He shifted gears. "She wants to come home, Sara. I don't know how much longer she'll be around. How can I say no to her? I want her home, too."

"Do you have any idea how much care she'll need?"

"Of course I do. For God's sake, Sara, I've talked to the doctors. I've arranged to have caregivers at the house fourteen hours a day."

"Okay, I guess."

"You guess? It isn't your decision to make."

Sara raised a staying hand to squelch his anger. "I know. I care about Nell, though. I want to make sure she gets the best care."

"She'll get the best."

"TLC Outreach?"

"Yes."

Her frown eased. "Okay."

Rem calmed down. Sara might be a pain in the rear end sometimes, but there was no doubting how much she loved his ma.

She touched his arm, her manner hesitant but also determined. "As far as Finn goes, here's the deal. You can tell Nell that he's her grandson on the condition that she understands that he isn't to know. And you can't tell him that you're his father."

"What the hell?"

"Those are my terms. For years, you didn't want to acknowledge him as your son. You can't change the rules on a whim."

"I want to be his father now."

"I can't risk that you'll hurt him."

"I'll take you to court."

"In the eyes of the law, I'm his only parent."

No way. "You didn't put my name on the birth certificate?"

"I had planned to, but you walked out on us."

She might as well have sucker punched him. It hurt. Finn was his son. He'd never claimed the boy, though, had he?

"Did you really hate me so much?"

"I've never hated you, Rem. Never. But I don't trust you to do what's right for my son."

Without waiting for a response, she strode away and Rem was left reeling. So, should he go ahead and tell the boy anyway, against Sara's wishes? Somehow, that didn't feel right.

He would tell his ma, though, when the time was right.

He returned to Ma's room to say goodbye.

Last week, on the day of her latest stroke, it had occurred to him that she was his only family.

Other than Finn.

He'd always thought her hale and healthy, but she'd shrunk, was small now, and he was in danger of losing her. Now he had this impulse, an inkling that had started after he became a full-time veterinarian, but urgent now that Ma was so bad, to start a family. He already *had* started one, though, and wanted to claim his son and get to know him.

He'd screwed up in not acknowledging him from the beginning. He was through screwing up. He was setting everything in his life right.

Sara had done a great job of raising Finn alone, so Rem would respect her wishes. For now.

"Ma, I'm going to see how that young girl is doing and then finish setting the house to rights for your homecoming tomorrow."

She tried that smile again, but must have known how bad it looked because she stopped. *Ma, you're breaking my heart.*

He squeezed her good hand. "I love you."

She nodded.

Rem rushed out because of the headache throbbing behind his sinuses. Maybe he was getting a cold. Or maybe it was just that he'd been up too late last night turning the dining room into a bedroom for Ma's return, including moving in the new bed he'd had delivered.

On the first floor, he found Randy in the emergency ward. "How are the girl and her mother?"

"Lucky, from what I hear." He punched Rem on the shoulder. "Heard you're the man of the hour for pulling her out of the wreckage."

Rem shrugged. "You would have done the same thing. Seriously, how are they?"

"You called it right. Mother's got a concussion, fractured ribs and a broken arm. Daughter's got burns to her scalp, hands and arms."

"Can I see them?" Rem needed reassurance that the two were alive and well. When the kid had been trapped…

Quit. Don't think about it.

Randy directed him to Intensive Care. "They're pretty doped up, but you can look in on them."

Rem stepped into the room. Nurses worked around the young girl's bed quietly, lending the room a hushed, expectant silence.

Her face looked peaceful in her drugged sleep, with the white bandages swathing her head.

His gaze drifted to the other bed, where her mother lay awake and watching him, her gaze only slightly unfocused by pain meds.

"Hi," he said with a wave of two fingers.

"Hi," she said. "Are you the one who saved my daughter?"

"Yeah." He squirmed beneath her admiring gaze. *Lady, I'm not a hero.*

He approached her bed. Under the bruises on one side of her face, he could tell she was a whole lot younger than he'd originally thought, probably younger than his own thirty-two years.

"What's your daughter's name?" he asked.

"Melody."

He had a snap memory of this woman screaming that as Rem dove into the burning vehicle. "I'm Remington Caldwell. People call me Rem."

She smiled, then grimaced as if her face hurt.

"I'm Elizabeth Chase. Liz," she said. "Did that happen at the crash?" She pointed to his wrapped hands.

He nodded.

"I'm sorry." She had a pretty voice, feminine and sweet.

"You're not from around here. Are you here to visit family?"

She shook her head and shadows clouded her eyes along with a dose of fear. Something wasn't right, but the woman wasn't saying more. Fair enough. She had a right to her privacy.

When he asked no further questions, she stared at him some more as though he were her hero, and he had to leave the room before he disappointed her by blurting out how wrong she was.

REM TURNED THE JEEP INTO his driveway and stared at his big old oak and the fields on either side of the entrance to his ranch.

Fire had scorched the fields, now sodden under the weight of the water the fire crews had poured on them.

The acrid scent of charred earth drifted through the open window.

The fire trucks must have reached his ranch shortly after he passed through Ordinary on his way to the hospital.

After last summer's drought, the town had installed solar-powered pumps in Still Creek where it ran along the highway.

Thankfully, access to water for the fire pumps wasn't an issue.

The results could have been so much worse. Those golden fields could have burned right up to the house and taken it down, too.

He had lost grain, though, and would have to replace it.

He climbed out and pressed his hand against the scar on the tree where the car had hit. Fire had blackened this entire side of the trunk. Still fresh, the odor of burning wood had replaced that of singed flesh.

His bandage came away sooty and black.

Above his head, bare limbs formed a stark spider's web against the blue sky.

Lucky he hadn't lost the whole tree. The other half

remained green. Thank God. He loved his land. Rem had an affinity with nature and this hurt. It really sucked.

The stag was gone. Maybe one of the firefighters had taken it home to butcher and freeze for the winter.

Out here in rural Montana, food didn't go to waste.

Rem shook himself out of his pensive musings.

Given Sara's reluctance to let him get to know his son, he had a lot to prove, a lot to do to persuade her that he was a responsible man.

Fired up, he drove to the house, ready to jump into final preparations for Ma's homecoming tomorrow morning.

One way or another, he would find a way to be Finn's dad, Sara be damned.

CHAPTER FOUR

SARA TOOK THE ELEVATOR down to the emergency waiting room. Finn waited for her there, listening to music in his headphones and sketching. Thank goodness he'd broken his left wrist instead of his right.

She should go home and make him lunch, but acid churned in her belly. How could she possibly eat after the bomb Rem had dropped?

Since his birth, she'd had Finn all to herself, had taken him to and from school with her, year after year until she finally became a nurse, her dream of medical school eliminated by her pregnancy. No regrets, though.

She'd kept him with her despite Mama's and Timm's arguments to leave him in Ordinary with them.

She made every decision about his life. If she could keep her son close enough to her, Sara could keep him safe. How could she possibly share him, especially with a man who had spent too many years wasting his life on the worst habits, and who'd made a mistake of the biggest proportions? He'd burned Timm and ruined her brother's teenage years. He'd ruined Sara's, too.

With her parents' attention firmly on Timm's operations and physiotherapy, and the illnesses brought on by a compromised immune system, Sara had faded into the background. Had disappeared. Had become another caregiver for her older brother.

But their care had never been enough. Timm had been

sick too often. He'd been scarred. Sara had felt so helpless, so useless no matter how hard she'd worked. She'd been only ten years old when the accident changed the landscape of her family's life. It had never been good again.

Then her oldest brother, Davey, had been killed by a bull, in the rodeo, and things had become even worse. Dad had turned more and more to the sedative of the bottle. He'd finally killed himself by driving into a tree on his way home from a bar in Monroe.

Sara had never been able to do enough to fix her brother or to save her family.

So…now she was a nurse. She'd learned how to take care of people and to help save them. Or was she just kidding herself? She hoped the work she did had value.

She stepped forward and called Finn's name. Time to take care of her son. Rem was not going to ruin what was already working fine.

Finn closed his book, took the buds out of his ears and showed her his cast. "You know the guy who pulled that girl out of the car?"

"Rem? Yes."

"Look what he put on my cast."

He'd signed only his first name, a big flamboyant *Rem,* but he'd drawn a smiley face beside it—with a lopsided grin and devil's horns. Sara couldn't help laughing. She had never doubted his charm.

On the drive home to Ordinary, Finn didn't put his earbuds back in, nor did he open his sketchbook. His MP3 player sat idle in his hand as he stared out the window.

Sara glanced at him, worried. He looked pensive, the way he'd been lately just before asking her questions she'd rather not answer.

"Mom," he said, turning to her.

"Yes?"

"Father's Day is coming up."

"I know." Nuts. Every year, Finn became more and more curious about his father, more troubled by his lack of one. The issue seemed to be pulling him further and further away from her. She felt that separation like a physical ache.

"On Father's Day, all the kids are allowed to bring their dads to school. Everyone's talking about it. There's gonna be a big party in the gym. I'll be the only one there without a father."

"The only one for sure?"

"Yeah," he mumbled.

"How can you possibly know that?"

"Everyone's talking about their dads."

"But I know there are single mothers living in town. How about Stacey Kim's daughter, Joy?"

"She's in high school."

"Oh. I guess she is by now." Sara came up with more names, but the kids were either too young for school or were in high school. Of all the rotten luck for Finn. A fluke of demographics left him isolated.

As the new kid in school, life was hard enough on Finn. He already stood out too much. Adding the weight of his being the only kid without a father at the party was so unfair; but he had no idea of the kind of damage Rem Caldwell had done to the Franck family. Sara had no idea what additional harm Rem could still do while trying to father Finn.

Her parents had spent her adolescence warning her away from Rem, from the boy who'd been her best friend before Timm's birthday party. One small mistake. Such big consequences.

"Why don't you have a photograph of my dad?" Finn's question caught Sara by surprise.

Why hadn't she prepared herself for this? But what preparation could there have been?

"I didn't know him for that long."

"How long did you know him?"

She swallowed around a lump that was the lie she'd told her family and the entire town—that she'd met a man at a party and they'd had unprotected sex. Finn was still so young for that explanation.

"Well?" Finn asked. "How long?"

He wasn't going to let it go.

"One night," she answered.

Finn's chin dropped. "You had a one-night stand?"

"Yes," she whispered.

"That's so uncool, Mom. *So* uncool."

He stared out the window silently for a moment and Sara hoped that was the end of it.

"So, why didn't you find him and tell him about me?"

"The name he gave me was false." Was she going to hell for telling her son so many lies? "I discovered that when I tried to track him down."

"So, there's some guy out there who doesn't even know I've been born?" His voice had risen in anger. "That makes me feel really rotten, Mom."

Sara brushed her hair back from her forehead, but her hand shook. This was so hard. How long could she continue to lie to her little boy?

"Finn, I'm sorry."

He didn't respond, so she continued, "I made a mistake one night, but it gave me you and I'm not sorry for that. Can you forgive me?"

Wasn't that sweet freaking irony, such hypocrisy on her part to beg her son's understanding when she hadn't forgiven Rem a single one of his many transgressions?

"I'm not even supposed to be alive!" He turned to her

with an accusation that cut through her defenses. "I'm a big mistake!" he yelled.

His anger fueled hers.

"Stop right there." She didn't shout but she wanted to. "You're the best thing that ever happened to me. *Ever.*"

Finn crossed his arms over his chest, but his fury seemed to seep out of him. His lower lip jutted forward, but rather than looking petulant, he just looked sad.

"I'll *never* have a father."

She shook her head, unable to tell him "no" out loud. She'd come close with Peter Welsh in Bozeman, a sweet, smart, handsome doctor. But after that one night when she slept with Rem last summer, after he'd been stabbed, Sara hadn't been able to sleep with Peter again. She'd broken off their relationship.

As much as she tried to forget Rem with other men, she couldn't deny her feelings for him, even if she wouldn't act on them.

It didn't look like marriage was ever going to be in her future. So, yet again, she was on her own. Independence suited her just fine.

They turned down the road to the old Webber home. It had been vacant for more than a dozen years, had been for sale for ages.

This past spring, Sara had bought it.

She and Finn could live here, just the two of them, and not worry about having to depend on anyone else. Not emotionally, and certainly not financially. This little house was hers and only hers. She'd earned it and deserved it.

The property abutted Still Creek, and the spot where she and Rem had created Finn on a blanket under the stars.

Refusing to consider why it had been so important to her to buy *this* property, she turned and studied the house.

A smallish bungalow, it would be more than enough for the two of them.

The siding was dirty, the wraparound veranda needed a coat or two of paint, the eaves troughs needed cleaning and the gingerbread appointments had fallen apart. But the bones were good. Just right.

She and her son had lived in tiny cheap apartments, some dingy, most crowded, none in the best parts of town. On the rare occasions that she dated and developed a relationship with a man, she never brought him home. Not to those places in which she felt no pride.

Now they had a house where she could give her son safety and a permanent roof over his head. It didn't look like much but it was all hers. Amazing how proud that made her feel.

She pulled the key out of her purse.

"Let's go inside," she said.

She pulled the cleaning supplies she'd picked up yesterday from the trunk. Because of his broken wrist, Finn could carry only one pail filled with bottled cleaners.

She opened the door of her house and stepped in.

The rooms smelled stale. She could fix that. She could fix anything here.

As she walked through the hushed rooms and opened windows, the house breathed in fresh air and seemed to come to life. She could bring a spark to this place.

She handed Finn a broom. "Sweep up. I'll wash the kitchen and the bathroom. Unless you'd rather scrub the toilet and I'll sweep."

"I'll sweep," he mumbled without cracking a smile.

The ancient bathroom fixtures still worked. One of the Webbers had fitted the old claw-foot tub with a showerhead and a track on the ceiling from which to hang a shower curtain. She hung the new yellow-and-mauve-striped curtain that she'd picked up in Bozeman before the move.

This house was hers. All hers. She hadn't told anyone about it yet, not even Mama. This was her own private secret. In time, she would tell everyone, but not until she fixed it up the way she wanted to. Then she would throw a big party and be *proud* to have her family here.

She heard a sound in the doorway and looked up. Finn stood there with a scowl on his face.

"Mom, when are we going to move here from Oma's house?"

"Soon. When I'm off work, I'll gradually move over some of the boxes from Oma's and then have our furniture shipped from Bozeman."

"So, like, only you and me will live here? Right?"

Sara looked around. A fresh coat of paint on the walls would brighten the space beautifully.

"Mom, right? Only you and me?"

"Hmm? Sorry! Yes, only us."

Finn stared out the window above the sink. "What is there to do out here?"

He'd stumped her. "We'll come up with stuff. Anything you do at Oma's can be done here."

She was worried, though. With her working two jobs and Finn being supervised by only Mama, would he get into trouble, as he'd started to in Bozeman? He had no friends here. Who was going to fill that void when he finally did make friends? Good kids?

Or would he follow in his father's footsteps? She refused to allow it.

"How am I supposed to become friends with kids in Ordinary when I live way out here?"

If she had to drive him everywhere, then she could control who his friends would be.

She packed the supplies into a hall closet. Finn followed her down the hallway like a lost puppy.

"Mom, are you *listening* to me?"

"Yes." She couldn't hide her frustration. "Don't be so negative about this, Finn. Give the place a chance."

Finn stomped out of the house and to the car. Sara locked up and followed him. Why did he have to question everything she did these days? Was this a lead-up to adolescence? If so, she was going to go nuts before it was over. Seriously. Stark raving mad.

On the trip into Ordinary to the Franck house where they currently lived, Finn fell asleep. Taking advantage, she touched his nape.

Such a beautiful boy.

It was her job to protect him and she took that seriously. When they got home to Mama's, Sara spent the afternoon checking out every class, course and organized sporting activity around Ordinary and Haven, to replace that swimming course Finn should have been in three afternoons a week. She glanced at the calendar. She'd have to cancel the basketball league she'd signed him up for, as well. That left too many days empty—too many days he could fill with mischief—and there was nothing left to register him for.

CHAPTER FIVE

AT ELEVEN O'CLOCK THE following morning, an unforgiving sun followed Rem out of the house and to the corral where his horse Rusty ambled lazily, kicking up puffs of dust with his hooves.

What was taking Ma so long to get here? He'd expected her half an hour ago.

He'd already been out to the hospital this morning with a bag of nice clothes for her to wear home. He'd signed all the necessary papers, had packed up all of the cards the townspeople had given her. He'd found an elderly woman in another room who had no family and had given her Ma's flowers. Then he'd driven out ahead of Ma's ambulance. He'd expected them to be only a few minutes behind him.

He'd already had time to put the cards around her room, to give her something to look at all day.

He glanced around the yard. It looked good. Clean.

He'd taken Ma's pretty flowered cushions out of plastic in the storage shed and had spruced up her blue wicker chairs on the veranda. Rem's ancestors had built this two-story home more than a century ago, had built it with brick to last and with gingerbread trim that Rem had repainted white in May.

He'd put a fresh coat of blue paint on the veranda floor and stairs, too.

He'd started on the stable with more white paint, but had only finished the front and the corral side, both of which could be seen from the dining room windows. He still had to paint the far side and the back, but that would come in time.

Gracie lay on the steps like the grand old dame she was, a border collie with too much gray fur among the white and black. She spent a lot of her days sleeping, sometimes in the house, sometimes in the stable.

Two days ago, Rem had planted pansies across the front of the house, in yellow, purple and mauve. What did he know about flowers? If they lasted through the summer, he'd be surprised. They brightened the place, though.

At the rumble of an engine in the driveway, he turned.

The ambulance rode up the long lane, with neither siren nor flashing lights.

Ma. Home at last. Feeling like a kid getting a present, he ran to the steps at the front of the house. He'd missed having her here.

The ambulance swung around in the yard, backed up toward the house and stopped a couple of yards away from him.

The driver jumped out of the vehicle and came around the rear, nodding at Rem, his pressed white shirt almost blue in the sun.

"How is she?" Rem asked.

"Comfortable," the attendant replied while he opened the door.

"What took so long?"

"Half the staff came out to say goodbye."

Rem thanked his lucky stars that he lived in a close-knit community. Ma would have loved the attention.

Another attendant jumped down from the patient area and Rem caught his first glimpse of Ma, half sitting in the dark interior. She looked pale, her face immobile, her eyes a little scared.

His chest tightened. *Ma, I'll take care of you. You'll never go to a home to be taken care of by strangers. I promise.*

The attendants lifted the stretcher out of the ambulance and released the legs. Rem stepped close. He took Ma's hand in his, but it was the paralyzed one, so she might not have felt his touch.

Her eyes flickered to the pansies raising their colorful faces toward the sun and a weak smile cast the ghost of movement across her face then disappeared. She blinked.

On the veranda, she dropped her good arm over the side of the gurney and Gracie stood and licked her fingers. Her glance at the cushions on the chairs brought forth another smile. Rem was glad he'd worked so hard.

After the attendants wheeled her through the front door, Rem ran ahead to open the dining room doors. "In here."

He'd rented a comfortable hospital bed and had crowded Ma's treasured dining room set into the closed-in porch at the back of the house. For the past two nights, he'd worked until three in the morning to make Ma a comfortable new bedroom.

After they transferred her from the stretcher to the bed, Rem walked the paramedics out and shook their hands.

"Thanks, guys. I appreciate you taking care of her."

Any minute now, one of the caregivers should be showing up.

Sure enough, a small blue sedan rode up the lane just moments after the ambulance drove off. Ah, here she was, the first nurse.

Sara stepped out of the car, spit polished and as crisp as a new dollar bill in a white shirt and navy skirt. She pulled a bag out of the backseat and turned toward the house.

Sara? What was she doing here?

She approached the steps then stopped before climbing them.

"Hello, Rem," she said, her voice as cool as her gray eyes.

His expression flattened. "What are you doing here?" Even to his own ears, he sounded unhappy. "Checking up on me?"

"I'm here to work with Nell. I'm with TLC Outreach."

"No way. You're a nurse at the hospital."

"I have two jobs."

"What do you need two jobs for?"

"I have student debts to pay down."

Rem knew Sara well. Again, as with her reasons for returning to Ordinary to live, he got the feeling he wasn't getting the whole story.

"Why didn't they send someone else?"

"I volunteered."

"Why?"

"Rem. It's Nell. How could I not want to help her?"

Yeah, that part made sense, but, honest to God, this complicated things.

"There will be two of us caring for Nell," Sara explained. "You'll have one full-time nurse, and I'll be working part-time."

"We'll see."

Free of yesterday's emotional overload, Rem got his first good look at Sara.

She never changed. The conservative clothing did nothing to brighten a dull landscape. With her brown hair pulled back hard enough to draw tears, she looked all business. Would a little lipstick hurt?

Her legs, though… Her legs were her best feature, not long, but damned perfect. Her slightly pigeon-toed walk, that minor vulnerability in a capable woman, had always charmed him, as had her hint of an overbite.

She watched him with a solemn gaze in that unremarkable face. "I'll try to stay out of your way."

She climbed the steps to the veranda and gestured with her head toward the hallway. "May I see her?"

Rem stepped aside and she brushed past him.

"Ma's in the dining room," Rem said. "You remember where it is?"

She nodded. Of course she would. She'd been here last summer to nurse him after the stabbing at Chester's. That had been a rough time. He hadn't forgotten a thing that had happened between them in those days while he recovered.

On the day that Timm had driven him home from the hospital, Sara had arrived to take care of him. After Timm had left, Sara had crawled into bed beside Rem and had held him while he'd slept.

In those days that Sara had nursed him, Finn had stayed with her mom. Rem's own mother hadn't said a word about Sara being on the Caldwell ranch and spending so much time in Rem's room. He suspected that Nell would have loved for them to have married. Maybe last summer she'd hoped it was finally going to happen.

Anyway, Rem had needed a caregiver. Ma had already had a stroke and couldn't have nursed him back to health.

Then there'd been that night a week or so after the stabbing when they'd made love, carefully so he wouldn't hurt his healing wound. And tenderly, because they'd both known how easily that biker's knife could have killed him.

Getting close to him had scared her, though, and she'd packed up, had taken Finn and had run away to Bozeman. The woman was a coward.

When Sara passed him to walk into the house, something scented with lily of the valley swirled around her.

She used to smell like sunshine, fresh air and kid sweat. Now she simply smelled feminine.

Just inside the dining room door, he pulled up short, Ma's new appearance catching him off guard again. He kept expecting to see her old self, but she looked like she didn't weigh much more than a handful of green beans.

He felt his eyes water and blinked hard. Shoot.

When Sara saw his mother, her face lit up and she looked younger.

Sara bent forward and wrapped Ma in a hug. "I'm going to be one of your caregivers."

When she pulled away, Ma's pleasure in seeing her was obvious. She loved Sara, and wasn't that a kicker because it meant there was no way Rem was going to boot Sara out as one of Ma's nurses. Ma's joy would make having to put up with Sara worthwhile.

It also made him sad, made him rue that horrible day when Timm had been burned. If that accident hadn't happened, would Sara be living here now as his wife? Would he have been a father to his son all along?

What-ifs weren't worth a hell of a lot, though, were they? They just left a person regretful.

"I'm going to make you better," Sara said, smiling and rubbing Ma's hands.

Really, Sara? You do that and I'll kiss your feet.

When Sara pulled a nightgown from a stack of clean laundry Rem had put in the room last night and then started to remove Ma's clothes, he rushed outside.

The nitty-gritty of having Ma home overwhelmed him. He didn't have a clue how to take care of a sick woman.

His cell phone rang.

"Rem, it's Max Golden. Got a problem with a horse. Can you take a look at her today?"

"I can come now."

Rem ended the call and went to the kitchen to rummage in the fridge for a carrot or two.

He passed the dining room. "I have to go on a run to the Golden ranch," he said. "Will you two be okay?"

"Yes, just fine." Sara didn't look up. Her no-nonsense independence rankled. She didn't need him. She never had.

"Is my gun still in your car?" he asked.

"Sorry," she said, her glance a little sheepish. "I forgot to give it back yesterday. I'll get it."

"Is your car locked?"

She shook her head.

"I'll get it myself."

Rem checked his vet bag, then left the house. After he secured his rifle back in his Jeep, he drove to the Golden ranch.

When he entered the yard, Max met him in front of the stables and nodded. "Thanks for coming."

They shook hands and man-hugged, slapping each other on the back.

Old enough to be Rem's father, Max was a good friend, had taken Rem under his wing since Dad's death. He'd stood by Rem when he'd needed someone to talk to, to advise him.

Max was big, handsome with the gold skin and high cheekbones of his Native American ancestry, a hands-on rancher, and a recovering alcoholic. Rem couldn't be prouder of him. Max had fought the hard fight and had won. As far as Rem knew, Max had been sober for a while, close to a year if he had to guess.

"What's the problem?" Rem asked.

"Maggie's got ticks and the hands are all out on the range. I don't have time to take care of her. Can you do it?"

Ticks? Stunned, Rem asked, "You're going to pay me

vet's wages to clean Maggie?" Max was out of his mind to pay a vet to do a ranch hand's job.

"Yup."

"I can't charge you full price. I'll discount it."

Max pointed a stern finger at Rem. "You will not. I'm paying full fee."

"Is she the only one affected?" Rem stood in the doorway to the stable.

"Yup."

"Let's keep it that way. Put apple cider in the drinking water for all of the horses, including in their troughs. Make sure the others don't get it."

"Good idea. I'm heading into town in a minute. I'll pick some up."

Rem approached Maggie's stall and Max followed. "Hey, girl." She nudged his shoulder, remembering him from previous visits. He pulled a carrot out of his pocket and fed it to her.

There wasn't a single veterinary task that Rem was above doing, no matter how messy or dirty, but ridding an animal of ticks wasn't rocket science. Any ranch hand could do it.

He checked out Maggie's mane and hide. "She has ticks, all right."

"How's your ma, Rem? She going to be okay?"

"She's good. Came home this morning."

Max started. "I didn't know. Go on back home. You can do this another day. I only called 'cause I thought you could use the work. Didn't know you'd have Nell to take care of."

So, this was a pity call. Like a bad case of acid reflux, shame backed up in Rem's chest. Man, he shouldn't have told Max how worried he was about Ma's hospital bills.

"Sara's with Ma right now."

"Sara's home?"

"For good."

"I bet Adelle's thrilled about that." Max blushed.

Well, well, well, what was going on between Max and Sara's mother? As far as Rem knew, Max didn't date anyone. His wife had been dead for fifteen years or so, though. Was Max finally ready to move on?

"I gotta go," Max said, and left the stable. A minute later, Rem heard his car drive off.

"Come on, Maggie," Rem said. "Let's get started."

He led her to a corral behind the stable where he tried to put on a pair of rubber gloves. His bandaged hands wouldn't go in. He'd need his fingers free to work properly.

He unwound the bandages. The gloves abraded his palms, but there was nothing he could do about that other than to pad each glove with the gauze to cushion the burns.

When he was ready, he combed ticks out of Maggie's mane and tail, gently pulling insects out of her skin.

He filled a trough with a garden hose, added antiseptic and gave the mare a bath.

After washing her thoroughly, he rinsed her with cold water from the hose then brushed her coat until it shone.

She preened in the sun.

"You like the attention, don't you, girl?"

He checked her mane and tail again and found nothing. The brushing and bath should have rid her of the problem.

This was what he loved, making a living handling animals. It filled him with a sense of accomplishment.

At the end of Max's driveway, he leaned out of his driver's window and folded an invoice into Max's mailbox before driving home to his ranch.

When he got back to the ranch, Sara's car was gone and a different one sat in its place. He ran into the house.

Inside, he rushed into the dining room and found Ma awake. A middle-aged woman bustled around the room efficiently. Alice Betts. He recognized her from Ma's church. Good. Someone she knew.

At his entrance, Alice said, "Hi, Rem. I'll be here until Sara returns tonight to get Nell ready for bed."

Rem wondered at the niggling disappointment that Sara wasn't there. So what? He really didn't want her here, anyway.

SARA PUT PLATES OF OMELETS onto the table. Finn picked up a fork and dug in.

She and Mama had taken a few bites of their lunch when the front doorbell rang.

Finn jumped out of his seat to answer it.

"Sit, please," Sara said. "Eat your lunch. I'll answer the door."

Max Golden stood on the other side of the screen door. What on earth was he doing here?

She opened the door and invited him in.

"Max, what a surprise. Can I help you with something?"

He removed his cowboy hat and worried the brim with his fingers while his cheeks turned red.

"Is your mom home? Could I talk to her?"

"Sure. Mama, Max Golden is here to see you."

Mama stepped out of the kitchen and approached with a soft smile. She fingered the chain around her neck that Papa had given her a long time ago and blushed. Mama did everything softly, prettily. It was one of the reasons everyone loved her.

Without preamble, Max said, "It's been a year, Adelle."

"A year already?" Mama asked.

Intimacy sizzled between the two and Sara found herself *de trop*. She returned to the kitchen, but could still hear what Mama and Max were saying. There was nowhere for her and Finn to go where they wouldn't hear without walking back out into the hallway.

"Already for you, maybe," she heard Max say. "Felt like a lifetime to me."

A year for what?

"Can we try again?" he asked, and Sara thought, *Try* what *again?*

"Mom," Finn said. "You shouldn't be listening."

"You're right." She started eating and tried hard not to listen. When she heard Max ask, "Tonight?" she knew she had to make noise so she couldn't eavesdrop. "What do you do in your notebook, Finn?"

"Just sketch stuff."

"What kind of stuff?"

He shrugged. "Just stuff."

A year ago, he would have chattered about any of his interests, but now he was as closed to her as his sketch-book was.

Sara heard Mama shut the front door. A second later, Mama entered the kitchen with bright red cheeks.

"Mama, what's going on?"

Mama lifted her shoulders in a delicate shrug. "I have a date on Friday night." When she left the room, Sara ran after her.

"With Max? When did this start?"

"Last spring. But he was drinking. You know I don't like that."

With Mama's experience with Papa, why would she?

Mama leaned close and whispered, "He joined AA. He hasn't had a drink in a year."

"For you?" Sara gasped.

"For me."

Sara hugged her. "Oh, Mama, I'm so happy for you. You deserve to have a man adore you."

"Thank you, sweetheart." Mama walked upstairs, apparently forgetting that her lunch sat on the table.

Sara watched her go, wondering about the ache constricting her heart. It took her a minute, but she eventually figured out her problem.

I am jealous of my own mother.

Satisfied that Ma's care was being handled capably by Alice, Rem drove his SUV to Ordinary and parked on Main Street.

With a hunk of worry riding shotgun, he headed toward the newspaper office.

Ma's hospital bills were sizable and he had two salaries to pay—Sara's and Alice's. He needed money. Lots of it. More than he would make on the occasional visits to Max's ranch to rid his horses of ticks.

He needed to tame horses. That's where the good money was.

He scrubbed his hands down his face, hurting the burns on his palms.

He had to take out an ad in the *Ordinary Citizen.*

Rem stepped into the newspaper office.

After last summer's regression into his adolescent ways, a lot of people had still called him to work their animals. Others, though, had started using Pete McVitie from over in Haven. He had to convince them to come back to him.

Angel Donovan stood behind the counter reading the latest issue of her husband's paper.

"Hey, Angel," he said, glad to see her. After all of the trials Timm's life had presented him, Timm had finally found happiness with Angel.

"Hey, yourself," Angel said. "Where've you been, stranger?"

His gaze dropped to Angel's belly and he smiled.

"Lord. You're ready to pop any minute."

Angel propped one elbow on the counter and returned his smile easily. "Yep, someday soon we'll be heading to the hospital."

"I want to take out an ad. Can you do that for me or should I talk to Timm?"

"He's in the back room," Angel said. "I'll get him."

She waddled off and a minute later Timm appeared in the doorway. The top two buttons of his shirt were open, showing some of his burn scars. So he was no longer ashamed. Angel's influence, no doubt. Good. He used to be adamant about hiding them. Fortunately, the fire hadn't reached his face.

Rem set aside twinges of useless guilt and pointed to the paper spread out on the counter. "Can I take out an ad?"

"Sure." Timm took a form out of a drawer and handed it over.

Rem explained his problem.

"Do you want to advertise for vet work," Timm asked, "or for horse training?"

"Both."

"Okay. Let's keep it simple."

Between the two of them, they came up with ad copy.

Veterinarian and horse training work needed. I'm the best around. Am reliable and responsible. You need me. Remington Caldwell.

With that settled and paid for, Rem left town.

When he got home, he headed to the barn and fell onto

a bale of hay, resting his elbows on his knees and his head in his hands.

All he'd ever wanted in life was to handle animals, to train them and to heal them when they were sick.

Well, what he really wanted was to be the carefree spirit he had been before Timm's eleventh birthday party, but that was never going to happen.

All he could do now with Dad gone and Ma sick was hang on, to do his best. He was already trying so bloody hard; but what if he couldn't get enough people to trust him?

As if sensing his mood, Gracie appeared at his knee. Animals were great barometers of their owner's emotions. She licked his hand and sat carefully.

"You stiff?" he asked his ancient collie. "Arthritis bothering you?"

He scratched her ears and she closed her eyes.

"You're looking ragged."

Rem retrieved a brush from the far wall and brushed Gracie until she shone. He could pet an animal for hours and never grow tired.

At the burble of a car engine in the yard, Gracie's head came up.

Rem stood and walked to the open doorway.

Sara. She entered the house without noticing him.

He trudged across the yard and tiptoed into the house. Peeking into the dining room, he found her beside Ma's bed, talking quietly with Alice about Ma's care. She wore pink nurse's scrubs. She was stopping in before her shift at the hospital, even though Alice was on duty.

Her worry for Ma was sincere. Despite his resistance, it was right that she was here for Ma.

Pink looked good on her. She'd put her hair up in some kind of tight bun, though, as usual. Too bad.

Rem tried to remember the last time he'd seen Sara with her hair down, but couldn't. It must have been years ago, when she was a kid.

But a memory arose, warm and fluid. The night they'd first slept together, when Finn had been conceived, she'd lain in the moonlight with her hair spread out around her on the blanket they'd brought with them to Still Creek.

Her hair had turned to soft gold in the pale light. Moonlight had gilded her bare skin. She hadn't been plain then. Or practical. Or no-nonsense. She'd been beautiful—a teenaged girl on the brink of womanhood. Rem had helped her along her journey that night.

When Sara noticed him in the doorway, she stepped forward, whispering because Nell still slept.

"Where did your bandages go?"

He'd forgotten about his hands. "I had to put on gloves to handle one of Max's horses this morning."

Taking antibiotic cream, gauze and tape out of her bag, she told him to wash and dry his hands well then join her on the veranda. He found her sitting on a wicker chair.

"Can you wrap my fingers separately? So I can still use them?"

She spread cream on his burns, taking her sweet time for a woman who prided herself on efficiency. Then she started to wrap his right hand in gauze, holding each finger delicately while she wrapped it. A soft sunset bloomed on her cheeks. So, she was affected by their closeness, too.

What an unholy mess.

What was this crazy dance they played? Why did it wreak havoc with every intention he'd ever had where Sara was concerned?

He was through with her, damn it.

She lifted his hand closer to her face to wrap the gauze around back and her warm breath caressed his wrist. With that ever so slight overbite, she worried her lower lip while she worked. He wanted to taste that mouth, nibble that lip himself.

None of that. He'd decided he wouldn't have any more to do with her. *Yeah, but you also didn't think you'd have to.*

While she worked, she said, "I'll try to stop in on Nell before I go to work every day." Her voice sounded unsteady.

"This is out of your way. Alice seems competent." He bit his lip, mirroring her actions, and she stared at his mouth. *Stop.*

As though she'd heard him, her gaze flew back to his hand. Cripes, she hadn't even finished one. He knew then exactly what was going on. On this veranda, at this moment, there was no Nell, no Finn, no Timm, just the two of them and she was taking advantage of this rare time and space.

He caught her peeking from under her lashes.

Yeah, he knew she also liked looking.

Why couldn't they be like this all the time?

She bit off a piece of tape, then started on the other hand.

Tomorrow, they would be enemies again because the fact remained that there *was* Finn and there *was* his mom and there *was* Timm. And the tragic accident that had left them all scarred.

Something seemed to stir on her face. Regret, perhaps, and sadness.

She finished his second hand too quickly, as if suddenly understanding that she was playing with fire.

She gathered up her supplies and stood with them jumbled in her palms, flattening the roll of tape in her grip.

When she drove off, Rem stared at the driveway long after the dust her car had stirred up settled back to earth.

CHAPTER SIX

AT A LITTLE PAST NINE, Sara returned to get Ma ready for the night. Alice had left at nine on the dot and Rem was sitting with Ma, keeping her company.

"I asked at the hospital to leave early. Otherwise I wouldn't get here until nearly eleven."

"Thanks," Rem said. "Is Finn already in bed?"

"Not this early." Sara moved around Ma's new first-floor bedroom with a lot less energy than she'd had earlier.

She'd been here first this morning and had then spent hours at the hospital. Rem knew how hard nurses worked.

He'd seen them maneuver the patients who couldn't move on their own, lifting and turning to bathe and dress them in clean gowns. Most of them weren't as small as Ma was these days.

For a tiny woman, Sara worked hard. Too hard. There were dark shadows under her eyes.

"Mama makes sure Finn gets ready for bed," she continued, yawning, "but he's allowed to stay up until I get home."

"Even if you get home late?" As hard as he tried, Rem couldn't quell his curiosity about the boy.

Sara shot him a look of exasperation. She didn't like him asking about Finn.

"Finn good boy?" Ma asked.

"Yes. Great." Sara tidied an already neat bedside table

and frowned. "Well, he used to be anyway. Now he's starting to become a teenager."

"Teenage boy. I 'member." Ma grimaced playfully, if a little grotesquely.

Sara grinned. "They're nothing but trouble."

"If you're going to talk about me as if I'm not here, I'm leaving." Rem crossed his arms over his chest and pouted, giving a good imitation of a sulky preteen. Ma laughed and his heart lifted.

Sara washed and dried Ma's face with warm water, then got out a toothbrush and toothpaste.

Feeling like a fifth wheel, Rem left the room.

Outside, he looked up at the early moon rising in the darkening sky and wondered what to do with this bit of spare time.

It was one thing to tell himself he was over Sara. It was another to stick around while she was in his house.

He got into his SUV and drove into Ordinary, but didn't get out on Main Street.

Last summer, he drank too much and too often in Chester's Roadhouse and had nearly been killed there.

It was now Chester's Bar and Grill. Chester and his new wife, Missy Donovan, ran a respectable restaurant. Missy was Timm's new mother-in-law. Rem's memories of that building weren't good, though, especially given his meeting with Sara at the Christmas party, and he drove by without stopping.

On the other side of town, he picked up speed and realized what was calling him. He wanted to visit the young girl he'd saved, and her pretty mother.

After driving out to Haven, he parked and entered the hospital.

"Hey, Rhonda," he said as he approached the nurses' station.

"Hi, Rem. Your mother make it home okay this morning?"

"She's good. Listen, can I see the little girl who got burned? Just for a couple of minutes?"

"Sure. She's still in ICU. Don't stay past ten, okay?"

"No problem."

As he walked away, she called, "Don't wake her if she's asleep."

"Got it."

He snuck into the room quietly. Melody was sleeping and Rem felt a dip in his energy. He'd been looking forward to seeing her more than he'd thought.

Her mother's bed was empty.

At a noise behind him, he turned and there she was in a wheelchair.

"Hi," he said quietly, as though he were in a chapel instead of a hospital room. "You out for a stroll?"

Timm Franck stepped into the room behind her.

"Hey, Timm. What are you doing here?"

"He's trying to interview me," Liz said. A frown marred her forehead. "I don't want to be interviewed."

"Rem, help me convince her," Timm said. "It's just a small local paper. The townspeople would love to know about Melody and Liz, where they're from, where they were heading when they had the accident."

"No. Please, no." Liz frowned. "I don't want to share all of that." Even more than just seeming unhappy, she looked scared.

"Timm." Rem's voice held a warning. Timm was a reporter, and a good one, but he needed to back off on this.

Timm's lips flattened, but he accepted Liz's decision with grace. "Fine. I understand."

He left the room.

Rem turned to Liz. "How's Melody doing?"

"Better than we'd first thought when we got here yesterday." Her eyes misted. "She's a fighter."

Liz tried to lever herself out of the wheelchair, but winced.

"Those ribs have got to be sore. Let me help you." Rem put an arm under her knees and the other across her shoulders and lifted her into the bed. She smelled like roses and felt like an enticing bundle of femininity.

After he got her settled, he stepped away, unnerved by that flash of physical awareness.

He shouldn't have come out here to act on his attraction to this woman. He couldn't do this right now. He needed to concentrate on Ma and making enough money to pay for Alice and Sara.

Thinking of Sara, he sobered and felt an odd quirk of guilt. That somehow he'd been unfaithful to her by being attracted to this warm woman.

Crazy thought.

He owed Sara no fidelity.

After saying good-night to Liz, he found Timm waiting for him at the hospital entrance.

"I'd love to know what's going on with that woman." Timm tapped his notebook with his pen.

"Your reporter instincts are kicking in?"

"Big-time. That woman's afraid of something. There's a story there."

"You need to respect her wishes, Timm. Don't go digging up dirt on her. Not every story needs to be told."

"I won't. I'll just do a straight report of the accident without background on the victims."

"Good." They headed to their vehicles.

On his way back from Haven, Rem called Sara to tell her he'd be there in a few minutes and she should head home to bed. He passed her at the end of his driveway.

She flashed her lights then scooted onto the highway into Ordinary. He honked and turned in.

10:15 p.m.

Ma slept soundly in her hospital bed.

Rem mounted the stairs and got ready for bed. He lay on his back, pillowing his head with his hands, and stared at the ceiling. Ma was home. Day One was over, and they'd all survived. Thank God.

God? Rem didn't know what he believed in, had maybe left all of that behind with childhood, but right now, he'd honor any deity who let his mother live for a few more years.

The next time he opened his eyes, the bedside clock said 3:00 a.m. He'd fallen asleep without realizing it. So what had woken him? There it was again, a sound so faint he couldn't identify it.

When he tried to sit up, his arms didn't respond. He'd been sleeping for four hours with his hands under his head. They were useless, fast asleep while his mind raced.

Downstairs, alone, Ma would be vulnerable if anyone decided to break in. Who would do that, though? This was rural, small-town America. Ordinary didn't experience a lot of crime.

Finally, his hands recovered enough that he could pull his pants on. He stood, swung his arms and bit back a curse when the blood rushed into them.

Stealthily, he crept downstairs then stopped when he heard a barely discernable voice.

"Help."

Ma!

He jumped down the last few stairs and ran barefoot into the dining room.

"Ma! What happened? What's wrong?"

"Pee! Now!"

Tossing clean towels and nightgowns from the dresser, he scrambled for the bedpan. "Where does Sara keep the damned thing?"

If Ma had an accident, he would be the one cleaning up and he just didn't think he could change Ma into a fresh nightgown.

"There," Ma shouted more forcefully than he'd heard her since this last stroke.

He turned on the lamp and looked where she pointed— to the bedside table—and grabbed the bedpan.

Handing it to her, he said, "I'll give you privacy," and hurried from the room to wait in the hall.

Shuffling, rustling noises came from the room and Rem imagined Ma throwing aside bedclothes and her gown to get the bedpan in place.

A moment later, he heard an odd groaning noise then thin screaming from deep in Ma's throat.

"Can't," she cried.

"Cover up, Ma. I'm coming in."

He rounded the corner into the room and stopped. With her left hand, Ma had managed to get the blankets thrown off and the pan as low as her stomach while her right arm lay useless beside her.

She hadn't even been able to pull up her nightgown.

"Help," she whispered, and Rem rushed to her side.

How stupid of him. He should have known she would need help. Idiot.

He rushed to her side and pushed the bedclothes to the foot of the bed. Grasping the hem of her nightgown, he drew it to her knees.

He hadn't seen her legs in years. Tiny veins covered them and her feet, the skin dry and nearly transparent.

Her legs were thin with disuse, the muscles flaccid. He remembered when they used to be strong, with firm calves. She'd always been a hard worker and had helped Dad with everything that needed to be done on the ranch.

He pulled the gown up to her thighs but stopped there. He hesitated and glanced at her face.

Her eyes pleaded with him, but he didn't know for what. For him to stop baring her? He couldn't do that. She had to go and he had to help her. Or for him to go fetch a woman to help her? He couldn't call Sara—or anyone for that matter—at three in the morning to come help Ma with this.

He picked up the pan from her stomach and gently inserted it between her legs. She flinched. No wonder. The metal was cold.

She opened her legs to accommodate it and Rem looked away. While he pulled Ma's gown up to where it wouldn't get wet, he studiously peered at a painting on the wall that some relative had painted a generation or two ago, of the house.

He tried to slide the pan under her, but she couldn't lift her butt high enough on her own to do it.

Rem stared at the image of a border collie—one of Gracie's ancestors, no doubt—and the corner of the barn that showed in the painting.

Ma should be allowed to preserve what little dignity she had left. Grasping a corner of her nightgown so he wouldn't touch her skin, he lifted her with one hand under her buttock. The barn used to be green. He hadn't remembered that. She was so light. He got the pan into place. The barn was white now. He threw a bedsheet over her and left the room to give her what little privacy he could.

In the hallway, Rem leaned back against the wall beside the dining room doorway and swiped one hand down his face.

His hands shook. How quickly Ma had become helpless. How easily.

He was crazy to keep her here. Sara was right. He should have put her into the convalescent home. That thought stuck in his throat like a lump of lard, though.

Bad enough that Ma had to be manhandled, exposed, by people who knew and loved her. But there was no way he'd leave her in some impersonal institution to be shoved around by strangers.

Rem filled his lungs with fresh determination and entered the room.

Ma's face was turned away from him, as though she, too, found that old painting fascinating.

Averting his gaze, Rem lowered the bedsheet and lifted the full pan away. He placed it carefully on the bedside table then pulled Ma's gown down past her knees. He covered her with blankets, including that functioning left hand that was curled into a white-knuckled fist, and tucked them in tenderly around her.

Tears leaked from the corners of her eyes. He'd never seen Ma cry. Stalwart, practical, unsentimental Ma was crying and he didn't know what to do about it.

He scrambled to turn off the bedside lamp to shade Ma's vulnerability and his own grief, both of them too exposed in this harsh landscape of illness and dependence.

Leaning forward, he skimmed his lips over her forehead with the briefest touch. "Love you, Ma."

He picked up the full bedpan and left the room, but not before Ma whispered, "You, too."

In the downstairs bathroom, Rem punched the wall. Where was the dignity? The pride? Where was the reward for having lived a full, productive life?

Ma'd been a good person all of her life, a hard worker who'd never complained, yet fate had pulled this rotten trick on her.

Rem cursed fate and God and whoever else was controlling this situation, then went to bed with a renewed determination to make Ma's life as comfortable as possible. And to find ways to make her happy.

Now or never.

Rem stood at the bottom of the stairs. Morning sunlight streamed in through the beveled glass panes beside the front door, shining rainbows on the hallway walls.

Sara would be stepping through that door soon to bathe Ma and get her ready for the day.

Before Sara arrived, though, Rem needed to tell Ma about Finn.

He hadn't gone back to sleep after helping Ma. Instead, he'd lain awake, trying to figure out how to lift her spirits and the only thing he came up with was telling her she had a grandchild.

Yeah, now was the right time. She would be ecstatic.

He entered the dining room.

Ma was already awake, staring at that painting, her jaw tight. Maybe she hadn't gone back to sleep, either.

"Hey, Ma."

She nodded, barely. She turned to look at him and the bleakness in her eyes stunned him. Now was definitely the time for good news.

Here goes.

He sat on the dining room chair he'd left in the corner in case of visitors.

"Ma, I have something to tell you."

He must have sounded serious because she watched him warily.

"It's good news," he blurted. "Real good."

She relaxed fractionally.

"You know Sara's son, Finn?"

"Yes."

Wow, this shouldn't be so hard, but the words stuck in his throat. This was huge. What if the shock made Ma worse? What if she had a heart attack? Were strokes and heart attacks related? If she were prone to one, would she be vulnerable to the other?

He'd already started, though, and she waited for his good news. No turning back now.

"When Sara's son, Finn, was born, Sara and I decided it would be best if we didn't tell people that I'm…that I'm his father."

Nell's eyes widened.

"You have a grandchild, Ma."

The nondroopy side of her face got real tight. The corner of her mouth turned white. She blinked, then blinked again.

"Finn yours?" She pointed toward him with her good hand.

He nodded.

With difficulty, she raised that hand to her chest.

"Mine? Grandchild?"

"Yes."

"Why you never tell me?" Damn. She was furious. He'd thought the news would make her happy.

"I didn't want people to know."

"Me. Why never tell me?" She slapped her chest. "Mine!"

"I thought I'd be a bad father. I would have screwed him up like I did everything else back then. I thought he'd be better off without me."

"Without me, too."

"I'm sorry, Ma. I never thought about how you would miss him. I only wanted to protect him from me."

"Want to see."

"I don't know if Sara will let him come to the ranch. She doesn't want to tell him about me."

"Want to see." Lord, how could one semiparalyzed woman sound so strong, so adamant?

"I'll ask Sara," he said, doubting it would ever happen.

"I *tell* Sara." She sounded determined. Maybe Ma could do the impossible.

"She doesn't want my son to have anything to do with me."

"Just me then."

"You can ask her, but she's stubborn."

As he left the room he muttered under his breath, "Almost as stubborn as you are."

Out at the stables, he hunkered down against the wall and pulled a cigarette out of his pocket. Smoking was the one bad habit he still hung on to. He hadn't been able to quit, especially in times of stress.

He was definitely stressed. That hadn't gone the way he'd expected. He'd been naive. Of course Ma would mourn the years of Finn's life she hadn't shared.

No matter what Rem did, he couldn't seem to stop screwing up.

He lit the cigarette and inhaled a lungful, the action calming, the smoke hot in his throat.

One of the barn cats came out of the stable and curled around his feet.

Sara's car appeared in the driveway. He thought of walking over to warn her about Ma's mood, but no. He was tired of taking the flak for everything that went wrong in her life—and his. He'd done it for too many years.

They'd both screwed up all those years ago when they'd made love and hadn't used protection. Let her face the music as he'd had to.

SARA GOT OUT OF HER CAR.

Rem crouched beside the stables in the shade, smoking, with a cat curling around his ankles. So, he still hadn't quit. He should have by now.

Watching her through narrowed eyes, he took a long hard draw on the cigarette held firmly between his index and middle fingers.

While she watched, he exhaled through pursed lips. Oh, those lips.

The smoke circled around his head like a wreath, hinting of sainthood. Ha!

A disgusting habit, smoking turned her off—totally— yet Rem made it look sexy.

He leaned one elbow on his knee and rested his thumb against his temple. A thin tendril of smoke drifted upward while he stared at her legs. The ghost of a smile kicked up the corner of his mouth. He sank his other fingers into the cat's fur. The cat just about turned herself inside out at his touch.

I know how you feel.

Rem looked like a saint, all right. A saint with decidedly unholy thoughts.

Leaving him to damage his lungs with nicotine and the eighty-one carcinogens in the cancer stick he held like a lover, she stepped into the house. Didn't matter to her if he killed himself.

Knowing herself too weak when around him, she had to stay well clear. Bandaging his hands yesterday had been murder.

She walked to Nell's room, smiling, because she always looked forward to seeing her.

Nell glared at her. What? Sara stopped on the threshold of the dining room without entering.

"Is everything all right?" she asked warily.

"You. Here." Nell pointed to the side of the bed, a dictator in a damaged body.

Feeling like a small girl caught in a lie, Sara approached the bed with caution.

"Why you not tell?" Nell said.

"What?" An uneasy feeling crawled up Sara's spine. Had Rem followed through on his threat?

"Finn."

Sara hung her head. It hadn't been her idea to hide Rem's parenthood, but she felt shame nonetheless. She'd worked hard over the years to maintain the fiction that Finn's father was a one-night stand.

While Sara had been lying, though, she'd unwittingly hurt a good friend in the process, robbing her of her grandchild for twelve years.

In a way, it was good to get it out in the open with Nell. Now she could set aside the guilt she carried.

"My grandchild." For a woman with half of her face frozen, Nell managed to convey an awful lot of disappointment.

"Yes," Sara said, giving in to the inevitable. "Finn is your grandchild."

"Want to see."

"He doesn't know that Rem is his father."

"Should." My goodness, Nell was furious.

"He can't."

"Yes."

"I can bring Finn to visit on one condition."

Sara could see that Nell knew the condition before she named it.

"No tell," Nell said.

"That's right. Do you promise you won't tell him that Rem is his father?"

Nell hesitated. "Then he can't call Grandma." She hit her chest with her fist. "I'm Grandma!"

"I know."

"Want to see."

Sara held firm. "Then do this for me."

Finally, Nell nodded. "'Kay."

"I have to work today, but I'll be off tomorrow. I'll bring him then."

"Good."

Sara helped Nell to go to the washroom, washed and changed her into a fresh nightgown, then started her leg exercises.

"Sara," Rem called from the doorway. He hooked his index finger in a "come here" gesture and she joined him in the hallway with the full bedpan.

"You told her," Sara said, her voice tight. Yes, Nell should have had a relationship with her grandson, the only grandchild she had, but the decision to tell her should have been both of theirs.

"I told her—" a hard edge to Rem's tone dared her to object "—because she had a bad night and I thought it would cheer her up."

"That didn't happen."

"No."

Sara didn't mention that she was bringing Finn with her on Thursday. She'd find a way to keep them apart while Finn was here.

He pointed to the bedpan Sara held so casually. "She had to go in the middle of the night. It was embarrassing having to help her. For both of us."

Sara nodded. "I can appreciate that. You both need to relax, though. It's just a fact of life."

"Yeah. How long will you be here?"

"About an hour. Why?"

"I need to run into Ordinary for a few things. I won't be gone longer than that."

She nodded, then walked to the bathroom to clean out the bedpan and then start on breakfast for Nell.

In Ordinary, Rem entered the only flower shop in town. The grocery store carried a few cheaper bouquets, but Rem wanted something really nice.

Ma deserved pretty things in her room. Even though Nell wasn't sentimental, Rem wanted her to have flowers anyway.

He looked at a dozen red roses. Beautiful, but too formal for Ma.

There were some big, blowsy pink flowers he'd never seen before, but they didn't suit Ma.

The birds of paradise with their aggressive spikes of color seemed too outspoken for her.

Finally, he found a small bunch of tight, pretty flowers in different dark primary colors. Contained and complete, they reminded him of his mother.

"What are these?" he asked Sharon, the owner of the shop.

"Primroses."

"I'll take 'em." He pulled his wallet out of his back pocket. "This the only bunch you have?"

"I have more, but I haven't made them into posies yet."

"Posies?"

"Small bouquets."

"Can you make me a couple more?"

"Sure. Mixed colors like that?"

"Let me see what you have."

He chose a bunch of bright yellow primroses for another posy. He didn't know whether Ma liked yellow, but he remembered a couple of yellow dresses she'd worn when he was younger and the color would spruce up the room.

Sharon made up a third posy of pink primroses.

Rem paid for them and left, feeling good. No way could he make up for keeping Finn a secret, but that's not what these were for anyway.

He drove back home and entered Ma's room. He heard Sara in the kitchen washing dishes.

"Ma, do we own anything to put these in?"

She glanced at the flowers and then at him with suspicion. "Why buy? Guilt?"

"No. I want to give you nice things."

She stared for a while then said, "Curio. Bottom shelf."

In the screened-in porch at the back of the house, Rem rummaged through the cabinet he'd moved there to accommodate Ma's bed in the dining room. He found two vases the right size and brought them to the kitchen to fill with water.

Sara had already left the kitchen. He heard her car start up and drive away.

He filled the two vases and a drinking glass and arranged the flowers in them. He put the yellow ones on the windowsill to catch and reflect the sunlight. The pink ones went on the dresser. The multicolored posy went on the bedside table to partly obscure that offensive bedpan.

He glanced at Ma. She was asleep. Or was she? Her eyelids flickered.

Rem left the room, but stayed in the hallway for a minute. He peeked around the corner. Ma's eyes were open and staring at the primroses beside the bed. She reached out her good hand to touch them and managed to snag one out of the bunch. She wrapped her fingers around it and dropped her hand to her chest.

She closed her eyes and, for the first time since coming home yesterday, looked at peace.

CHAPTER SEVEN

SARA STOPPED OFF AT THE newspaper offices her family owned to touch base with Timm. Angel was due to give birth any day now.

Timm stood behind the counter, talking to a pair of cowboys Sara didn't recognize. They looked like father and son.

"I need to get a horse tamed," the older man said.

"Remington Caldwell's the best around," Timm responded. "No need to advertise. Call Rem. Here's his number." Timm jotted down a phone number on a slip of paper and handed it to the man.

Sara smiled. Could she somehow use this to her advantage? "My brother's right," she said, and the men turned to her. Definitely father and son.

"Yeah?" The son's smile echoed the father's. "Is he some kind of horse whisperer?"

"You could say that."

"Mare's pretty wild," the younger one said.

"Rem can handle her."

"Wonder if he could start today. The sooner the better."

Sara got an idea. A really, really good one. It was dishonest, but so what? She needed *something* to work in her favor for a change.

Before Sara could change her mind, she said, "Well, I know for a fact he's busy today." *Liar, liar, pants on fire. You don't know any such thing.* "He's available all day tomorrow, though." *I hope.* "I'm sure he'd be happy to come out to your ranch then."

She could take Finn out to visit Nell without having him exposed to Rem. Perfect.

"What do you think, Jake?" the father asked. "I'll be running errands all day tomorrow. Will you be around to show him the horse?"

"No problem," Jake responded.

"I'll call him as soon as we get to the ranch."

They doffed their hats to Sara.

"Thanks."

"Appreciate the info."

"Welcome to the county," Timm said. He waited until the cowboys left, then turned to Sara with narrowed eyes. "What are you up to?"

Sara put on her best innocent face. "Nothing. Just helping Rem."

"I don't believe you."

Sara shrugged and kept her mouth shut. Rem would be away from the ranch on Thursday. She'd get Finn out there for a couple of hours and then scoot him back home before Rem returned.

"I'm not going to get the truth out of you, am I?"

"Nope." Sara grinned.

The phone rang and Timm answered. Judging by his responses, the conversation had to do with a problem in town. Last summer, Timm had been elected mayor of Ordinary. As far as Sara knew, he did the job well. People respected her brother.

When he hung up, she asked, "How's Angel?"

Sara couldn't wait to be an aunt.

"Ready to pop any minute. She had a lot of Braxton-Hicks contractions last night. That doesn't mean much, but she's tired today."

"Is she at home?"

Timm nodded. "I made her promise she'd nap today."

"Good. I'm going to talk to Mama again. She should be at the hospital when the baby is born."

"Good luck with that. She still hasn't warmed to Angel."

"I know, but I don't get why Angel's reputation as a teenager bothers Mama so much now."

Timm's eyes flickered away from her, as though he were hiding something.

With a healthy dose of suspicion, she asked, "What haven't you told me?"

"It's too outlandish—a little nuts on Mama's part."

"*What* is?"

"At one time she thought Papa was infatuated with her and might have done something about it."

"Angel *slept* with our father?"

"God, no! Don't be creepy. I asked her about Papa once and she never even knew he had a crush on her. I think it was just something Ma suspected."

"I'll talk to Mama and see what I can do."

Sara turned to leave the office.

"Sara?"

She pivoted back. "Yes?"

"That woman in the hospital and her daughter? Do you know anything about them?"

"Not much. Why?"

"They don't know anyone in town. I found out last night that the only visitor they've had is Rem. No cards. No flowers. Liz said her daughter's been really low. Depressed. We should do something for them."

"I'm working today. I'll go down to visit on my dinner hour."

"I'd go back in to visit, but I'd only make Liz tense.

She's afraid I'm going to write an article with too much of her personal information in it."

Sara's spirits lifted. Finn couldn't take any classes because of his wrist, but he could do a good deed at the hospital. He could spend time with Melody and stay out of trouble. She could kill more than one bird with this stone.

"I'll get Finn to visit the girl," she said. "They're close to the same age. Tell Angel I said hi."

She left the office with a renewed sense of purpose.

In the past, Sara hadn't been fond of Angel. Since Timm married her last summer, though, Sara had made the effort and it had been worth it. Angel was proving to be a great wife, seemed to be as crazy about Timm as he was about her. If only Mama would come around.

Time to convince Mama to give Angel a chance. Like that would go smoothly. Mama could be stubborn. So stubborn.

Sara marched into the house.

Mama and Finn were in the kitchen, Mama playing a game of solitaire, and Finn bent over his sketchbook—two people in the same room, but in their own private bubbles. Last summer, Finn would have been playing cards with his oma, but he'd been withdrawing from all of them.

Sara stepped into the kitchen. "Hi."

Mama immediately stood to help her make lunch.

Finn grunted and kept working on whatever the secret project was in his sketchbook.

Sara kissed the top of his head, and he bent forward to cover his sketch. Sara knew he drew cartoons, but that was the extent of her knowledge. Finn used to share everything with her.

She got a whiff of sweat. Her little boy was becoming a man.

"When was the last time you showered?"

Finn shrugged. "I dunno."

"March upstairs right now and don't come down until you're clean."

"Aw, for Pete's sake." Finn slammed his sketchbook shut and stomped out of the room, making sure to tuck the book under his arm and take it with him.

Not that Sara would have peeked if he'd left it on the table. Who was she kidding? Sure she would. She was dying to know what her son was working on.

"Wait a minute," she called, and ran into the hallway with a plastic bag and tape. She covered his cast and taped it until it was watertight.

Finn ran upstairs.

She pulled sandwich fixings out of the fridge.

"Mama, I stopped off and saw Timm. Angel's going to have the baby soon."

Mama shrugged, but Sara wasn't fooled. She saw her reluctant interest.

"How soon?"

"Any day."

"What does that have to do with me?"

"Mama, Angel is a good person. She makes Timm happy."

"Men are easily swayed by sex." Such derision in her tone.

"Oh, for God's sake, Mama, it's more than just sex. They love each other. Angel's reputation is ancient history. She was a wild teenager, yeah, but she's different now."

"How do you know?"

"I've gotten to know her. I like her. Timm's a smart guy. You should trust his judgment."

"He married her without my blessing." Through a crack in Mama's veneer, her hurt showed. They used to be close, but Timm had distanced himself from Mama after marrying Angel. "What kind of son does that? He married her without me at his wedding."

"You were invited," Sara murmured softly. "You chose not to attend."

Mama slathered too much mustard on a sandwich, tearing the bread, but remained silent.

"Mama, are you sure Papa had a crush on Angel?"

Mama dropped the knife to the counter and it slid into the sink. The noise echoed in the suddenly quiet room.

"I—I don't know for sure."

"Maybe it was your imagination. Papa loved you. Why would you even suspect that?"

"All of the men in town liked that girl."

"Come on, Mama. That doesn't mean Papa did. Did he tell you that?"

"No. We just had some…problems for a while. That girl worked in the store beside the newspaper office."

"That's it? That's your proof? Oh, Mama, that's unreasonable."

Mama shrugged. "Maybe."

"Timm says Angel never even knew Papa had a crush on her."

"She could be lying."

"Or maybe she's telling the truth. I can't believe you're going to have a grandchild you won't even get to know."

Mama still didn't answer and Sara gave up. Damn stubborn woman.

Finn returned to the kitchen with wet hair and smelling of the spray deodorant Sara hated. But it was trendy so of course Finn wanted it. She braced herself for the next confrontation on her list.

After she cut the bag away from Finn's cast, Sara left the room and phoned Randy at the hospital. She made arrangements with him to drive Finn home at the end of his shift, then returned to the kitchen.

"Finn, you're coming to the hospital with me today."

"What?" He sounded outraged. She almost smiled. "Why?"

"Just for a couple of hours, to visit that girl who was hurt in the accident the other day."

"Why?"

"Because she and her mother don't know anyone in town. She was in a bad accident. She nearly died and she's depressed. It would be good for her to spend time with someone her own age."

"Aw, Mo-om."

"It won't be for all afternoon and evening. Randy will drive you home."

When Finn didn't respond, she asked, "Did you have plans?"

Reluctantly, he shook his head.

"It's settled then. We'll leave after lunch."

An hour and a half later, Sara led Finn into the intensive care unit at the hospital, every bit as determined to get him in there as he was determined not to be there.

"Put yourself in her shoes," she coaxed. "She's a stranger. She doesn't know anybody. She's lonely and scared."

Finn shrugged her hand off his shoulder.

"Treat her well. Okay?"

"Okaaayyy." Like a giant put-upon two-year-old, he sighed and entered the ICU.

FINN DIDN'T LIKE hospitals. They smelled and they were boring—when they weren't scary.

This one smelled like all the others. He was okay when he had to sit in the waiting room—no big deal. But here in the ICU, it smelled like they used really heavy-duty cleaners.

He wondered what odors they were trying to cover. Blood? Vomit? It creeped him out.

Couldn't they at least spray something pretty to make it smell better?

The room the girl—Mom said her name was Melody—was in wasn't as bright as the hallway, and Finn stopped inside the door to let his eyes adjust.

Melody was sitting up in her bed with a big white bandage wrapped around her head, watching him and his mom. She didn't look curious, just tired. And really pale. Except for the dark circles under her eyes.

Mom went to talk to the woman in the other bed. He recognized her as Melody's mother, the one who was on the road when they came to the accident.

One side of her face was all bruised.

Finn stepped to Melody's bed before Mom could tell him to. She'd probably go ape-shit if he didn't. He shoved his hands deep into his pockets, squeezing his arm against his side so his sketchbook wouldn't fall.

He had a deck of cards in his back pocket. Mom said he should teach her how to play Polish poker. Lame.

He used to play with Oma last summer, but he was too old for that now.

Mom said he should play it with Oma again this year while Mom was at work, but Finn just wanted to sketch and listen to music. What was so wrong with that? Why did Mom have to get mad about it?

The girl watched him.

He stopped at the end of her bed. "Hey," he said.

"Hey," she answered. "Who are you?"

"Finn." He gestured with his chin toward his mom in her nurse's uniform. "She's my mom."

"She works in the hospital. Why are you here?"

Finn watched his mom wave and leave the room. "She thought you were getting bored." He had no idea how long he was supposed to stay here.

"I am." She pointed to his wrist. "What happened?"

"I broke it skateboarding."

"Does it hurt?"

"Not right now. Look." He pointed to the only signature on his cast. "You know Rem, the guy who saved you? He signed it here."

"Hey, that's awesome." She smiled. "I like his devil's face."

"Does your head hurt?"

"Yeah. They have to give me lots of meds."

Finn pulled the deck of cards out of his pocket and tossed them onto the food tray beside the bed. "My mom thought maybe you'd like to play cards." He shrugged as if he didn't care what she decided. "We can play if you want."

"Do you know how to play poker?"

"Melody," her mother said, and she didn't sound happy.

"Mom. I'm really bored. Why can't I have fun?"

"You're too young for poker."

"Not for Polish poker," Finn said. "I've been playing with my grandma since I was a kid. There's no betting or anything."

"See, Mom?" Melody said. "It's okay. Show me."

It sounded like she was ordering him to play. Finn didn't like that. "You're bossy."

"I am not."

Her mother laughed. "Yes, you are, Melody. You always have been."

"I'll show you how to play," Finn said, "but only 'cause I want to. Not because you're *telling* me to."

"Whatever." She motioned him to come closer, pulling the tray in front of her.

"Sit on the bed," she said, and Finn did, with the tray between them.

He dealt the cards and taught her the rules of the game. She liked it, but couldn't pick up the cards because of the bandages on her hands and wrists. She could hold them, though, so he picked up any cards she needed and passed them to her.

Finn hadn't played since last year. He'd forgotten it was fun. Maybe he *should* play with Oma again.

Melody seemed to get tired fast.

"How old are you?" she asked.

"I'll be twelve in nine days. You?"

"Almost twelve, too. My birthday's in September."

"Really?" She was eleven? She looked about nine years old, but she acted older. "How come you're so small?"

She frowned. Man, he shouldn't have blurted that out.

"I was born with a hole in my heart."

"Really?"

She nodded and didn't look very happy. Crap. He was supposed to be making her feel better, not worse. Mom would kill him if she found out.

"That's cool. I've never met anyone before who had that."

"You think it's cool?"

"Uh-huh."

"I had it fixed when I was little, but I'm still smaller than most kids my age."

She looked a bit better, but she kept squinting.

"Does your head hurt now?" he asked.

She nodded. "It's too soon for more meds, though."

Finn needed to distract her fast. "I saw Rem pull you out of the car, you know."

She sat up. "You did?"

"Yeah. Your hair was on fire. He put it out with his hands. He was awesome."

"I want to meet him."

"My mom knows him."

"She does? Maybe she could bring him in one day."

Finn puffed out his chest. "I know him, too. I'll ask him."

"He was here last night, honey," her mom said. "You were already asleep."

"Were you scared in the car?" Finn asked.

"Yeah, really scared."

They were quiet for a while.

"What's in there?" she asked, pointing to his sketchbook.

"Nothing." He shrugged. "Just some sketches."

"Did you do them?"

"Yeah."

"Can I see them?"

Finn's throat got tight. She might not like them. Maybe she would think they were stupid.

"Please?" Melody said. She'd gotten kinda "up" when they played cards, but she was looking low again.

He opened the book to the first page and held his breath. If she laughed or made fun, he was walking out of here, even if Randy wasn't finished work yet and couldn't drive him home. He'd rather sit in the waiting room for an hour than stay here with a girl who thought his drawings were stupid.

Something that could have been excitement flickered in her eyes. "Wow," she said. "*You* drew this?" It looked as though she really liked it.

"Yeah."

"You're good. Show me more. Tell me what it's all about. Is it a story?"

"Yeah, about a bad guy and a princess and the hero who saves her from the bad guy."

"No way! She has to save herself. That's what girls do. They don't wait for boys to take care of them. Tell me the whole story."

He did. After he described what the princess was like, she shouted, "She would totally save herself."

She was so excited, Finn grinned. "Yeah, I guess she could. I should change it so she does."

Melody leaned back against her pillow. She looked tired, but happy. She smiled at him and he smiled back.

"Can I sign your cast?" she asked.

He handed her one of the pencils from his back pocket. She had trouble holding it, though, and looked like she was about to cry.

"Here," he said. "Hold it like this and just do a smiley face like Rem did." He wrapped her fist around the pencil, the way a little kid would hold it.

She smiled. Even with the bandages on her head, she was cute. She drew a circle, then added eyes and a cat's nose and mouth. She added two big ears that were attached to each other and he realized it was a big *M* for Melody. He grinned.

He had a new friend, his first one in Ordinary.

CHAPTER EIGHT

On Thursday morning, Rem couldn't believe his good fortune. Yesterday afternoon, a man had phoned, someone new to the area, wanting to hire him to work with a difficult horse.

At first when he'd received the call, Rem had thought the ad was paying off already; but, no, Timm had recommended him. His buddy had come through for him.

"Ma," he said, "I won't be gone long. I'm picking up a horse to tame. The trailer's already hooked up to the Jeep." He made a point of training horses here at his own ranch, so he could work around his vet calls.

Nell peered through the archway to the living room and through the front window, anticipation clear in her eyes. "Sara?"

She seemed awfully keyed up about seeing Sara today. "She called to say she'd be about twenty minutes late." He tucked his fingers under Ma's armpits and lifted her to a sitting position, adjusting the bed for comfort.

"Is that good? Are you comfortable?"

"Yes."

Ma had called him down in the middle of the night again to go pee. Apparently, she'd been calling for a couple of hours.

"On the way back, I'll stop in town for a baby monitor. Then we won't have to worry about my not hearing you during the night."

"I'm not baby."

"I know, Ma, but you have to admit it's a good solution."

Nell graced him with one of her shallow nods.

Rem plucked a dead blossom from the primroses beside the bed and tossed it into the trash.

He was antsy to be on his way, to get started with the horse. "I gotta go. The rancher's son is only there for the morning. I don't want to miss him."

"When Sara here? Time?"

Rem glanced at his watch. "It's twenty after eight, so probably a little past eight-thirty. You won't be alone for more than ten or fifteen minutes. Okay?"

"Yes."

Rem turned to leave, but Ma's good hand plucked his sleeve. "Want to go there."

She pointed to the living room.

"You want me to carry you to the sofa? I'm not sure your back is strong enough to support you on the couch."

"Not sofa. Bed. There."

"You want me to move the bed to the living room? Why?"

"Two windows. Can watch."

She would be closer to the front window to see whoever came and went. But she would also have the side window, directly across from the corral. She wanted to watch him tame the horse.

Oh, Lord. Rem felt prickles behind his eyes and in his sinuses. Years ago, before he'd left for college, whenever he worked with horses Ma used to take time out of her busy days to lean on the corral fence and watch him sweet-talk wild or difficult animals.

Now, Rem was doubly glad he'd insisted on bringing the mare home with him.

He answered her earlier request. "Sure. I'll take care of that later. You have everything you need?"

"Yes."

Rem ran out of the house to his Jeep where the horse trailer he'd hooked up last night waited to be filled.

He drove slowly down the lane, studying the ravaged fields on either side.

Yesterday, he'd cleaned out the manure pile behind the stable and had spread it over those burned fields.

Nature had a reservoir of strength for which humans rarely gave her credit. Sooner or later, something was going to sprout—probably nothing more than hardy perennial weeds. As soon as he knew the soil was viable, he'd pull the weeds, spread seed and start again.

Rem felt a lifting of his spirits. The land did that to him. It would heal, as would Ma, and life would be good again.

WHEN SARA FELT FAIRLY certain Rem would have left for the other ranch, she herded Finn into the car and drove out of town.

"I don't understand why I hafta see this old woman." Finn had been complaining to her all morning—first, for waking him up so early and, second, for making him come to the Caldwell ranch with her—and Sara was tired of it already.

"She's bedridden and bored. Having a visitor will be good for her."

"Why does it have to be me? I visited Melody yesterday. Why can't I just hang out at Oma's today?"

Sara's frayed nerves were taking a beating. *She* didn't want Finn on the Caldwell ranch and *he* didn't want to go, so why was she putting them both through this?

Maybe coming back to Ordinary had been a mistake

after all. The longer she was here, the more frustrated she became.

She shouldn't have volunteered to tend to Nell in the first place; but, really, how could she not? She loved Nell.

Before she'd given birth to Finn, she'd thought she was the luckiest girl on earth to have a great mother, and soon a mother-in-law who she already liked so much.

Then the dream had crumbled when Rem had walked out on her and her baby. Now Sara was involving her son with that family and she was terrified of Rem's every move.

At least he wouldn't be here today.

Time to introduce Finn to the woman he would never know was his grandmother.

As soon as they entered Nell's room and Sara saw the older woman's eyes light avidly on Finn, she knew she'd done the right thing in bringing him. Nell ate up her grandson with a greedy gaze chronicling every detail about him, from his too-long hair to the jeans that sat low on his hips and hung over his shoes, the hems threadbare from rubbing on the ground.

"Come here," she ordered, and Finn looked at his mom.

Sara whispered, "Go ahead."

Finn stepped into the room.

"Closer," Nell said, clearly frustrated by her own inability to speak complete sentences.

Finn didn't flinch, though, and stepped up to the bed.

"Sit."

Finn pulled a dining room chair close to the bed.

Nell studied him while he sat with a wary expression. "How old?"

"Eleven," Mr. Talkative answered.

Oh, Finn, give an inch.

"When twelve?" Nell plucked at the bedsheet with her

good fingers and Sara realized the woman was both excited and nervous. She hadn't considered how Nell would feel today. Had only worried about Finn.

"Nine days."

Wow, two words.

"What you do on birthday?"

Finn shrugged and looked at his mom.

She shook her head. "We haven't made plans yet." She'd thought she might take him to a movie in Monroe and then out for a burger.

"Here," Nell said.

What did Nell mean?

"Really? We can have a party here?"

Nell nodded.

Wow, Finn had understood her?

Thoughtfully, he said, "Sick."

"Sick?" Nell frowned.

"That means cool," Finn responded, and Nell's frown faded. "Are there horses?" he asked.

"Yes. You ride?"

"No, but I want to. I was supposed to start lessons the other day, but then I broke my wrist."

"How?"

"Skateboarding."

Nell nodded. "You ride at party."

"Amazing."

Sara stepped into the room. "Nell, are you sure about this?" Rem would be there. No. She didn't want that. But Finn looked happy and Nell looked happy, and what Sara wanted didn't seem to matter anymore.

"Yes, have here."

With her left hand, she pointed toward the front door.

"You," she said to Finn, "go see Rusty. Horse. In stable."

"Can I, Mom?"

"Sure."

"Only couple minutes," Nell said.

"Cool." Finn ran out of the house.

"Pee. Now."

Sara helped her with the bedpan, then cleaned and washed her for the day. She changed her into a fresh nightgown.

"These flowers are so pretty," Sara said. "Did someone send them to you?"

"Rem buy for me."

"Rem?"

Nell watched her steadily. "He good man. Has good heart."

For the next fifteen minutes, Sara helped Nell with her arm and leg exercises, all the while glancing at those flowers. So thoughtful. So loving.

Once, she'd heard someone say that the way to tell what kind of husband a man would be was to watch the way he treated his mother. Sara shook that foolish thought out of her head.

When Nell showed signs of flagging, Sara said, "I'm going to throw in a load of laundry. Do you want to lie on your side for a while?"

"Yes."

Once Sara had helped her into position, Nell seemed to have recovered some strength. "Call Finn back," she ordered.

"Okay." Sara went out to the veranda. "Finn!"

He ran out of the stable, his expression more animated than Sara had seen in a while.

"Wow, great horse, Mom."

Finn entered the sick room and Sara followed him to gather together Nell's dirty laundry.

"What you do?" Nell asked Finn.

"I'm in school. Seventh grade in September."

"No. There." She gestured toward the sketchbook in Finn's hands.

"Drawing."

"Want to see."

Sara held her breath. Would Nell accept a no? Finn hadn't even shown his oma what he was up to.

"I don't show it to no one."

Sara grimaced. Finn used to have good grammar. Where was he getting all of these bad habits?

"Anyone," Nell said.

"Yeah, I don't show it to anyone."

"Show me."

Finn looked at his mom. Sara shook her head. She wouldn't force him to do it. He had a right to his privacy.

"Please," Nell said.

Finn shrugged. "Sure," he said and Sara's jaw dropped.

He opened the sketchbook to the first page and Nell stared at the drawing. Sara had no idea what he'd been sketching and couldn't see it from her vantage point, but Nell was captivated by it.

With her left hand, Nell touched the page. "Who that?"

"Andivort."

"Who Andivort?"

"He's the evil wizard."

Evil wizard?

Nell touched the page again. "Who?"

"Lady Serena. She's the girl the wizard wants, 'cause she's beautiful and smart, but she hates the wizard and calls him names."

Finn was writing a story?

He turned the page and said, "This is Sir Jon. He'll rescue Lady Serena from Andivort's castle."

"No." Nell wagged her finger. "Save self."

Finn grinned, and Sara's mouth fell open again. For months, his facial expressions had all been negative—disinterest, anger, sullenness.

"Yeah, that's what Melody said, too."

He'd shown his drawings to Melody? And now Nell? Sara was his mother—why didn't *she* rate?

"She said no way would she wait around for some guy to spring her. She'd beat up the wizard, or she'd use her brains to escape somehow."

"Smart girl."

"Yeah, she's pretty cool."

"She sick?"

Finn laughed. "Yeah, she's sick."

"Who is she?"

"Melody?" After Nell's shallow nod, Finn said, "She's the girl from the accident, the one who got burned."

"She *really* sick?"

"Yeah. She's got burns on the top of her head."

"Getting okay?"

"I think so. She gets tired easily, though." He picked at a hangnail. "She still has bandages on her head. I don't know what the burns look like."

Nell nodded. "What you listen?" She pointed to his MP3 player.

"Just music."

"Who?"

"Green Day."

"Want to hear."

Finn gently inserted his earbuds into Nell's ears and turned the music on.

Nell's eyes almost popped out of her face, and Finn rushed to turn the music down. "Sorry!"

With the good side of her face, Nell laughed. Finn

laughed, too, and Sara couldn't believe what she was hearing.

"Good voice," Nell mumbled.

"Yeah, that's Billie Joe Armstrong. He's amazing. I wish I lived in New York so I could go see the musical he's in."

Stunned, Sara listened to her son string together more sentences than he'd said to her in the past week.

Nell listened to the music, her head bobbing, then reached her left hand to pull out the buds.

"More story," she said.

Finn opened his book again then looked at Sara.

Nell stared, too, and Sara got that they wanted her to leave.

"Humph." She took the laundry and flounced out of the room. They got to have fun while she had to work. *Story of my life.* Hadn't that always been her role ever since Timm got burned? The kids she knew had played sports, or had hung out and listened to music, or had smoked cigarettes behind the school, while Sara had been at home doing laundry or cooking meals, or reading to Timm while he recuperated.

It had seemed to take so long. Timm would no sooner recover from one operation then they'd start another.

By the time he was well enough to start leading a semi-normal life, Davey was killed by a bull and Papa started drinking even more heavily. The family stayed locked in a holding pattern for years. That darkness colored all of Sara's adolescence.

Twenty minutes later, with a load of laundry in the washer and a tray of food prepared for Nell's breakfast, Sara entered the dining room and slammed to a stop on the threshold.

Finn, her little boy, stood in front of the dresser against the wall, taking bills out of a wallet.

Nell lay on the bed with her eyes closed.

Sara had caught her son stealing and felt sick.

"Finn, how could you?" Sara pressed her hand against her stomach.

Finn glanced up and his expression closed up instantly when he saw his mother's suspicion. The newfound openness was gone.

"You think I'm stealing?"

"What would you call it?"

"Mrs. Caldwell told me to take it."

"Why?" Her son had become not only a thief, but also a liar.

"To buy paint."

"*Paint?* What on earth do you want paint for?"

"Me," Nell said, her eyes open now and boring into Sara. "I told him."

"See?" Finn cried. "Why didn't you listen to me, Mom?"

"Because of those boys in Bozeman."

"Mom, *they* stole. *I* didn't."

Sara brought her fears under control. "You're right. I'm sorry, Finn."

He turned to Nell. "I took thirty-five dollars. Okay?"

"That enough?"

"For sure."

Finn brushed past Sara, pushing her out of the way with a rough shoulder.

"I'll wait outside." He stomped out of the house.

Sara felt about two feet tall. Finn had never stolen in his life and she shouldn't have jumped to conclusions now.

Nell still watched her with a disapproving glare. "Good boy."

Sara sighed. "I know. That was a lapse in judgment on my part. He got involved with the wrong crowd before we moved back to Ordinary."

"But *he* not steal?"

"No. He was with some other boys, older kids, when they were caught shoplifting, but the store's security tapes showed that he hadn't taken a thing."

"So why you think he steal here?"

"Because I'm afraid I don't know him anymore. He's becoming a teenager. He's moody."

"You afraid he go wild?"

"Yes."

"Like father?"

Sara didn't want to admit that that was exactly what she was afraid of, not when Rem was Nell's son.

"He not go wild like Rem. He not burn someone. Make no big mistake that change life."

"I know," Sara said, and put the tray of food in front of Nell. She scooped up a spoonful of oatmeal. "I'm in trouble with my son, aren't I?"

"Deep," Nell said before taking the oatmeal from Sara.

When Sara finished feeding Nell and helped her to lie down again, she heard the sound of a car engine in the yard. Who was it?

She stepped out onto the veranda and her heart sank.

Rem. Pulling a horse trailer.

He hadn't gone to work on the other man's ranch. He'd only gone to get the horse.

The proverbial shit was about to hit the fan.

Finn jumped up from where he'd been sitting on the grass and ran to the back of the horse trailer.

"Hey," Rem said to Finn, then looked at Sara, his gaze accusatory.

He approached her. "Why is Finn here?"

"Nell wanted to see him."

"Is that why you were late this morning? Timm told

you I was picking up the horse and you waited until I was gone to bring Finn here?"

She often forgot how well Rem knew her. She nodded.

"So Ma could spend time with him without me around?"

With one brisk nod, Sara confirmed his suspicions. "I'm the big bad bogeyman who's doing everything wrong today."

"Did they get along?"

As much as Sara wanted to deny it, she couldn't lie. "Like crazy."

"Really?" Rem smiled. "Was Ma happy?"

"His visit did her a world of good."

Before Rem could comment further, they were interrupted by the bloodcurdling sound of a horse screaming. Finn!

"What the—?" Rem ran to the back of the trailer and Sara rushed after him.

Finn had opened the rear door and the mare was freaking out.

"Hey, hey," Rem soothed, easing into the trailer and up beside the horse. "Finn and Sara," he said, keeping his voice low and calm, "go stand on the veranda. Now."

Only when they'd complied did Rem back the skittish horse out of the trailer and into the yard.

He led her into the corral, locked the gate then joined them on the veranda.

"What were you doing?" he asked Finn.

"I just wanted to see her."

A breath gusted out of Rem. "Okay. But you need to ask first. Next time wait for me."

"Yeah," Finn said, a sullen little boy again, the excitement he'd shown with Nell gone.

"You like horses?" Rem asked.

Finn jammed his hands into his low pockets and shrugged. "Yeah."

Rem grinned. "You want to learn how to ride?"

On the flip of a coin, Finn's face transformed from disinterest to animation.

"Yeah!"

Rem looked Sara in the eye while he said to Finn, "You can come out here anytime you want and I'll teach you."

"No," Sara blurted.

Finn spun to face her. "Why not, Mom? You told me I had to keep busy to stay out of trouble."

"Yeah, why not, Mom?" Rem parroted, his voice ripe with sarcasm.

Finn looked from one to the other, understandably confused by their animosity.

"Because—" She couldn't come up with a convincing reason. "Because you would get bored."

"Get real, Mom."

Damn you, Rem, Sara thought as the situation rapidly spiraled out of her control. "Fine. Do what you want."

IT WAS GOOD TO SEE HIS SON on his ranch, even if he couldn't tell him the truth.

As long as Finn was here, Rem was going to put him to work.

"Hey," he said. "You want to help me with something?"

"With the horses?"

"No. With something in the house for my ma."

"Yeah," Finn said, though with much less enthusiasm.

Sara had done a good job with him. He didn't want to work inside, probably wanted to start learning how to ride straightaway, but was being polite about it. The kid was all right.

Rem turned to Sara. "Ma wants to move into the living room. I have to borrow Finn for a couple of minutes. I need some muscle to help me move the big stuff."

"I can help you move all of it." The kid had puffed up a bit, maybe because Rem wasn't treating him like a kid, but Rem really could use his help. Moving the dining room furniture out to the back porch on his own the other night had been a trick.

Sara's nod was reluctant, but she must have recognized his predicament.

She and Finn followed him inside.

Ma was awake.

"Nice." She gestured ever so slightly toward the front window.

"The mare's a real beauty," Rem said. "Can't wait to start with her."

"What are you doing with her?" Finn asked.

Rem turned to answer, but his words caught in his throat. Looking at his son, he saw shades of his own father. He missed the old man a lot. Was this how people got over the loss of parents and grandparents? By focusing on the reflections they saw in their children? By grieving the loss, but celebrating the new?

Finn waited expectantly, so Rem finally answered his question. "I'm going to tame her. You saw her. She's hard to handle."

"Yeah." Finn tucked his thumbs into his front pockets and Rem realized the boy was unconsciously mimicking him.

Sara approached the bed. "Nell, you want to move to the living room?"

"Yes."

"I guess the first thing we need to do is to make some space in there."

"Finn," Rem said, "how about if we carry the sofa into

the hallway to start. We'll move it into the dining room once Ma's bed is out of there."

They moved the sofa easily. The boy was stronger than he looked.

Rem stared around the living room, trying to sort out the best configuration.

"Ma, I'm going to close these doors." The French doors that led from the hallway had never been closed in Rem's lifetime. "If I do that and then back the bed right up against them, you'll be directly across from the side window. You'll have a great view."

Nell nodded. She seemed tired, but she watched them intently, especially Finn.

Rem was glad he'd told her. It had been the right thing to do. Sure, the visit was tiring her out, but she had nothing else in her life right now.

Rem planned to push Ma's relationship with Finn to the max, and Sara and her resistance could take a flying leap.

They shifted the furniture out of the way and then wheeled the bed through the archway between the two rooms and backed it up against the French doors.

Rem had guessed right—her view was great.

Nell pointed to the wall on her left.

"Start there."

Finn nodded. Rem had no idea what the two were up to.

"Down," Ma said, and Rem stared at her. He wasn't following her.

Finn stepped to the wall and removed the painting that was hanging there. "You want all of them down?" he asked.

Nell nodded.

Finn removed every painting from every wall. "Where do you want these?"

"Take them out to the back porch," Rem said.

A buzz of excitement shimmered in the kid.

"What's going on?" Rem asked Sara.

She shrugged. "Beats me. Nell and Finn have cooked up something they aren't sharing with me."

The ghost of a smile curved the good side of Ma's mouth. She was tired, but so happy, and Rem counted his lucky stars.

He ran to the dining room, picked up the bedside table and carried it to the living room, gingerly so he wouldn't knock off the primroses.

Setting it beside the bed, he remembered his intention the other night of making Ma as comfortable as possible, of spoiling her. It was working. Ma's spirits were improving.

When Finn came back from the porch, Rem asked him to bring the other two pots of flowers. He did and put one on the coffee table and the other on the windowsill that faced the corral, directly in Ma's view. Smart kid.

After they got everything set up to Ma's satisfaction, Rem said, "Looking good," and grinned. He and Finn high-fived.

"Can I come back after lunch and hang out for the afternoon?" Finn asked.

"No," Sara shouted before Rem or Nell had a chance to respond.

Rem watched her fear run circles around her face and curl her hands into fists.

"Why not, Mom?" Finn asked.

For a moment, Sara looked lost. She obviously didn't have a single good reason—not one she dared share with the boy, at any rate.

Relax, he wanted to tell her. Exposure to Rem wasn't going to kill the kid.

"You don't have to leave," Rem said. "You can have lunch here."

"I need to get paint for a project." Finn stared down his mom, daring her to object. "Will you drive me into town?"

"I can," Rem interjected.

"No!" Sara shouted again. "I'll take you," she added, her tone moderated. "We'll stop and have lunch with Mama. Rem, can you please feed Nell?"

He nodded.

"Can we go now?" Finn asked.

"In about ten minutes."

Sara nodded and left the room. Rem followed her to the small laundry room behind the kitchen.

"Why can't I drive him into town?"

"You know why."

"This is gonna happen, Sara. You might as well give in."

"No." She slammed wet clothes into the dryer. "I don't want any of this."

She sounded more desperate than angry.

"I know, but frankly, this really isn't about you. Far as I can tell, that boy wants to be here."

"He's not 'that boy.' His name's Finn."

"I know his name," Rem barked. "Stop making stupid statements and even stupider judgments."

He strode out of the room.

CHAPTER NINE

THEY DIDN'T GET IT. Not one of them understood.

Sara hated that she was so close to tears. She didn't cry, for heaven's sake. Ever. And her heart was beating like a drummer with lousy rhythm. The turmoil she'd fought against so well since Timm's accident, and that great darkness that had been growing since last summer, were clogging her chest.

Sara's grip on the steering wheel made her knuckles ache. She struggled to calm herself, but couldn't.

Finn sat quietly in the passenger seat. He hadn't said a word since getting into the car.

Her little boy was growing up. He wanted to spend time with his grandmother and father more than he wanted to be with her. It didn't matter that he didn't know that Nell and Rem were his family.

Sara should have been his closest family, the one person Finn wanted to spend time with.

And Sara wanted to retreat to her house, but wouldn't have time today. She hadn't had time yesterday. She wanted to go there and hide for a while, to forget about work and responsibility and just *be*.

That wasn't going to happen, though. The truth was that hiding from responsibility was never an option for her. She had to face it head-on.

"Finn, I'm really sorry I misjudged you in Nell's room today."

He didn't answer.

"You don't have to go back there today." She tried to sound reasonable.

"I'm not going back 'cause I *have to*." The disdain in his tone hurt. "I *want* to."

"You can go another day. It doesn't have to be today."

"What's wrong with going back, Mom? I don't get why you're being so weird. You keep telling me to get out of the house and make friends."

Yes, she was. The *right* friends. Good kids his own age. Not a pair of adults who had the ability to rip apart the fabric of Sara's well-ordered life. Who could tear her son from her safe embrace where she would keep him forever if she could—as last year's ten-year-old, happy with his mom and his life.

She hated the dissatisfaction in her son that was driving him to strangers.

So what if they were Finn's relatives? He didn't know that, and they had the potential to send Sara's structured relationship with her son into a tailspin.

"Where can I get paint in Ordinary?" Finn turned away from staring out of the window to look at her.

"Scotty's Hardware."

"Where can I get artist's paintbrushes in town?"

"I don't know. Maybe Scotty has some."

Finn nodded, tucked his buds into his ears and played Green Day so loudly Sara could hear it, effectively shutting her out until they entered town.

What was he planning? What was it that Nell had agreed to? Obviously painting and, equally obviously, on Nell's walls. But *what?*

She pulled into a parking spot in front of Scotty's and entered the store with Finn, then watched while he picked up paint cans and some narrow brushes.

With only one functioning wrist, he couldn't carry it all, so Sara helped him load the car.

After lunch with Mama, they drove back to the ranch, Finn giving her the silent treatment all the while.

AFTER SARA AND FINN LEFT, Adelle sat in the living room and wondered why she was hanging around this house alone.

Sara was going to stay at Nell's to feed her dinner and then get her ready for bed. That meant neither she nor Finn would be home until late.

The afternoon and evening stretched out in front of Adelle. Sick of her own company, she thought about TV, cards, reading. Nothing appealed.

Last year, Timm had pestered her so much to get out and socialize, but she'd been afraid to. She'd dated Max once, but he'd been drunk by the end of the night and that had terrified her.

Apparently, she'd been too involved in her own problems to realize what the rest of the town already knew—that Max drank too much. After the trouble she'd had with Karl and alcohol, she wasn't prepared to go through it again. Even if she found Max so decent, so attractive, it hurt to turn him away.

She'd refused go out with him again until he sobered up. He'd joined Alcoholics Anonymous and had called to tell her so. He wasn't allowed to start a new relationship for a full year, but promised that the day the year was over, he was going to come back for her.

The year was up and Adelle found that she couldn't wait until tomorrow night to see him. She'd spent enough years alone. Now that the prospect of having something more was so close, she was impatient to start. They'd already had to wait a year.

She picked up the phone to call Max, then dropped the receiver back into the cradle. *Coward.* She couldn't remember the last time she'd reached out to a man. She'd only ever had one lover, Karl, and she had married when she was twenty-five. But her parents had been strict. She'd been a virgin on her wedding day.

The clock on the mantel ticked steadily and drove her crazy. She used to find it soothing, but not anymore. Now it made her too aware of the passage of time, of how many hours she'd been alone since Karl's death.

Oh, for pity's sake, call the man. See if he's free.

She picked up the phone again and this time dialed his number before she could chicken out. Her heart beat faster than the ticking of the clock.

Max answered on the second ring. "Hello?"

His voice sounded even deeper on the phone than in real life.

"Max?"

"Adelle?" She'd surprised him. She could hear it in his tone. "Is everything okay? Are we still on for tomorrow night?"

"Yes. Tomorrow night is fine. I was just wondering..."

"Yes?"

"If you aren't busy now, would you like to come over for a coffee?"

"Now?" It sounded like he was smiling.

"We can wait until tomorrow night, if you like."

"No! Now would be good." He hung up without waiting for a goodbye.

Adelle ran upstairs and put on lipstick. She spritzed perfume on the back of her neck and on her wrists. She put on her favorite white sweater with the subtle beadwork on the front.

The front doorbell rang and she ran downstairs. Who

was here? It couldn't be Max, not this soon. She'd have to get rid of whoever it was. But through the open front door, she saw Max standing on the veranda. She opened the screen door. "How did you get here so quickly from your place?"

"I was at the Co-op picking up some things for the ranch."

"I'm sorry. I shouldn't have bothered you."

He closed the front door behind him and the hallway shrank. He was so tall, so big. So handsome. She loved the golden color of his skin.

He took her chin in his hand and leaned forward.

Oh, goodness. He was going to kiss her—and he did—with smooth, warm lips. He tasted good, like cinnamon candy.

He didn't try too much, just rested his lips on hers, then stopped kissing her and nuzzled her neck.

It had been so long since a man had touched her. Karl had been dead for five years and there had been trouble between them long before that.

"You smell good," Max said, and pulled away to look at her. "And you weren't bothering me. I'm glad you called."

"Yes, me, too."

"I like the way you talk. I like your German accent."

"I'm surprised I have any left." He touched her cheek with one finger. "I came here when I was only ten. I shouldn't have any accent left at all but it was my mother tongue, so I guess…" She was babbling. "I'm nervous," she blurted out, then covered her mouth with her hand. She was a silly woman.

He took her in his arms. He smelled like a working man. No cologne. No sweat, either, clean but manly somehow.

His arm across her back, at her waist, he pulled her flush

against him and she felt her body respond. Oh, it had been too long.

"Max," she whispered. "You feel good."

"So do you, Adelle. I've waited a long time for this." He kissed her again and this time it was deep and passionate. His tongue explored her mouth thoroughly and his arms pulled her closer so she could feel his response.

Suddenly, she was tired of all of the time she'd wasted mourning her husband longer than she should have. She'd loved Karl, but he was dead and she wanted life.

When Max stopped kissing her, she said, "I choose life, Max."

He laughed, the corners of his dark eyes crinkling. "What?"

She couldn't believe what she was about to ask, but the years were ticking by and she was over sixty. She wasn't getting any younger. "Would you think I was too forward if I said I want to sleep with you?"

His eyes nearly popped out of his head. He smiled. "Adelle Franck, I thought you were a shy woman."

"I was—I am—but I want you. You said you've waited a long time for this. So have I. Tomorrow night we can go out for dinner or coffee or whatever you want. This afternoon, I want you to stay here with me."

He took her hands in his and kissed them. "Adelle," he breathed, "I want you so badly I'm afraid of messing up."

"I'm afraid, too, but I want you right now."

She took his hand and led him up the stairs to the room she'd shared with her husband.

Karl, she prayed, *I'm sorry to replace you, darling, but I need this man.*

"Do you mind if I close the curtains a little?" she whispered. "I…I am not as young as I used to be."

"Adelle, my lovely girl, do whatever you need to do."

That afternoon, she adored his body, his size, his skill. His knowledge of what a woman would like. She liked it all. She felt herself come alive, as though awakening in the spring.

Afterward, they dressed in the dim bedroom.

"Come downstairs," she said. "We need to eat."

Max helped her to fix a simple meal—eggs, toast and tomatoes.

"Adelle, can I ask you something?"

"Of course."

"Why didn't you date after Karl died? Or did you, and I just never heard about it?"

"No. There have been no dates. No men. Not until you and today."

He smiled. "I'm glad, but why did you wait so long?"

"Because of Karl's drinking. Because he crashed into a tree and died while he was drunk. I was ashamed. I thought the whole town would think we were terrible people."

"No. Never. Karl was a good man. So much happened to both of you, though. Timm got burned. Later, after Davey was killed in the rodeo, the townspeople felt compassion for you and your family."

"Are you sure?"

"Yes. What did you think of me when I was drinking? Did you think I was terrible?"

"No, but I regretted that I couldn't get to know who you really were. And, of course, it reminded me too much of bad times with Karl."

"I'll never drink again."

"I'm glad. Why did you drink?"

"It runs in my family. My father drank. I had it under control until my wife died. Then I drank every night, then every afternoon. That went on until that night you and I went out, and you said you wouldn't see me again unless I was sober."

He took her hands in his. "I've been attracted to you for a long, long time. Even when you were still married to Karl."

That took her by surprise. "You were? To me?"

He spread his palm on the side of her neck and his thumb traced her jaw. "I like how classy you are, how proud and how beautiful. Last year, when I disappointed you on that date, I thought the time was right. I had a good reason to quit." He turned over her hand and kissed the palm.

"You've shown your strength, Max. You stopped drinking. I know from watching my husband how hard that is to do."

"Adelle, I want to make love to you. Now. Do you have candles? I want to see you this time."

She thought of her aging body. Her round stomach. Her heavy thighs. "This is so… I'm not used to…"

Max framed her face with his hands, gentle for a big man.

"Please," he whispered.

Adelle went to the pantry and gathered the hurricane lamps she kept ready for emergencies. She handed two of them to Max and took two more for herself. Then she grabbed a box of matches and followed him upstairs.

In her bedroom, they undressed by candlelight and lay down. Adelle discovered that, where love was concerned, age really didn't matter.

"EASY, GIRL," REMINGTON CROONED to the pretty strawberry roan who was eyeing him warily. "I won't hurt you."

With a flick of her red tail, the mare shied away, but

not as far as she had for the past hour. Endless dust beat up from the dry earth of the corral.

Rem glanced down the driveway. Still no sign of Finn. He'd expected him back by now. God, he felt like an adolescent waiting for his date to pick him up. Pathetic.

He returned his attention to the mare.

"Good girl. Come closer." Rem kept his tone low and even, as he had since this game had begun. The mare had yet to learn that he had endless patience—with animals at any rate.

He used his sleeve to clear the sweat running into his eyes. Since the shirt was almost as sweat-drenched as his forehead, he hauled the garment over his head, wiped his face with a dry spot near the hem then tossed it onto the white wooden gate.

He shifted closer. The horse stayed where she was. Rem reached a hand toward her and she finally let him touch her face with the tips of two fingers, then four, then his palm. Hallelujah.

He stroked her velvet nose.

"You've got the prettiest brown eyes." Leaving his hand flat and still on her, he murmured nonsense for a few minutes, giving her a chance to get used to him before he stepped away.

Shuffling backward, he slipped through the gate and closed it behind him.

The mare took one step toward him, her big brown eyes wary but wistful then stopped. Good. Although she was still skittish, she'd enjoyed his touch and wanted more.

"Tomorrow, Lady. That's enough for one day." Rem measured success with animals in the smallest increments.

The rumble of a car's engine caught his attention. Sara and Finn were back.

After the car pulled to a stop, Finn ran to the corral. Sara watched uneasily without coming closer.

"What did you do with her?" Finn asked, avid curiosity lighting his face.

"Just talked to her. Crooned. Touched her a little, as much as she would let me."

Lady tossed her mane.

"One hand on her muzzle today, brushing her down by the end of the weekend, riding her next week. You've got to take it slowly."

"Does it work?"

Rem nodded. "It has in the past. Let's see how Lady does. I never rush this process."

Rem was tempted, though. God knew he needed the money.

"Why not?" Finn asked.

"Pushing it is nuts. Without trust, the mare will balk."

From his vantage point leaning on the outside of the gate, Rem watched Lady run around the perimeter of the corral, pulling just out of reach every time she passed him, like a coy girl flirting.

Rem laughed. So did Finn.

The next time she came around, Finn put out one hand and Lady came close enough to sniff it, stunning Rem. When Finn moved his fingers to touch her, she shied away, but came back to memorize his scent.

The kid had something inside him that the horse liked. Trusted.

Rem turned to look at Sara, who still stood beside the car, watching them.

He lifted one eyebrow, as if to say, *Remember, Sara? Horses used to trust me right away, too, when I was a kid. Like father, like son.*

She clearly understood his look. She didn't say a word, but her stricken expression spoke volumes.

Rem couldn't worry about her pain now. His son was on his ranch and Rem was a kid in a candy store. His son, who he'd missed parenting for so many years, was on the Caldwell ranch learning horses the way Rem used to as a kid.

Finn was here, with Rem, tasting his heritage. Where he belonged.

AMAZING.

The summer wasn't going to be boring like Finn had been afraid of.

He couldn't believe Rem was going to teach him how to ride *and* Mrs. Caldwell was going to let him paint on her walls.

He liked her, even if she was old and couldn't speak right. Weird how her stroke killed only half of her.

Finn carried the supplies into her house, making a few trips because of his busted wrist. Man, this was going to be good.

He walked through the house and into her living room. When she heard him, Mrs. Caldwell opened her eyes.

"Hey," he said.

"What you got?"

"Paint and brushes."

"Colors?"

"Black and red and yellow. The walls are already white so I didn't need to buy any of that. I'll just leave the white areas blank and the wall will show through."

"What red for?"

"Andivort's shirt."

"What yellow?"

"Lady Serena's dress."

She gave one of her weird little nods.

With only her eyes, the old woman followed everything he did. To the left of the archway into the dining room, he set the cans of paint down beside the wall. That's where he would put the first cartoon frame.

Then he'd paint more clockwise around the room.

"Wash first."

He turned to Mrs. Caldwell.

"What?" he asked.

"Finn," Ma said from the dining room where she'd picked up the broom and swept the floor. "Manners."

Why didn't she just leave him alone with Mrs. C.? Finn turned back toward the bed and said, "Pardon?"

"Wash first."

Finn shook his head. "I don't get it."

"She wants you to wash the wall first."

The woman blinked, so he knew Mom was right. "Why?"

"Paint doesn't stick to dirty walls."

"Oh. Where can I get stuff to use?"

"I'll show you."

He followed his mom to the kitchen where she filled a bucket with water and cleaner then handed it to him.

He carried it back to the living room and washed the entire wall to the left of the archway. His arm got tired about halfway through because he could only use his right, but he didn't care and kept going.

He figured he could fit maybe three frames on that wall before jumping to the other side of the archway.

Mom followed him in with newspaper and the broom.

"Just a sec. Let's clean the floor so you don't get dust in the paint."

"'Kay." Mom seemed to be excited about the painting, too.

When she finished sweeping the floor in front of that wall, Finn put down the newspaper and moved the supplies onto it.

He opened the can of black paint and started on the outlines. On the internet, he saw a lot of anime, but the style he was more drawn to was the old comic books he'd found one time in a secondhand store—about King Arthur and the Knights of the Round Table.

When Mom was in school they shopped for everything at secondhand stores. Even after she'd finished and worked full-time, they scrimped like crazy so she could buy that house.

Maybe now that they were living in Ordinary and it was cheaper than the city, they could get new stuff for a change. He really wanted a pair of Vans skateboarding shoes for his birthday—brand-new, not just a pair of running shoes some other kid had already worn.

While he worked, Mrs. C. kept making noises behind him. He didn't know if they meant she liked what he was doing or that she didn't. She never told him to stop, though, so he kept painting.

At one point, she fell asleep.

He finished the first frame in a couple of hours. It was a lot harder than sketching in a book. In his sketches, he only drew with black pencil.

In color on the wall, though, the painting looked sick. Amazing.

After he closed the tins of paint and washed the brushes in Mrs. Caldwell's laundry tub in the basement, he returned to the living room.

Mrs. C.'s son, Rem, was there staring at the wall and Finn tensed. Maybe he wouldn't like that Finn was painting on the wall. Finn wondered if it was Mrs. C.'s house or Rem's.

"Who are these people?" Rem asked, pointing to the wall. He didn't look mad. Just interested. Finn relaxed his shoulders.

"The big, evil-looking guy is called Andivort. He's holding Lady Serena's arm so she won't get away."

"She looks familiar. Did you use a model?"

Finn shook his head, but stared at what he'd drawn. Without realizing it, he'd changed her face from his sketches. Not a lot, but now she looked like Melody, maybe a grown-up version of how she would look someday.

Weird.

"What comes next in the story?" Rem asked.

"No!" Mrs. C. said, really loudly. "No tell."

Finn grinned. "Your mom wants to guess the story before I paint it. I'm only painting one frame at a time."

Rem brushed his jaw and nodded. "Kinda hard to tell what's going to happen from only one drawing."

"What you call?" Mrs. C. pointed to the drawing.

"In animation it would be called a cel. *C-E-L.* Someday, I want to study animation and make movies. That would be sick."

Mom stepped into the room carrying a full laundry basket. When she saw the drawing her eyes widened. "Where did you learn to do that?"

Finn shrugged. "I just know how."

"That's incredible." Mom looked at him as if she thought he was pretty special.

He felt his cheeks get really hot. He'd been mad at her for a long time—he was still mad—because she wouldn't tell him who his dad was. Now he found out she didn't even know his real name. How lame was that? So stupid.

What was he supposed to say to kids in town if they asked about his dad? *He* didn't even know his dad's name. Embarrassing.

She made him mad because she bossed him around so much, wanted to make him too busy. As if there was any trouble he could get into in such a small town.

But here she was excited about his drawing. He liked that Mom was happy with something he did. It made him feel warm. But he was confused, too. He missed the way things used to be between them. Like, they used to be almost friends. Now it felt like he was angry all the time and Mom was always tense.

When Mom started to put the laundry away, Rem said, "I can help you with that."

"It's my job," she said, her voice a little hard. "You're paying me to do this."

Something real weird was going on between those two, a vibe he didn't understand, and Finn wanted to know what it was about. He planned to watch and listen until he did.

SARA CLEANED UP THE KITCHEN. Dinner was finished and she'd already got Nell ready for bed.

Rem, Finn and Nell were playing Polish poker. Finn had taught them how.

After putting the last plate away, Sara hung up the dishcloth. Her feet ached and she was tired. She'd missed going to her house two days in a row and it bothered her. She needed her private place.

A well of dissatisfaction had dogged her all day. She didn't understand where it was coming from and wanted it to quit already. Her life was fine.

As if to mock her and her sadness, laughter sounded from the card players. She stepped into the living room and stopped, surprised by the joy on their faces, her son's and his father's and his grandmother's.

When was the last time *she* had felt carefree?

The only time she could remember was that night with

Rem, when she'd forgotten about her family's problems for a few hours and had felt cherished. They hadn't been careful, though, and Finn had been conceived. Then there had been years of struggle.

Even now she worked two jobs because she insisted on paying Mama rent until she moved into her house, while also making the monthly mortgage payments.

Her life was and had been all about work for as long as she could remember, and she was tired. Sick and tired.

Had she robbed Finn of a carefree life? He hadn't had any holidays outside of coming home to Ordinary. There'd been no trips to Disneyland or to the Grand Canyon. No karate lessons, hockey leagues, skiing in the Rockies or swimming in the ocean.

No wonder he looked up to a guy like Rem, who knew how to have fun.

Face it, Sara, to a boy Finn's age, you're downright boring.

She stood in the archway between the dining room and living room and watched these three people she loved—yes, even Rem despite his flaws—and felt so alone, so left out, and so lifeless and gray.

Her cell phone rang and she answered it.

Timm was yelling into the phone.

"Timm, slow down. You're talking too fast. I don't understand what you're saying."

"Angel's having the baby. We're at the hospital. Her water broke."

"Are you serious?" As if someone had turned on a big, honking lightbulb, fresh blood raced through Sara's veins. "I'll be right there."

Grinning, she closed the phone.

Three people stared at her with their mouths open. "Angel's gone into labor. Timm just took her to the hospital."

"Great!" Rem said. "You want to go be with them?"

"Yeah, I really do," she said. Then she remembered she was here on Rem's dime. Alice had needed today off and they'd arranged for Sara to take her place, which meant all day and evening, too—her shift and Alice's—because she had to get Nell ready for bed. "You're paying me, though. I can't just leave."

"Sure you can," Rem said, and he smiled. "Come on, Sara. This is special. You have to be there."

"Okay. Finn, we'd better get going. I want to be there when the baby comes."

"Do I have to, Mom? Don't those things take a long time? You said it took you sixteen hours to have me."

"He can stay here," Rem said.

Sara looked at Finn. "Finn, are you sure? If it goes really late, you'll have to sleep here."

"That's okay, Mom. I want to stay."

She didn't know what to do. Was leaving him with Rem okay? Rem wouldn't break his promise not to tell, would he?

"Sara, Angel could be in labor for hours, or even days." Rem was the voice of reason. He knew what she was afraid of and was reassuring her with his tone. "Finn shouldn't be there the whole time. Let him stay here. Tomorrow I'll teach him to ride, or something."

She should resist, should resent that Finn wanted to be here instead of with her, but she was too excited about this baby.

"Okay, I'll call and let you all know how she's doing."

Before she left, though, she couldn't help herself and turned to Rem to say, "Keep him safe."

"I'd never do anything to hurt him." Rem's smile was soft and, for a rare moment, she felt in harmony with him.

She nodded and left the house and sped to Ordinary to

pick up Mama, to persuade her to come meet her second grandchild.

She ran into the Franck house shouting, "Mama, where are you?"

Sara checked the living room and the kitchen. She had just put her foot on the bottom step of the stairs when Mama came out of her bedroom, tying the belt of her robe at her waist, her feet bare.

"Sorry, were you asleep? It's still pretty early."

Mama didn't say anything, just stared at Sara with eyes that were a little bit scared, with a look that was slightly embarrassed.

Her hair was a mess, her cheeks and neck red, as though someone had been nuzzling—

Mama wasn't alone. She had a man in her bedroom. For the first time in thirty-one years, Sara had no idea what to say to her mother.

CHAPTER TEN

"LET'S GET YOU ON A HORSE." Rem headed to the kitchen and Finn ran out of the house and straight to the stables.

Between working at the hospital and taking care of Mrs. C., Ma hadn't had a chance to rebook his first horseback-riding lesson at that other ranch, the one that he'd missed because of Melody's car accident.

Anyway, he'd rather be taught by Rem any day. The guy was cool, even if he was weird around Mom and Mom was even weirder around him.

Rem saved kids from burning cars and tamed horses and fixed them if they were sick. He was amazing.

Finn rushed to Rusty's stall. Man, he was excited. He felt like a kid, and how stupid was that when he was almost twelve, but he didn't care. He just wanted up on a horse.

About five minutes later, Rem entered the stable and led Rusty out into the aisle. He showed Finn how to talk to the horse and how to saddle him.

"Always treat a horse with respect." Rem gave Rusty a baby carrot from his pocket. "If you do, Rusty will be your friend and treat you well in return."

He took the saddle off Rusty and had Finn redo it. The saddle was heavy, but Finn managed pretty well.

"The important thing to remember," Rem said, "is that even when he's your friend, you're still the boss. Once you're up on Rusty, *you* will be in control, not him. Got it?"

Finn nodded and Rem walked him through how to control the horse. Unbelievably cool.

Finally, he let Finn get up in the saddle and it was better than he had imagined. Even though he was farther up from the ground than he'd thought he'd be, he wasn't scared! It was amazing.

Rem led him around the corral for a while and then let Finn go on his own.

"How do I make him go faster?" he asked.

"Relax, kid. You'll get there eventually. You need to get to know Rusty first and how to handle him. How to keep control."

Finn rode for an hour.

"Hey, look," he shouted. "Mrs. C. is watching."

"Mrs. C.?" Rem smiled. He seemed to like that.

Finn waved to her and she lifted her left hand as far as she could.

Rem showed Finn how to unsaddle Rusty and then how to curry him before leading him to his stall.

"Can I ask you something?" Finn said.

"Sure. Shoot."

"How come my mom is so mad at you?"

Rem paused with his hand still on the latch to Rusty's stall and looked at Finn over his shoulder. He seemed like he was really fighting with himself. "Let's go get some drinks and sit on the veranda," he finally said.

Finn followed him to the house and waited while Rem went inside. He came out with colas and a bag of cheese snacks. Great. Finn was starving.

Rem opened the bag and handed it to him. "You know your uncle Timm got burned when he was a kid, right?"

Finn nodded. "Yeah, I saw his scars once. His whole chest was burned. It must have hurt real bad."

"Yeah, he was out of commission for a few years." Rem

took a long swig from his can of pop, then pulled a cigarette and matches out of his shirt pocket.

"You smoke?" Finn asked.

"Only sometimes. When I'm stressed."

Finn got a bad feeling. "Talking about Uncle Timm makes you stressed?"

"Talking about his accident does." He lit his cigarette.

"You were there when he got burned?"

"No one ever told you what happened?"

"No and it's always bugged me."

"I burned him."

Finn felt as though Rem had punched him in the chest. "How come? Didn't you like him? I thought you were his friend. Why would you want to hurt him?"

Rem held up his hand, as if telling Finn to stop thinking for a minute.

"It wasn't on purpose. It was a terrible accident. At Timm's eleventh birthday party, I had a can of foam streamers. You know the stuff I'm talking about?"

"Yeah, so?"

"So, I was only ten, about a month shy of my own birthday. I didn't know the streamers were highly flammable."

Rem took a hard drag on the cigarette and blew the smoke in a long stream. "When his mom brought the birthday cake in and put it in front of Timm with all the candles lit, I sprayed the foam at him and it caught fire. So did Timm."

"Man, that's awful." Finn felt sick. "God. That's bad."

Rem smiled but he didn't look happy. "Yeah. It was the worst thing I've ever seen. Timm was in recovery for a long time after that."

"So that's why my mom seems mad at you a lot."

"I used to think she had a right to be. These days, though, I think she should be over it by now."

Finn stared at the fields that went all the way to the road. What if he'd been burned on his last birthday? His life would never be the same. He couldn't skateboard, maybe couldn't sketch if his hands got burned. Wow. Poor Uncle Timm.

"Are you mad at me now, too?" Rem asked.

"Yeah, a little. It was a dumb thing to do. Or maybe I'm just mad that it happened at all."

Rem jumped off the veranda and stubbed out his cigarette on the bare soil. He put one foot on the bottom step and rested his hands on his knee.

"Timm was my best friend. Your mom was my—" Rem stopped and smiled sort of ruefully.

"Your what?"

"My little buddy. She was a year younger than us, but followed us everywhere."

Rem smiled again and this time it looked real. "I had to fish her out of scrapes all the time, just because she wanted to do the same stuff we were doing, but she wasn't as big."

Finn couldn't see it. "It's hard for me to imagine Mom as a kid having fun."

"Your mom works way too hard. She needs to learn how to relax."

"Yeah, you got that right. What kinds of scrapes did she get into?"

"We used to climb trees." Rem jerked his thumb over his shoulder toward the road. "You see that big oak?"

"The one that got burned by the car?"

"That's the one. Timm and I used to climb it. Stupid, yeah, with it so close to the road, but we'd climb on the field side. Never the road side."

Rem took off his cowboy hat and dropped it onto the top step. "One day Timm and I climbed up and your mom followed. It was her first time climbing a tree. We knew what we were doing. She didn't."

He shoved the hair off his forehead and wiped the sweat away with the sleeve of his shirt.

"We got down and ran away, but she couldn't."

"Did she cry?"

"Naw." Rem grinned. "It wasn't in her nature to cry."

"What did she do?"

"She stood on one of those branches and held on to the one above her head and just watched us. She didn't say a word, didn't have to, because she knew I would come back to get her."

"How did she know that?"

"Because I always did."

"ANGEL'S HAVING HER BABY, Mama."

Caught between the sensual haze in that bedroom with Max and out here with the cold reality of her daughter's censure, Adelle wanted to be a million miles away.

This wasn't how she would have chosen for Sara to discover her mother was still a sexual creature.

"I'm going to the hospital," Sara said. "Um…do you want to come?"

Adelle shook her head, mute in her shock, unable to form a coherent sentence.

"This is your grandchild." Sara's voice sounded harsh. "You should be there."

"Not right now, Sara. You go alone."

Sara hesitated, but finally turned away. Before she stepped out the door, she said, "You need to come to terms with this, Mama. That baby will need her grandma."

Sara closed the door harder than she needed to.

Adelle felt more than heard Max step out of the bedroom once Sara was gone. She turned to find him fully dressed.

"Adelle? Do you want to talk about this?"

"This?" She felt lost. Ungrounded. Her daughter had caught her with a man and she felt ashamed.

"Your daughter is a grown woman. She should be able to accept that her mother is, too."

"I don't know, Max."

"Why did you make love with me this afternoon?"

"Because I was tired of wasting time."

"Before Sara caught us, how did you feel?"

"Wonderful. Carefree. Sexy. Better than I have in years and years."

"You hold on to that thought while you get freshened up and dressed. I'll make us a pot of coffee and we'll talk."

Adelle took a quick shower and dressed, then applied makeup. She needed to cloak herself in normalcy and her everyday routines.

When she entered the kitchen, Max was staring out of the window and the setting sun turned his Native American skin even more golden. He was beautiful. She wanted to drag him back upstairs to bed, to feel his masculine beauty and virility and strength against her again. He made her feel alive and vibrant.

Without a word, he approached her and kissed her. Thoroughly. Not like an old married couple kisses, but like a passionate, earthy, energetic couple.

He drew back and stared at her with hard-won compassion and perception. "We are lovers, Adelle. There's no turning back. We've wanted each other for a long time and there's no shame in taking what we want. Do you understand?"

She smiled. "Yes, I do. I want to keep making love with you until we are cross-eyed."

Max laughed and held her so tightly she could barely breathe, but she didn't complain.

He stepped back and poured them coffee, then sat at the table. "Tell me why it sounds like you don't want to get to know Timm and Angel's baby."

It all felt so petty now as she explained her fears about Karl and Angel.

"In all the years I've known her, I've never known Angel to sleep with a married man. Or one as much older than her as Karl was. You've misjudged her, Adelle."

She covered her hot cheeks with her hands. "Have I disappointed you?"

"No, but I don't want you to miss out on your chance to know your grandchild."

He stood and took her hand. "Let's go to the hospital."

She followed him out the door.

SARA DROVE TO THE HOSPITAL with that feeling of being off-kilter that had been dogging her for a year, only now it was worse. She'd just caught her mother—

She shied away from thinking about that. Her life was changing too much and too quickly. Her brother was married and becoming a father, her son was growing up and away from her too fast, and her mother was getting it on, most likely with Max Golden. Sara couldn't imagine who else it would be.

At the hospital, Sara tracked down her brother and Angel and knocked on the door of the birthing room. She felt timid because as much as she and Angel got along now, she had no idea whether she would be welcome at this time.

Timm opened the door with a worried frown. Behind him Angel called from the bed, "Sara, get over here and help me," her voice tinged with a good dose of panic.

"What's wrong?" Sara ran into the room. She glanced

at the doctor and recognized Dr. Simpson, who didn't look particularly worried.

So, no complications. Just a first-timer's anxiety.

"It hurts. That's what's wrong," Angel grumbled. "Why don't men have to go through this?"

Sara grinned. "Angel, trust me. It will all be worth it once the baby gets here."

When Angel had another contraction, Timm came up behind Sara and gripped her shoulders. "Does it always hurt this much?"

Sara took Angel's hand and squeezed. "She's doing really well. Relax, Timm."

Sara stayed for the next half hour, talking to Angel, distracting her from the pain, asking her about the preparations they'd made in their apartment for the baby.

"We painted the room yellow and pasted up pictures of baby ducks." She gasped and held her breath.

"Breathe," Timm ordered. "Come on, Angel, like we learned in class."

Someone knocked on the door. Timm walked over and opened it.

"Mama," he said, clearly surprised.

Mama entered, her steps tentative, her smile cautious.

"Mrs. Franck, why do they make the women do all of this work? You raised a strong boy. Why can't Timm have this baby?" And just like that Angel broke the ice.

Mama smiled. "It is the woman's job."

Another contraction hit and Angel whimpered, "Tiiimmm."

He rushed to her side and grasped the hand Sara wasn't already holding. "I'm here, honey."

Sara wondered if Angel was bruising his hand as much as she was bruising Sara's.

The contraction dragged on while Angel bit her lip and seemed to go inside herself to control the pain.

It passed and Angel panted.

"You're doing well, honey," Timm said. "I'm proud of you."

If Sara didn't know better, she would have said Timm's eyes looked misty. He wasn't the emotional type, though.

"I love you," he whispered to Angel. She whispered the same thing back and stared into his eyes, and they might as well have been alone in the room.

Sara looked at Mama and raised an eyebrow. *See? I told you.*

Mama nodded. She saw it. Finally.

Timm rested his forehead on Angel's and she seemed to draw strength from him.

Another contraction hit and Sara turned to Dr. Simpson. "They're coming fast."

The doctor nodded. "Yep. She's close. You and Mrs. Franck had better leave now. I need to check Angel's dilation."

Timm said, "I'll call you if we need you."

Sara kissed Angel's cheek. "You go, girl. Do us women proud."

She stepped away from the bed and Mama filled her vacated spot with the speed of a racehorse, nearly pushing Sara out of the way.

Wrapping her arms around Angel, she whispered, "I will be right outside praying for you."

"Thank you," Angel whispered back and, in that quiet moment, a tenuous bond formed between the two women.

Angel swore a blue streak as another contraction hit, and Sara and her mother ran out of the room, giggling when Angel called Timm a stupid, horny donkey for knocking her up.

Just before the door closed behind them, they heard Timm laugh.

"She is so...so...so passionate!" Mama said.

"Yes, she is, and she devotes that passion to Timm. He's a lucky man, Mama."

"I see that now."

They found Max in the waiting room and Mama said, "Sara, Max and I are together. You must get used to him being at the house. I care for him deeply."

Sara enfolded her in a hug. "Good for you, Mama." She turned to Max and said, "Mama is special. Take care of her."

"I will." He smiled softly at Adelle.

Oh my, he's drunk on love these days, Sara thought.

Mama draped one arm around Sara's shoulders and threaded the other through Max's. "Let's go drink terrible hospital coffee and wait for this new baby who I plan to spoil and spoil and spoil."

They met Angel's mother, Missy, with Chester.

"We got here as soon as we could," Missy panted. "How is she?"

Sara filled her in on the situation and calmed her down.

"Who's taking care of the restaurant?" Max asked.

"No one," Chester responded.

"We closed for the night, but had to wait for one couple to finish their meals."

An hour later, Sara's new nephew, Karl David Franck, was born, and he was the cutest little button.

When Sara held him, she was transported to the hospital room after Finn was born.

Karl snuffled and moved his little arms and legs. Another precious creature had entered the world. Despite her background in nursing and science, Sara recognized it as a miracle, just as she had when Finn had been born. People thought it was only science, but wasn't science a miracle?

She pictured Rem on the day he'd come to see his son for the first time, and how terrified he'd been. Then she thought of him now, of how he was with Finn today. There was no comparison. They weren't the same man. Sara, on the other hand, hadn't changed one bit.

She'd refused to adjust her opinion of him despite evidence of change. Irrefutable evidence. Like the way he treated his mother, decorating her room with flowers, and refusing to let her be tended by strangers, even though it meant more responsibility and more stress for him. And how his ranch was spick-and-span and perfect. And how he treated his son with respect, how he had fun with Finn. Not crazy dangerous fun, but simply admiring his drawings, playing cards with him and teaching him how to ride.

Sara realized that when he'd said he'd keep her son safe, she had trusted his word.

Something tore open inside her, exposing a gaping vulnerability that she'd been hiding from herself.

She wanted more than she had, so much more than she'd allowed herself for years. She wanted a man in her life, wanted a new awakening like her mother was having, wanted another one of these precious miracles, only this time it would be easier. There was no more school, none of the stress she'd lived with through Finn's childhood. She owned a house now and had a good job.

In Bozeman, with Peter, she'd come to understand that even if she couldn't accept who Rem was, she couldn't be with anyone else. She'd had a few lovers and had enjoyed them over the years, but last summer's experience with Rem had effectively ruled out any other relationships.

She wanted to come alive.

She'd buried her desires beneath the single-minded

strength she'd needed to get through every day as a student and a single parent, and beneath the determination to put one foot in front of the other day after day, month after month, year after year.

She realized what she'd hidden from herself for the past year, since Rem had proposed last summer. That she wasn't happy. That she wasn't fulfilled. That she wanted a partner almost as much as Finn wanted a father.

Returning to her family, to Mama and Timm, hadn't been enough. She wanted a family of her own, like the one Angel and Timm had just started.

She remembered Finn as a newborn and a wave of longing hit. *I want to do this again. Finn should have a brother or sister. And I want to share it with someone this time.*

Not just any man would do. It had to be Rem.

She'd come home to Ordinary thinking the move would make Finn happy, that he would be happy with her family. But the move hadn't solved *her* problems. In fact, holding this beautiful newborn bundle, she knew that she'd made things worse, because Rem was here, and she had to admit that she still loved him. Really, truly, deeply loved him. There had been other lovers, but there had never been another man for her.

It always came back to Rem.

She'd rejected him, though.

That ship has sailed, sweetheart, and it ain't ever coming back.

She'd messed up last summer.

She said goodbye to her family, hoping no one would pick up on her change of mood, then drove out to pick up Finn from the Caldwell ranch, all the while dogged by a deep sadness.

She was alone because she'd wasted years carrying a

grudge against her son's father and had never healed from an accident at a birthday party over twenty years ago.

She had to find a way to fix her life.

ON SATURDAY EVENING, Sara cleaned the kitchen after dinner then went to the dining room. Nell had her eyes closed, was humming to music playing on the pink iPod Rem had bought her.

As if Sara needed any more proof that he'd changed from wild, crazy boy to hero.

Finn was nowhere in sight and the house was quiet. It looked like he'd completed one more frame while she'd been working in the kitchen.

Wondering if he was in the stables with Rem she headed over, but found only Rem there organizing tack and whistling through his teeth.

"Have you seen Finn?"

At the sound of her voice, he turned.

"Last time I saw him," Rem said, "he was in the back porch sketching and listening to music. Ma okay?"

"Yes."

He'd pushed his cowboy hat onto the back of his head and his dark hair fell across his forehead.

"Sara?" he said, and she realized she'd been staring.

Her view of her life had shifted since she'd held Karl, and she saw Rem through new eyes.

"Was there anything else you needed?" he asked.

Yes. You.

That ship has sailed, sweetheart, and it ain't ever coming back.

She'd messed up badly.

Red-faced, she turned and strode to the house as fast as her legs could carry her.

She needed to get Finn for the drive home and walked

to the back porch, but he wasn't there. She sniffed. Cigarette smoke. Coming from the side of the house.

She stepped outside.

Someone coughed and it sounded suspiciously like her son.

She rounded the corner and stopped, her mouth open.

Her son stood hunched over a cigarette, taking puffs from it and choking.

"Finn!"

He jumped and dropped the cigarette. It smoldered on the ground amid dry grass.

Sara stamped it out with her heel then kicked dirt over it.

"What on earth possessed you?"

Finn hunched his shoulders and withdrew into himself.

"No, don't you pull that adolescent crap with me. Where did you get the cigarette?"

"I took it."

"From where?"

"I found Rem's stash in the drawer of Mrs. C.'s china cabinet."

"You are never to do this again, do you hear me?"

"Why not? It's not so bad. It's cool."

"It's *not* cool. It's dangerous. It turns your lungs black and it will eventually kill you."

"Rem smokes and he seems fine."

So, Finn had seen Rem smoking.

"Get in the car," she ordered.

She marched around the house and rushed to the stables, but Rem wasn't there. At the far end, the last rays of golden sun poured in through the open back door.

She stomped down the aisle. Even before stepping outside, she smelled cigarette smoke yet again. Rem leaned against the wall watching the sun go down while he smoked.

"Do you know what I just found?"

Startled by her presence and harsh tone, he straightened.

"I caught Finn smoking." There was no mistaking her tone for anything other than fury. She pointed in the general direction of the house and then at the cigarette in Rem's hand. "He stole one of your cigarettes."

"Oh," he answered.

"That's it? That's all you have to say for yourself?"

"Kids experiment, Sara."

"I don't want him to. He said he thinks you're cool and you smoke, so to him that means it's okay."

Rem's lips flattened. He dropped the cigarette and crushed it with his boot, burying it as she had under a layer of dirt.

"Done," he said, meeting her gaze. "I won't smoke again."

He looked serious and her anger deflated. "Really? Just like that?"

"Really. If you think my influence is hurting him then, yeah, I'm done with it."

She turned to go, hesitated, then walked away nonplussed.

How could she believe his promise? How could he quit so easily?

She got in the car. Rem followed her across the yard.

Finn sat in the passenger seat, sulking, and watched him approach.

Rem leaned his arms on the open window.

"Finn, your mom's right on this issue. I wasn't a good role model when I smoked in front of you. I'm quitting. I'll be throwing the rest of my smokes in the garbage as soon as I go inside. See you later, kid." He tapped the window, then entered the house.

"Really, Mom, he just quit?"

She nodded. "It seems so." He was so determined that she believed him. If he promised his son that he would, then he would. "Yes. He just quit."

FINN AND HIS MOM LEFT THE ranch and were driving to the hospital to visit Angel and Karl.

He couldn't believe Rem was going to quit smoking just because Mom didn't think it was good for Finn. What a cool guy. He wanted to be a good role model for Finn. Sick.

Mom wasn't saying anything about the smoking, though, and that was strange. Usually, she'd be giving him heck, but right now, she just seemed strange, sort of lost or confused or something.

He didn't know what to think of that. She'd been weird a lot lately.

"Mom, Rem told me about Uncle Timm."

"He did? What did he say?"

"That he burned Uncle Timm. You shouldn't still hold that against him."

"Why did he tell you about it?"

"Because I asked him why you were mad at him and he said he used to think you had a right to be."

She was quiet for a moment and then said, "Maybe not."

"Definitely not, Mom. He was only my age—younger, even. He didn't do it on purpose. Kids make mistakes."

"Yes, they do." The light from the dashboard made her look real pale.

"Mom, are you okay?"

She took a deep breath and then let it out in a whoosh. "I'm good. Thanks. Can we stop talking about this now?"

"'Kay."

"Let's go see the new baby."

One thing Finn was sure of, he wasn't going to smoke again anytime soon. It tasted like crap. Why did people bother?

The new baby looked like a baby. Finn didn't get what the fuss was about.

He left the room and went to see Melody. She wasn't in the ICU anymore, so she must be doing okay. A nurse told him her new room number and he visited her there.

"Hey," he said when he walked in.

She was looking out the window but turned at the sound of his voice—with a great big smile. She seemed happy to see him.

He guessed he was happy to see her, too.

He pulled out his sketchbook and showed her his latest sketches, before bringing out the cards. He liked spending time with her. All of a sudden he had new friends. Strange ones—a sick kid in the hospital, a guy who ran an awesome ranch and wanted to be a good role model for Finn, and an old lady with a half-dead body who was funny and cool.

He felt good.

"Do you want to come to my birthday party next weekend?" he blurted out. "It's going to be on a ranch." He wanted her to be there.

Her smile was radiant, totally amazing.

SARA DROVE HERSELF AND FINN HOME from the hospital. Finn was happy because the hospital had agreed to figure out some way to let Melody attend his birthday party.

Sara was glad to see him in a good mood and so relieved that he was making friends with a lovely girl like Melody instead of with troublemakers.

What about her own happiness, though? What was she willing to do for herself? She had to do something to fix what was broken in her life and move on.

She needed Rem.

Now was the time. Despite Rem claiming the ship had already sailed, she was going to turn herself into a siren and woo him back to shore.

Like you have any idea how to be a siren.

I'll figure it out. Finn needs his dad. I need a lover and it has to be Rem. If he asks me to marry him again some day, even better.

Poor man was going to be so confused with this one-eighty Sara was about to pull.

So was she, a little, but it felt vital that she try this. She was barely in her thirties, yet had become a dried out, old crone. This decision felt right. She wanted to sleep with Rem *and* she wanted another baby.

REM ROLLED OVER IN BED to answer the phone.

What time was it? It felt like the middle of the night.

He felt around for his watch—12:15 a.m.

"Rem, it's Will Holden. I got a horse here with laminitis. Can you come?"

He couldn't leave Ma. Trouble was, laminitis needed to be treated right away. A horse in that condition was an emergency patient.

The horse needed him and he needed the money.

"I'll be right there, Will."

Rem hung up and called Sara. She answered on the second ring.

"Who is it?"

"Rem. I need to get out to the Holden ranch to treat a horse. Can you come stay with Ma?"

"I'll be there in twenty minutes."

SARA JUMPED OUT OF BED and dressed.

Before she left the bedroom, she stopped and glanced at her clock. After midnight. Rem would probably only be gone for a couple of hours. Was she really ready to be so close to him in the middle of the night and not do something about it?

She'd been handed a golden opportunity.

Rummaging through her underwear drawer, she found what she was looking for near the bottom—a pretty silk-and-lace nightgown, pale pink and almost see-through.

Mama, of all people, had bought it for her. Probably wishful thinking on Mama's part, hoping that Sara would attract a husband and give her more grandchildren.

Sara threw it into a bag with her toothbrush and left the house.

At the Caldwell ranch, Rem stood beside the Jeep waiting for her.

"Thanks," he said. "I'll try to be fast."

"I might nap upstairs if you don't mind."

"Get the monitor out of my bedroom and take it with you to Ma's room. You'll hear her if she needs you."

He sped off and she entered the house.

Nell was sleeping soundly so Sara went upstairs. She stepped into Rem's bedroom and looked at the monitor on the bedside table.

Nope, she wasn't sleeping in Nell's old room. Sara was going to sleep in Rem's bed.

She took off her clothes and slipped into the negligee. How wickedly soft it felt against her skin. It whispered around her.

She climbed into Rem's bed, pulled the bedsheet and quilt over herself, surrounding herself with his scent. And waited for her lover.

A LITTLE AFTER 4:00 a.m., Rem turned into his driveway, tired and achy.

Laminitis could kill a horse. If all went well in the horse's recovery, Rem had saved the one he'd just tended.

Yawning, he climbed the stairs, went to the bathroom, brushed his teeth and washed his face. He trudged down the hallway to his bedroom, stripped down to nothing and climbed into bed.

Man, it felt good. He rolled to his side and his hand touched something soft. What?

He reached farther and touched warm silk covering a breast.

He threw off the bedcovers and jumped out of bed.

"Who— What—?"

Sara lay on the far side of his bed in something pale, lacy and sheer, watching him.

"What the hell are you doing here?" Rem stepped well away from the bed. "I told you to use Ma's room."

Sara stretched, then slowly crawled across the bed, her nightgown tangled around her gorgeous legs. It rode up as she got close to the edge.

She stood and the remnants of pale moonlight barely limned her body, but he saw enough. Too much.

One faint dark circle pinpointed a breast. His hand still felt its imprint. Lower, a dark triangle tempted him.

"You know where Ma's room is, right?" He stalked to the door and pointed down the hallway.

She passed close to him and her butt touched his hip. He sucked in a breath and sprang away.

"Oh, I see," she said. "Down there."

She smiled up at him and Rem hadn't seen her look so soft or tantalizing in a long, long time.

"Sorry, my mistake." She waved two fingers over her

shoulder. "It's so late I might as well stay until morning and get Nell ready for the day."

He nodded, but couldn't speak, because a tempting wraith walked his hallway.

She stopped at the far bedroom and the barest hint of moonlight streaming through that room's window lit the pink confection floating around her.

"If you need me, I'll be right here."

Then she was gone and Rem fell against the doorjamb, unsure what had just happened.

With any other woman, Rem would think she'd been waiting for him, but not Sara. Sara didn't have a seductive bone in her body. She'd also made it more than clear that she didn't want him. So it all added up to an honest mistake.

Still, it took Rem a while to get over that mistake. His bed smelled soft and powdery like her and he found his hand reaching across the sheets of its own volition, hoping to find a silk-covered breast.

CHAPTER ELEVEN

LAST NIGHT, SARA HAD been too bold. She needed to be subtle. The trouble was, being an honest, forthright person, she didn't know how to be subtle. Or how to seduce Rem without jumping his bones.

She had to figure out an effective next step.

After she got Nell ready for the day, she drove home and showered, making sure to use plenty of her lily-of-the-valley powder afterward.

Maybe she should buy something heady and sexy, but that would probably be overkill. No, she had to come to Rem from an angle rather than head-on.

Finn lay on the sofa with his eyes closed and his buds in.

She lifted one out of his ear and his eyes popped open.

"You coming to the ranch today?"

"Yeah." He jumped up from the sofa.

She liked to see his enthusiasm, was adjusting to having him at the ranch so close to Rem. Every minute he spent there was a minute he stayed out of trouble.

"Get your stuff together. I'm leaving in ten minutes."

Mama sat in the armchair watching a morning TV show. She'd been spending a lot of time at Max's ranch. Why wasn't she there now?

"Mama, where's Max today?"

"He had to drive to Billings on business."

"Don't stay here alone. Come out to the ranch with us."
Sara was happy. She had a plan, a new direction in life.

Last night, waiting in Rem's bed, she'd been fired up,
thrilled by the chase.

At the Caldwell ranch, Mama went straight to the house
to visit with Nell. Nell's face lit up with the joy of having
a new visitor.

Finn set up his painting supplies.

Sara sent him out to see Rem in the stable while she got
Nell ready for the day. After breakfast, she would enlist
Mama's help with Nell's range of motion therapy.

Just having Mama there talking to Nell, and Nell having to respond, would help to improve her speech.

Left hemisphere strokes, which Nell had suffered, often
resulted in aphasia; so Sara had asked Rem to pay for a
speech therapist to come out twice a week.

With right hemiplegia, they needed to work on Nell's
ability to use her right hand to feed herself.

Sara made Nell a healthy shake for breakfast, chock-full
of antioxidant berries and protein powder to build muscle. She put it into a plastic tumbler with a wide straw and
brought it to the living room where she instructed Mama
in how to help Nell learn to use her right hand to drink it
by herself.

She went out to the veranda and called Finn in. "You
can start painting now if you want."

She put in a load of laundry. Who would think that one
stroke-hampered woman could make so much dirty laundry; but then, Sara changed her nightgown twice a day.
While the load was in the washer, she poured herself a
glass of lemonade and walked to the veranda. She'd noticed that Rem had brought Lady out into the corral.

Sara wanted to watch him work his magic.

He was a man who knew how to seduce. He did it with women. He did it with balky horses.

She angled a wicker chair so she could see him clearly. *Watch and learn, Sara.*

First, she noticed how gentle he was. Persistent, yes, because he had a goal, but gentle in his persuasion.

He talked to her quietly, cooed sweet nothings and encouragement.

He touched her and, from this distance, his touch looked non-threatening, quiet, so when Rem moved away, the mare followed for more.

Around the corral, he'd placed the equipment he eventually wanted Lady to wear. He held pieces out for her to smell. He placed them on her body, so she could get to know them.

And then, he stopped and left the corral. Lady stared after him, stepped forward, stopped, stepped forward again until she came right to the fence. He put his hands on her again, petted her nose and neck, and she was happy.

Sara remembered something Rem had once said to her. At the time she'd thought he was joking, but now she wasn't so sure. Now, she saw that it was real and that it worked.

Always leave them wanting more.

She had to learn how to do that.

At that moment, Rem turned and met her gaze, almost as though he'd known all along that she'd been watching him. She didn't look away, not as she would have done before now. She stared back, openly, honestly, curiously.

She stood and stepped toward the veranda railing and ran her fingers along it, slowly caressing it. Rem's gaze followed her fingers. She brought them to her chest, feathered them along her collarbone.

He watched every gesture.

Lifting the last of the lemonade to her mouth, she drank it and licked her bottom lip. His eyes tracked the movement of her tongue.

She turned and entered the house.

Always leave them wanting more.

THE FOLLOWING MORNING, Sara arrived early and made a pot of coffee with a dash of vanilla in it. She also made homemade cinnamon buns with icing sugar glaze.

The way to a man's heart...

Tired of waiting for Rem to make his first appearance of the day—he must be sleeping in—she walked upstairs and heard water running in the bathroom. He was showering. Ooh, opportunity.

Quickly, she ran downstairs, retrieved a bucket and cleaning supplies, then rushed back up. Outside the bathroom, she caught her breath before opening the door.

Rem wasn't showering. He stood in front of the sink with the water running, his tight butt wrapped in a towel, his back bare, shaving. In the small circle he'd cleared on the steamed-up mirror, she saw his eyes widen and he nicked his skin with the razor.

"What are you doing in here?" The shock on his face amused Sara.

She took her time staring at his back and behind. Gorgeous, gorgeous man.

He watched her in the mirror and she eventually met his gaze after looking her fill.

"Oh, I'm so sorry," she said. "I just wanted to clean. I'll come back later."

He looked bewildered, poor man, and his breathing seemed unsteady.

She stepped out, closed the door softly behind her and walked downstairs smiling. She'd never cleaned his bathroom. It wasn't in her job description, but he wouldn't realize that.

Fifteen minutes later, she called Rem and Finn for breakfast.

Sara and Finn met in Nell's room where she'd laid out plates for everyone.

Five minutes later, Rem entered the room, his face covered with tiny bits of tissue covering red dots of blood, where he'd nicked himself even more after she'd left. Goodness, she *had* rattled him.

"What happened to your face, man?" Finn asked, laughing. "Looks like you turned it into chopped liver."

"Funny. Ha-ha." Rem glared at Sara and she stared back, feigning innocence.

Over the next couple of hours, she waylaid him more than once, bumping him by mistake or stepping a little too close.

She'd also "forgotten" to button her shirt as high as usual and caught him looking.

That night at home, she searched through her wardrobe for her shortest skirt. Rem had always liked her legs. Or she guessed that he did since he'd spent a fair amount of time over the years staring at them.

Unfortunately, she'd never been in the habit of wearing her skirts very short.

She chose the shortest she owned and spent that evening raising the hem by one inch. Not much, but she was determined to be subtle.

She didn't really know if her campaign was working. She had nothing to compare it to.

When she arrived on the Caldwell ranch the following morning, Rem was already up and out in the corral working with Lady. Sara wondered if this was to ensure she wouldn't surprise him in the bathroom again.

She drove around the yard in a wide arc so she could back up against the front of the house. She wanted the driver's side to face the corral. Opening her door, she put one leg out, then turned back into the car to talk to Finn.

"You go on inside and see Nell. I'll bring in the groceries."

When Finn got out of the car and ran into the house, she continued to lean over, as though looking for something in the backseat, while she shimmied to hike that hem higher up her thigh.

When she turned around, put her other leg out and stood, she caught Rem watching her. Lady butted his shoulder with her nose, but Rem didn't notice. He continued to stare at Sara's legs.

She reached into the backseat for a couple of bags of groceries that she'd strategically positioned behind the passenger seat rather than hers. She had to reach so far across the seat she could feel her skirt ride up.

Read 'em and weep, buddy.

Arms full, Sara took her time mounting the steps to the veranda. Her hips might have swayed more than usual.

Once inside, she ran to the living room to peek out the side window at Rem. He stood stock-still in the middle of the corral, still watching the veranda steps she'd just sashayed up.

He shook his head, turned to Lady, then once more checked the veranda over his shoulder. Hoping for her to come back out, perhaps?

It was amazing the difference one little bitty inch made.

"Good morning." Nell's voice startled Sara and she jumped.

She'd forgotten about Nell. "Oh. Nell. Good morning. I'll go start on breakfast."

She carried the groceries to the kitchen with a self-satisfied grin.

Watch out, Rem. I'm coming for you.

THE WOMAN WAS EVERYWHERE. He couldn't avoid her, not even at night.

He tossed and turned and spent hours dreaming of her and he was damn tired of it.

She was off-limits. She'd made that abundantly clear.

So why was she crowding his thoughts? Most of the stuff that had been happening with her seemed innocent enough, but yesterday morning in the bathroom, the way she'd looked at him had made him feel dirty and, man, he'd liked it.

After she'd left, his hands had been so shaky he'd massacred his chin and throat while shaving.

Beneath his confusion and crazy-minded desire, a fine anger simmered.

She had rejected him—fine, he understood that and had accepted it—but it wasn't fair of her to look at him like that unless she was willing to follow through. She either wanted him or she didn't. Which was it?

Besides, he'd already laid down the law with her. Nothing would ever happen between them again. Sure, he still wanted her, but he'd controlled his urges just fine. Until now.

The woman was driving him crazy. Why did her legs look even better today than usual? Man, she had great thighs.

Thighs? He didn't usually see her thighs. In fact, her skirts weren't normally that short. Was she playing with him? Why?

He worried that issue all day.

At suppertime, she called him in.

Adelle was visiting Ma again, this time with Max. The two of them and Finn balanced plates of sandwiches on their laps. He went to the kitchen to get his own.

Sara was there, just making up two plates. One for her and him, he guessed.

He went to the counter to pick up his plate, but she said, "Wait. I forgot to put mustard on your sandwich."

She leaned over to fix his sandwich and touched his arm with her breast. He lost it.

"That's enough!" he shouted, and tossed his plate onto the counter, sending food flying. "I've had it with you."

He grabbed her hand, pulled her outside and dragged her around to the back of the house.

He pushed her against the house and crowded her, pressing himself full-length against her. Her eyes widened. "I don't know what game you're playing or why, but if you want it that badly, lady, you're getting it."

REM'S LIPS MET SARA'S and she gave in, surrendered, instantly. No fighting back. He tasted like fresh air and hot sun.

Insistent and wild, his kiss inflamed her. More. She wanted more.

Entwining her fingers in his hair, she pulled him closer as his leg slid between hers.

For ages they kissed, tangling and grasping at moments, gentle and giving at others.

She welcomed the pressure of his knee against her. She pressed back, gave as good as she got.

Why had she denied herself for so long? All this time, she and Rem could have been tearing each other apart with passion and melding back together with love.

"What are you doing?"

The shout drew them out of the kiss. Her brain drugged

by passion, it took Sara a moment to realize it had come from the back porch.

Finn stood on the steps watching them.

Rem watched Finn and shook his head, his eyes unfocused. "I don't know." He turned to her for an explanation.

Sara had never faced this before. She'd been careful with her boyfriends. She didn't think Finn had ever seen her kiss a man.

She realized that while she wanted Rem in her bed awakening her slumbering body, she'd avoided thinking about Finn, how she should deal with the issue of parenthood. Of Rem as a father. She hadn't thought anything through clearly. She'd just wanted and, for once in her life, was taking.

Was this the right time to tell him that Rem was his father? She didn't know, couldn't figure out what she saw on Finn's face. He was closed up, shutting her out once again.

One thing she did recognize, though, was a dawning suspicion. She might have run out of time. In trying to seduce Rem, had she alerted Finn to possibilities?

Rem must have seen something in Finn, too, because he said to her, "I don't know what's going on here, but I want to tell Finn the truth."

She looked at Rem. *Now?* Is this how her great, big secret would finally come out? She was so scared. How would Finn take it? All of that lovely desire she'd had for Rem dissipated, all of the happiness dried up. She'd lied to her son for too long.

"No," she told Rem. "I should."

"Please," he said. "I have a right to tell him."

"He barely knows you. It should come from me."

"Stop!" Finn shouted, awareness sharp and painful on his face. "Do you guys think I'm stupid?" He pointed an accusing finger at Rem. "He's my dad, isn't he? I saw pictures of Mrs. C.'s husband and wondered why he looked like me. I'm right, aren't I?"

Sara nodded, jerkily, as though someone else was pulling her strings.

"I can't believe you never told me!" he screamed at her, and the look of fury and hatred on his face chilled her.

She stretched a hand toward him. "Please. Wait. I can explain."

"Don't touch me. Don't ever come near me again."

He ran through the too-long grass of the backyard to the stable.

Sara fell onto the bottom porch step and covered her face with her hands. "What have I done?"

She felt Rem's hand on her hair. "I'll go talk to him."

"I should come, too."

"No. You should stay away from him right now."

"He hates me."

"He doesn't."

"The way he looked at me, Rem." She shivered. "I stole so much from him."

Rem pulled her into his arms. "We both did. We made mistakes, Sara."

"We sure did," she mumbled.

Rem gasped and his chest stiffened under her head.

"What's wrong?"

Then she heard the pounding of a horse's hooves and raised her head. "Finn?"

"Crazy kid. We'll follow him." He ran to the Jeep.

The second she jumped in, Rem took off. As he swung around the outside of the corral, she banged against the passenger door and then managed to get her seat belt on.

"Where are we going?"

"He didn't come out through the front of the stable, so he must have opened the back doors."

"He's only been riding once, right? What if he falls off?"

"We'll deal with that if it happens."

"He's going to kill himself." She wrapped her arms across her stomach.

"Calm down. That's not likely to happen."

"How can I fix this, Rem? How can I make him love me again?"

"He loves you. He's just mad at you."

He pointed to a silver line of trampled grass. "Look. We'll follow that."

They bounced over a bump in the field and Sara's teeth knocked together.

"What's been going on with you lately?" The steering wheel bumped out of his hand and he gripped it. "It took me a while to figure it out, but you've been hitting on me. Why?"

"I wanted to sleep with you."

"Why?" Rem looked at her and then back through the windshield. "When did you come to this decision?"

"The night Karl was born. I caught Mama with Max Golden."

"Yeah?" He grinned. "They finally got together?"

"You knew about it?"

"I got the impression he liked her. So he asked her out."

"I don't think they ever *got* out. They set up a date for Friday night, but I found them in bed at Mama's house on Thursday evening. They moved fast." She twisted the fingers of one hand in the other. "Where's Finn?"

"We'll find him."

He swerved around a hummock. "I still don't get it. Why did that make you want to sleep with me?"

"I had a boyfriend in Bozeman. I thought we would get married some day, but after that night I spent with you last summer, I couldn't be with him again."

She felt her cheeks pink up and rubbed her forehead. Now that she had to tell him the truth, it embarrassed her. "I...don't...want...anyone else." She turned to him with a helpless shrug. "Only you."

"So you were trying to seduce me?"

"You told me our ship had sailed. I wanted to bring it back." She held back on telling him about wanting another baby and a future with him. Far too much information, far too soon.

The breeze had picked up since the afternoon and whipped strands of hair out of her ponytail and around her face. Had Finn put on a jacket? Was he cold?

"He's so mad at me. Maybe he'll never talk to me again."

"He will." Rem's voice was so quiet Sara almost missed what he said. "Trust me. That boy loves you."

"I don't know, Rem. We'll see."

"There!" Rem pointed to the silhouette of a riderless horse against the setting sun.

Rem gunned the engine and stopped just shy of Rusty. He slammed on the brakes, jumped out of the vehicle and ran to get the horse.

Sara got out and called, "Finn! Where are you?"

"Here."

She followed the sound of his voice and found him sitting on the far side of an oak, his left arm, still in its cast, resting on his thigh. It would have been useless to him when he fell.

Thank goodness full darkness hadn't yet descended.

"Are you okay?" She'd give him a piece of her mind later, but right now she needed to know he was safe.

"I hit my head on a rock when I fell off Rusty. It hurts."

She ran to him and landed on her knees beside him. Rem followed right behind her. "Let me see." She felt around and found a lump the size of her palm on the back of his head.

"Honey, look at me. Can you see properly?"

"The stuff on my right side looks wavy."

"Can you stand?"

"Yeah."

Rem helped him to his feet.

"Do you feel nauseated?" he asked.

"No."

"Dizzy?" Sara asked from his other side.

"Uh-uh. Not dizzy. Not normal, though."

They took him to the Jeep and helped him into the backseat.

"Do you need me to sit back there with you?" When Finn said no, Sara climbed into the passenger seat.

"Let's get him to the hospital." Rem tied Rusty to the back bumper.

"Yes." Sara turned around to study Finn. "If you need to be sick, say so. Rem can stop."

"'Kay."

Rem drove back across the graying fields, slowly so Rusty could keep up and so Finn wouldn't be knocked around any more than he'd already been.

Sara wanted him to race, to fly, because dread was balling up in her stomach, but of course they couldn't.

The porch light shone like a beacon in the gathering darkness.

At the back of the stable, Rem untied the horse and led him to his stall. He closed the back doors.

On the other side of the corral, he parked the Jeep.

"Go ask your mom if she can stay with Ma while we take Finn to the hospital."

"I can take him myself."

"No, Sara. Not tonight. I'm coming, too."

She didn't want to argue. "Okay."

Adelle and Max came to the front door.

Sara climbed the veranda steps, so very tired.

"Finn fell off Rem's horse. He has a concussion. Can you stay with Nell while we take him to the hospital?"

"Of course." Mama turned to Max. "You go on home. I'll probably sleep here tonight."

"We'll be back as soon as we can," Sara said.

They drove to Haven in silence. Sara broke it occasionally to ask how Finn was. After each positive response, she lapsed into silence again.

That dark cloud of dread hadn't broken. Her anxiety persisted.

It's only a concussion.

I know, but...

Something wild and tumultuous beat inside her chest but refused to make itself known. It pressed against her lungs. She breathed shallowly because, with every minute that passed, that wild thing seemed to grow.

FINN SAT IN THE BACKSEAT again on the drive home and fell asleep right away.

Sara had called it right. A CT scan had confirmed a concussion.

He couldn't do a lot in the next week—no horseback riding, no skateboarding, no activity that might result in another fall. If he hit his head again, the situation could be dire.

Sara knew how rough he was going to feel for the next week or two. He was going to have wicked head and neck aches.

Speaking of headaches, her temples throbbed. She had

trouble swallowing and her eyes burned. Maybe tomorrow she should go to the doctor.

She was a nurse, for Pete's sake. She should be able to diagnose herself, but this felt nothing like any illness she'd ever had.

They pulled up to the house and Sara climbed out of the Jeep holding on to the door frame like an old woman. Thirty-one-year-old women didn't feel like this unless something was very wrong.

Despite the symptoms, she knew this illness wasn't physical, that these aches and pains were only harbingers of some amorphous thing yet to come.

Rem stepped around the Jeep. "You and Finn are staying here tonight. There's no point in going home at this hour."

Her refusal to fight him revealed how low her spirits were, how tired her body was. All she wanted was a soft bed to sink into.

Rem stood beside Finn while he got out, but their son was able to stand and walk on his own.

"There's a room at the far end of the house you can have. Turn left at the top of the stairs."

Finn barely mumbled okay.

To Sara, he said, "You can have Ma's room upstairs." Rem closed Finn's door and the one Sara had left open. He gripped her upper arms. "Are you okay?"

She wanted to lean on him—badly—but she'd been depending on herself for so long.

"I don't know how to give in, Rem. How to rely on someone else."

"Yeah, I know."

"My head hurts. Something's wrong, but I don't know what."

"I know, honey."

"Why do you keep saying that? You mean you know I'm feeling bad? Or you know what's wrong with me?"

"Both."

Over the course of the night, her ponytail had gone askew and the elastic was pulling her hair. Her temples ached. She yanked it out and rubbed the sides of her head.

"How do you know what's wrong with me?"

"I just know. I have a feeling."

"Rem, for God's sake, help me."

"You've been caring for everyone else for years. It's time to take care of yourself. Figure out what's wrong inside and fix it."

"Quit with the bloody riddles. I don't understand. What do you mean?"

Rem shrugged, his face smooth and serene like a stone guru, and she felt like slapping him to break his self-control. Somewhere nearby an owl hooted and sounded altogether too calm, exacerbating her frustration.

Rem's hands slid down her arms and he massaged her fingers. "Remember when you used to follow Timm and me around when we were kids?"

"Yes. What does that have to do with anything?"

"Remember how you always got into trouble because you were too small to do the things we were doing?"

"Yes. You would always help me."

Rem nodded. "I can't do that anymore. You're a big girl now. You have to rescue yourself."

"What the *hell* are you talking about? Rescue myself from *what*?"

"You'll figure it out, honey." He let go of her hands and headed for the stable. "I need to put Rusty to bed properly."

"Don't you dare walk away without explaining." She felt like tearing out her hair. "Come out and say whatever it is you're trying to say."

He turned back to her but he'd stepped away from the halo of the porch light and she couldn't read his expression.

"It will all work out, Sara."

"*What* will work out?"

He didn't respond, turned and walked away, and she picked up a clod of dirt and threw it at him. The action was petty, but so what? When the dirt hit his shoulder, she felt good.

"Your aim's a lot better than when you were a kid." He brushed off his shoulder and entered the stable, leaving her alone in the yard to watch bats swoop in front of the light spilling through the stable door.

Sometimes, she missed the noise of the city. Here, in this deathly still summer night, there was nothing to cloud her frantic heartbeat, nothing to obscure the roaring of her panic.

She went inside and together, she and Mama made a bed on the sofa. Mama would spend the night downstairs.

Sara slept in Nell's bedroom across the hall from Finn. She checked on him throughout the night, compulsive in her need to make sure her boy was okay.

The fourth time she checked, Rem came out of his room.

"How is he?"

"Okay. Sleeping well. The painkillers they gave him at the hospital are working. He'll be hurting in the morning, though."

The house creaked around them in the breeze that had flared again. Otherwise, silence.

Rem had pulled on a pair of jeans. His bare torso called to her. She knew how warm his skin was and, despite the heat of the night, she was cold.

He stared at her legs, even though there couldn't be much to see in the darkness of the hallway. He knew they were bare. He was the one who'd loaned her a T-shirt to sleep in.

She said good-night and backed into her bedroom then lay in bed and listened.

He didn't return to his room for a while.

Sara slept little for the rest of the night, but didn't get up again until she heard movement downstairs. When she came down, Mama already had Nell washed and her private needs taken care of and was in the kitchen cooking breakfast.

She thought Finn would probably sleep late, but in case he didn't, asked Mama to come into the living room for a few minutes.

Mama looked puzzled, but did as she was asked, turning off the burners before following Sara out of the kitchen.

In the living room, Sara pulled two chairs close to the bed and asked Mama to take one. Nell watched her carefully, perhaps already guessing what was about to happen.

"I have to tell you something, Mama. I've already made Finn angry and you probably will be, too, but it's past time for the truth to be told."

This wasn't easy. She hadn't thought about how lying by omission was still lying. Mama would be hurt that her daughter hadn't confided in her.

"I lied about who Finn's father is. I didn't have a one-night stand."

"Of course you didn't," Mama said. "You weren't the type."

"Did you guess? That Rem is his father?"

"I had an idea."

"Why did you never say anything?"

"I wanted to, but you and Rem must have had your reasons."

"Finn guessed yesterday. He's so angry with me. I don't know how to fix it."

Adelle looked at Nell. "Did you know?"

Nell nodded.

"I told her a week ago, but Finn didn't know until last night."

"So Finn rode away because he was upset?"

"I guess because I deprived him of having a father all of those years."

"Why did you do it?"

"We were so young. Rem didn't think he would be a good father and made it clear he shouldn't be in our lives. After that, I decided he was too irresponsible and that Finn and I were better off without him."

Sara looked at Nell. "Did Mama tell you that Finn has a concussion?"

Nell nodded. "Will hurt."

"Yes."

If Sara wasn't mistaken, a hint of compassion shone in Nell's eyes. Thank goodness, because she suspected that in the next while she was going to need every friend and every drop of support they could offer.

Rem entered the room. He must have already been out taking care of the horses because he smelled like the outdoors.

Finn showed up in the doorway, squinting.

"My head really hurts."

Sara got out the painkillers the doctor had prescribed last night. She poured him a glass of water.

"Take these. They'll help a bit."

"Thanks," he mumbled, obviously in a lot of pain or he would never let his mom this close. "Something strange happened in bed."

Strange? Sara stilled, instantly on alert. "What?"

"When I wanted to roll over, my neck was too weak to turn my head. I had to lift my head with my hands and turn it while I rolled."

"You hurt a lot of muscles and they're sore and compromised. That will pass in time."

"'Kay."

Not once during their conversation did he look at her.

So he was still angry. When all was said and done, she didn't blame him.

When Sara said, "We need to go home and shower," Finn stared out the window.

"I'm staying here," he said.

What did he mean, he was staying?

For how long? She couldn't bring herself to ask because she was afraid of the answer. She hadn't slept last night and had no reserves to draw on. If he said he never wanted to see her again, she might start to cry and not be able to stop.

Finn was her little boy, but right now she wasn't his mother.

"Okay," she said, taking a deep breath. "I'll bring fresh clothes for today."

"No. I mean I'm staying here for good."

For good. Her stomach cramped. She couldn't do this, couldn't walk out of this house and not take her boy with her.

Sara appealed to Rem silently, but he shook his head and raised his brows.

"If he wants to stay, he can."

"I want to get to know my *dad*." The mulish twist to Finn's lips made him look like a kid, but the anger was real and justified.

Sara covered her face for a minute and breathed into her

hands then dropped them. "I'll pack you a bag and bring it back."

She stood. "Mom, could I ask you to help Nell today?"

"Of course. Bring me back a change of clothing, too."

While she drove into town, packed bags for her mother and her son, delivered them to the ranch, drove back home and curled into a ball on her bed, she couldn't feel anything, not her hands or feet, or her heart. She was frozen and had no idea how to thaw.

CHAPTER TWELVE

REM FED FINN A COUPLE of slices of toast then took him out to the stable.

"We need to talk," he said.

Rem led him to the back office and indicated a stool beside Gracie. Finn sat.

"Does Gracie live out here?"

"Naw," Rem answered. "She's allowed in the house, but seems to pick the stables most days now that she's older. Maybe she likes the company of other animals."

"She's old? So, like, is she going to die soon?"

"Not if I can help it."

That answer seemed to satisfy Finn. He nodded.

Rem settled in an old office chair, the ancient leather creaking beneath him.

Rem couldn't figure out the best way to start the real conversation, how to tell his son why he'd walked away all of those years ago. Where was the instruction manual for this type of situation? For twelve years, he'd been a father but he hadn't fathered.

"I need to explain what happened when you were born. The last thing I want is for you to think I didn't want you." It suddenly occurred to him that might be exactly what Sara had told the boy.

"What did your mom tell you about your dad?"

When he swallowed, Finn's Adam's apple moved in his thin throat. "That they'd had a one-night stand and that he gave her the wrong name so she couldn't find him and tell him about me."

At least Finn hadn't thought that he hadn't been wanted. "Okay, here goes. I'm probably going to have to tell you more than I should for your age. But I really want you to understand."

"I'm not a kid."

You surely are. "I told you about the fire that burned your uncle."

Finn nodded.

"It screwed me up for a long time. As a teenager, I turned wild. Got drunk a lot. Went through a lot of girls."

"But it was an accident."

"I know, but when you hurt your best friend like that it hurts you, too. I didn't think I was worth very much. Thought all I deserved was a screwed-up life."

He cracked his knuckles because he was coming to the part when he had to tell Finn that he had walked away from him—even if he'd thought his reasons were noble. He needed to tell it so it made sense to Finn.

"Your mom was my little buddy. I lost her for a long time after the accident. She blamed me for ruining both Timm's life and hers. She had to do a lot for Timm and the family. She didn't get to go out with friends. Her life was so serious. She had no fun at all in high school. For her, everything was really dark and hard."

He could see Finn trying to process this information, to see his mom as a teenager.

"I watched her fade, almost as if she disappeared. I wanted to give her back some of who she used to be, so the summer before she was supposed to go to college, I pursued her. I thought I was giving her this great gift. Teaching her how to have fun again."

He leaned forward and pressed his thumbs against the

bridge of his nose. "It *was* only one night, Finn. She didn't lie about that. We weren't as careful as we should have been and you were conceived. When I found out, I freaked. I'd barely scraped through high school and my future was up in the air. I wasn't prepared. I still felt like such a kid."

"How was Mom? Did she want me?"

Rem smiled, warmly, glad there was some good news to share. "She was crazy happy. You brought her so much joy. I was the one who hurt her, not you. After she had you, I visited her in the hospital. She thought we were going to get married. I broke her heart that day. She didn't talk to me for a long time."

Rem tried not to think about that day. "Life handed me a challenge that I couldn't rise to. I didn't touch you, didn't hold you, because I knew I'd fall for you and then where would I be? Loving a kid I didn't deserve and couldn't do a good job of raising."

Finn had buried both fists in Gracie's fur. Rem could only guess how he must be feeling, but Finn kept silent.

In his stall, Rusty made throaty noises and, to Rem's guilty conscience, they sounded sympathetic.

"If it's any consolation, since you got home this summer, I've wanted to be your father. Your mom wasn't convinced she could trust me, so I've been trying to change her mind."

"She should have told me!" he shouted, apparently no longer able to contain his anger. "A long time ago. She didn't have to lie about not knowing his name. She could have told me it was you, but that you didn't want me."

"That would have hurt you. She thought she was protecting you. I left her in an impossible situation. I was sure I'd make a lousy father and, when your mom thought about it, she agreed."

"So how come you want to be my dad now?"

"I've straightened out. I need to make things right for you. You deserved a dad when you were growing up. I wasn't mature enough to do it then, but I am now. Besides, I like having you here. I like getting to know you." He stood. "Let's go back to the house."

Walking appeared to loosen Finn's tongue, because he started talking as soon as they left the office.

"I don't ever want to speak to my mom again. I'm kind of mad at you, too, but I want to get to know you. I'm really mad at my mom, though, 'cause she kept lying even after you wanted to tell me the truth."

When they passed Rusty's stall, he poked his head out to be petted. Rem could feel Finn watching him and asked, "You okay?"

Hesitantly, Finn asked, "Can I, like, hug you or something?"

Rem had him in his arms so fast he was afraid he'd given the kid whiplash. Finn made some remark, but it was muffled against Rem's shirt. He eased his grip and stepped back.

"Sorry," Rem said. "I've wanted to do that for a long time." To give his eyes a chance to clear, he turned to scratch Rusty's nose.

"I've wanted a dad for a really long time." Finn reached a hand to scratch Rusty's nose beside Rem's. To Rem's astonishment, it looked like a young version of his own. This feeling in his chest, this fullness—is this what Sara felt whenever she held her son? Rem hadn't understood what he'd been running away from.

Someday, he would have to tell Sara what he thought of her courage for sticking with Finn and raising him so well.

"Can I call you *Dad?*"

Afraid that he would collapse from all of the painful joy coursing through his veins, Rem simply nodded.

When he thought he could speak clearly, he said, "You know what would make Mrs. C. really happy?"

"What?"

"If when we go inside you call her *Grandma*."

Finn grinned. "I have two of them now."

Rem placed his hand on Finn's shoulder and they walked to the door. Before they stepped outside, though, he said, "I have a lot to make up for. I understand that, Finn."

"I have tons of questions, but I can't think of them all right now."

"I'll be here to answer them anytime."

Finn hesitated. "Some of them will make you angry."

"I doubt it. There's nothing you can say to me that I haven't already said to myself."

They walked across the yard and Rem thought he might be hovering a few inches above the earth. He had a son.

SARA BARELY SLEPT THE NIGHT her son stayed at Rem's ranch. She missed him.

After she arrived the following morning, Finn walked into the kitchen with his hands shoved deeply into his pant pockets, a typical posture for him these days.

She wanted to drag him into her arms, but knew he wouldn't tolerate that. He'd been distancing himself from her for a while, but now felt like he was so far away she might never get him back.

She tried to behave as though nothing were wrong, but couldn't pull it off.

When she asked, "How are you feeling?" her voice shook.

She could tell that he didn't want to talk to her. He was still suffering from the concussion, though, and he knew she might be able to help him. "Awful. The pain meds only last for a little while. Can't I take more?" He sounded angry and surly, as if she were the last person he wanted to see.

"When did you take them this morning?"

"About an hour ago."

"You can't take any more yet. Is it just your head or your neck, too?"

"My neck. I think that's where the headache is starting. My neck is really stiff."

"Do you want a massage?"

Poor Finn looked as if he couldn't decide which he wanted more—to stalk out of the room, or to let her take care of him.

She made the decision for him. "Come here."

She sat him at the kitchen table, then retrieved a headache balm from her bag. She massaged his temples gently, careful not to get any on his longish hair.

He stiffened at her touch but gradually relaxed.

She massaged down his neck, trying to loosen his tension.

"How high does it hurt?"

He pointed up into his hair to where the bump had almost disappeared. "Is it still tender?"

"Yeah. I forget about it at night and rolled over onto my back. It hurts as soon as I touch the pillow."

She put more balm on her thumbs and rubbed up into his hair, stopping just shy of the bump. It was definitely smaller but would still be tender for at least a week.

"What is that stuff? Am I going to smell like it all day?"

"Probably. It's menthol and eucalyptus. The scent is strong, but it's worth it. Trust me."

When she finished, he muttered, "Thanks," like a sulky little boy and walked out of the room.

His birthday party was on Saturday, only two days

away. She'd picked up a brand-new pair of the Vans skateboarding shoes he'd asked for. She sincerely hoped it would be a turning point. She didn't believe in bribery, but right now she needed an edge.

Thank goodness she had shifts at the hospital those two days and Nell to care for mornings and night, because the work would keep her sane. Exhausted, but sane.

When she wasn't working, she planned to go to her house to sit on the veranda and drink up the peace of the surroundings.

Secretly, she wanted Finn's birthday to be here and gone already, though. There was something bothering her about it. Asleep, awake, busy, inactive, she couldn't escape that ball of dread that still hurt in her stomach.

WHILE HE WAS MUCKING OUT the stalls, Rem heard Finn enter the stable.

He looked sullen or bored. A second later, he realized it was pain, both physical and emotional.

"Do you miss being at home with your mom?" Rem leaned the pitchfork against a stall and approached his son. Finn had now spent two nights here and the adjustment was bound to be tough.

"No," he answered, but Rem thought the boy might be lying. He and Sara had spent so much time, so many years together.

"It's great that she isn't bossing me around," Finn continued. "She wanted me busy all the time so I couldn't get into trouble."

Rem didn't think that was such a bad idea. "What do you have planned for the day?"

Finn shrugged. "Nothing."

Rem guessed it was up to him to keep Finn occupied now. He had no idea how. He did know he had a lot of work to do, though, and wouldn't mind the help. "Come on," he said. "I'll show you how to take care of horses."

Finn perked up. "'Kay."

In the middle of the morning, Rem got a call from Max. "Ticks again, Rem. On two more horses."

Pity call or not, Rem needed the money. "Be right there."

Hanging up, he turned to his son. "Finn," he asked, "you want to come with me on a vet call?"

"For sure."

Rem grinned. "Let's go."

Max stepped down from his veranda when they pulled up.

"Do you mind if Finn hangs out while I work?" Rem asked.

"Not at all."

"Didn't the cider in the water work?"

Max looked sheepish. "Um, I forgot all about it. I've been distracted lately."

Rem laughed and slapped Max on the back. Max still seemed distracted, but happy.

"Can you head into town for cider now?"

Max nodded. "Sure. Be right back."

Rem started working on the two horses, all the while telling Finn what he was doing and why. He even showed him how to pull ticks out of an animal's skin so he wouldn't leave parts of the insect in to cause infection.

Finn didn't turn up his nose at any of it, and again it was brought home to Rem just how much he'd missed by walking away from this boy.

SATURDAY ARRIVED CLEAR and cloudless.

Sara still didn't know why she was dreading this party.

Even before Finn had stopped talking to her, she'd been uneasy.

She was always glad for an excuse to make a fuss over Finn, was happy when he was happy, so what was her problem with his twelfth birthday? Timm had been burned on his eleventh, so there was no significance there. This wasn't some freaky mirror anniversary fear. And Rem wasn't about to blow foam streamers on his own son.

Everywhere she turned, her nerves tripped her up. She dropped a platter in the kitchen and it shattered. "Damn."

She cleaned up the best she could, then went to the living room to confess to Nell.

"What's wrong?" Nell asked as Sara stepped into the room. She gestured toward her face with her right hand. Good. She was trying to use it. "You look gloomy."

"I dropped your platter and broke it. I'm so sorry. I'll replace it."

"Which one?"

"The turkey platter."

"Always...hated that thing."

A laugh spurted out of Sara. "So, I'm forgiven?"

"Yes. You said makeup?"

Sara retrieved the makeup she'd bought for Nell and applied it.

When she finished applying a trace of blush to Nell's cheeks, Nell asked, "Better?"

"Better." Sara's smile felt wobbly, so she worked harder on her mood. She wanted Nell to have a good day.

"Do you want Peach Surprise or Pink Paradise?" Sara held out two lipsticks she'd picked up.

With an effort, Nell lifted her right hand and touched the Pink Paradise.

Sara smiled. "You're doing so well."

She applied the lipstick, then stepped away for a good

look at her handiwork. "Lovely." Despite Nell being in bed, Sara had dressed her in a white blouse and dark slacks, helping her to sit on top of the quilt so she could feel as much a part of the festivities as possible.

"Look like old woman," Nell groused, but a smile played around her lips.

"You're fishing for compliments, Nell. You look beautiful." Sara smiled and tidied the room.

Around her duties involving Nell, Sara had worked the past two days to clean the house.

Rem and Finn had scoured the outside of the house and the grounds. The Caldwell homestead and ranch looked grand.

Through the living room window, Sara and Nell watched Max Golden's truck pull into the yard.

Mama climbed out with the birthday cake she'd promised to make for Finn.

Rem arrived not long after. They watched him pull bunches and bunches of flowers out of the Jeep.

Nell sighed and said, "Too much money." Sara knew the truth, though. Nell might pretend to be unaffected, but she loved the pampering.

On impulse, Sara kissed her forehead and Nell smiled.

Rem carried the flowers into the kitchen, hollering for Sara along the way. All morning, Gracie had picked up on his excitement, running in and out of the house endlessly. She followed Rem inside again now. Sara unwrapped a chewy dog bone and put her out on the back porch out of the way.

Together, she and Rem cut stems and arranged flowers in vases.

On the last delicate bouquet of freesias, Sara stalled. Rem noticed and glanced at her. "Something wrong?"

"This birthday…" She shrugged. "It worries me."

"Sara." He leaned close and murmured low, "Nothing will happen."

He didn't have to ask what she meant. Had he been thinking about it, too?

His blue eyes darkened. "*Nothing* will go wrong. I'll make sure of it. Be happy for Finn."

He grinned, one of his heart-stoppers. "He says he's not a kid anymore. As if he's going to turn into a teenager overnight."

Picking up a couple of filled vases, he left the room.

Still, Sara was worried. Her funk wouldn't quit.

REM STOOD AT THE CORRAL and watched people arrive, most of them his and Sara's friends and their kids, because Finn was too new in town to have made many of his own yet. He checked out what they carried with them, looking for anything that might be a problem.

He hadn't told Sara, but he was nervous, too, which made no sense—it was just a kid's birthday party. But he thought Sara was close to figuring things out, and he knew how much she would hurt when she did.

She'd taken over the house and the yard. Rem had declared the stables off-limits. He didn't want kids messing with the horses.

Instead, he'd borrowed a sedate little pony named Penny from his neighbor Hank Shelter and had her safely ensconced in the corral. Rem would take charge of pony rides.

Finn ran in and out of the house just as Rem, Timm and Sara had done as children and the parallels were killing Rem. Finn had a good head of unruly dark hair and a tendency toward olive skin that would tan easily like Rem's. He had Sara's gray eyes, but unlike hers, Finn's weren't

cool. They were alive with mischief and a hint of recklessness today that terrified Rem.

A car he didn't recognize drove down the laneway.
When it stopped, Randy from the hospital got out of the
driver's seat.

The woman who climbed awkwardly out of the passenger seat had a white sling holding her right arm close
to her body.

Liz. In the past two weeks, all of the bruising on her
face had dissipated. Rem had been right. She was pretty,
strikingly so.

When Randy reached into the backseat and lifted out
a young girl, Rem's eyes watered. Melody.

They all approached Rem.

"Hey, man," Randy said.

"Randy. Hey, Melody, how are you, sweetheart?" He
pointed to the bandages on her head. "It's okay for you to
be here today?"

She nodded. "I'm good. I was allowed to come because
Randy is a nurse."

"Randy, thanks, man."

"No problem. I'll do anything for a free meal."

Randy handed Melody off to Rem. She weighed so little.

"Hey, kid," Randy called to Finn.

Finn ran over. "Melody, you came!"

"Of course. I wanted to. Look," she cried. "You have a
pony."

"Have you ever been on a pony?" Finn asked.

Melody shook her head.

"Can she go on Penny?" he asked Rem.

"I don't know, Finn." Rem carried her to the corral gate.
"What shape is she in?" he asked Randy.

"She can handle a pony ride with someone beside her. No problem."

When Rem entered the corral, Finn ran in behind him.

Rem put Melody on Penny and then walked her around the inside of the fence, while Melody's small hand sat trustingly on his shoulder. If he could rescue her from a burning vehicle, he could keep her safe on a pony.

When her energy started to fade, Rem lifted her from Penny's back. He carried her to Liz, but felt reluctant to let her go.

"How long can you stay?"

Randy answered. "She's good for a couple of hours."

Rem, with Melody in his arms, entered the house and Liz followed them inside.

When Rem brought Melody to the living room, Nell patted the bed awkwardly. "Here."

"Ma, this is Melody and her mom, Liz. Remember I told you about the car fire."

Nell nodded. "Yah."

"You talk funny," Melody said.

"Melody!" Liz admonished.

Nell just smiled her droopy smile. "It's okay," she said. She looked at Melody. "Yes. I talk funny."

Settled beside Nell, Melody glanced around and squealed. "Paintings! Finn's story. He said he was going to do this. Mummy, look."

Nell pointed to Lady Serena. "Looks like you."

Melody clapped her hands.

More guests arrived, some Finn's age along with younger siblings and the noise level went up in both the house and the yard.

With everything under control here, Rem went back outside to check on the pony rides.

HALF AN HOUR LATER, SARA went looking for Finn, as though she couldn't trust anyone else to keep him safe. She was running a party, though, and couldn't keep track of him every minute.

Where was he?

She found him beside the corral, watching while Rem walked the pony around the perimeter. Astride the pony, a small girl giggled and patted the horse, while Rem kept a good grip on her arm.

Rem glanced up and saw her. He frowned, slightly, as though he felt it, too, this tension that shimmered in the air.

The next two hours passed in a blur. The younger kids played organized games in the yard that the adults supervised.

Penny gave so many kids rides that Rem came in to collect three fat carrots to reward her.

Sara peeked into the living room. Melody and Nell watched from the window.

Sara had no time to socialize, barely had time to greet guests, let alone sit and chat with Timm and Angel. She had the chance to hold Karl for only a few brief minutes.

Sometime after Sara served the food, Nell fell asleep; Melody curled against her side and passed out, too.

Sara waited until Melody and Nell woke up, then called everyone in for cake.

She lit Finn's birthday candles in the kitchen and carried the sheet cake into the dining room. Finn sat on the sofa, waiting, but as Sara watched him through the wavering heat from the candles, his face morphed into Timm's and the party into that other one so long ago.

Her head filled with screams, flashes of fire and terrible smells, and the muted shock of the aftermath.

The cake slid to one side of the platter and would have

fallen if Rem hadn't been there to catch it. He shot her a concerned look, then started everyone singing "Happy Birthday."

He placed the cake on the coffee table in front of Finn and handed Mama the knife.

Leaving Adelle and Liz to hand it around, he strode toward where Sara still stood frozen in the doorway. He gripped her hand and led her out to the back porch.

The second the door closed behind them, he pulled her into his arms.

"It's okay," he whispered, his voice urgent. "*He's* okay."

"Rem, what's wrong?" She felt like she was on the edge of some kind of meltdown. "Why am I remembering it so badly today?"

"I don't know, sweets."

"Why am I feeling it this year?" Her voice shook. "Why wasn't it worse last year when he turned eleven?"

"Were there a lot of kids at his party last year?"

"No. I took him out to his favorite restaurant."

He released her and she rubbed a chill from her arms.

"Maybe the kids are the problem. Are you afraid one of them might do something?"

"I guess that's it. It must be."

But no. That darkness inside her grew. It wasn't the kids. It couldn't be Rem. He would take care of Finn if anything happened. So what *was* the problem?

Rem and his compassion unnerved her and she rushed back into the kitchen to distract herself with cleaning.

After the party broke up, Adelle sat with Nell in the living room. Sara listened to their soft voices and slumped into a kitchen chair. She didn't think she had the strength to drive home. The birthday party was over and nothing had happened, but still Sara vibrated with edginess.

She hung up the damp dish towel, put the last cake plates away in the china cabinet and joined Adelle and Nell.

Through the open living room windows, she heard Rem, Max and Finn talking on the veranda. Finn sounded happy, so at least Sara had done something right. She'd thrown a good party for him and he'd been overjoyed with his new shoes.

"You look tired," Adelle said. "Why don't I get Nell ready for bed before I leave?"

"Thanks, Mama, I'd appreciate it."

"I'm going to stay at Max's ranch tonight," Mama said. "Don't go back to the house alone. Stay here tonight."

"I don't know if Finn will want me here."

"It's not up to him. Just do it."

"Maybe you're right. I don't feel so well."

Sara kissed Nell's forehead. "Did you have a good day?"

"Won...derful."

Sara found Rem on the veranda and asked if she could stay the night in Nell's bedroom.

"Of course. You look beat."

She smiled wanly, said good-night and headed upstairs, washed up for the night, borrowed one of Nell's nightgowns from a drawer, got into bed and stared at the ceiling.

She heard Mama and Max leave and then Finn come up to bed. An hour later, she heard Rem go to his room.

She stared at the ceiling. And stared and stared while anxiety churned in her stomach.

Suddenly, she sat up and doubled over, panting. She couldn't breathe.

Something was very wrong.

Since lighting the candles on Finn's cake, her desperation had grown. It gnawed a hole in her psyche.

She needed Rem. Through the years, her life had constantly circled back to him.

It will all work out, Sara.

She had no idea what he was talking about. *Yes, you do.*

No, I don't!

If whatever this was didn't work out, if after all of her hard work things got worse again, like they had after Timm's accident, she wasn't sure she could survive.

She couldn't face that. Rem said she had to rescue herself, but she didn't feel strong tonight. She didn't know what she was supposed to rescue herself *from*.

She needed Rem.

Silently, she tiptoed out into the hallway. Finn's door was closed. She turned away to head toward Rem's room.

Here she was again at Rem's door, beside his bed.

Help me.

He lay still, one sheet covering his lower body and a quilt on the floor. Sara stood above him, careful not to block the pale moonlight gleaming on his chest. She wanted to devour his beauty, his strength.

She'd always thought she was the strong one, but she wasn't anymore.

Arms spread, Rem hogged the bed. One foot peeked out from under the sheet.

Sara lifted her cotton gown over her head and dropped it to the floor, where it puddled like a melting ghost.

Gently, she crawled in beside Rem and rested her head on his shoulder. His arm came around her and pressed her against his chest, warming her heart.

She was so cold.

She cuddled against him, tried to crawl inside him, needing the oblivion of the sex he could offer. He knew how to make her happy and safe and blissfully unaware of the darkness.

Still, he slept.

She rose above him and nibbled his lips. They reacted, allowing her to slip inside to persuade him to awaken. Or perhaps it was better if he slept. Maybe he wouldn't give her what she wanted if he awoke.

One hand roved across his chest, lighted on his nipples, traced the scar where the knife had cut him, spread across his flat stomach and then lower. His body rose to greet her.

Welcome me, *not some other woman you're dreaming about. Please be glad it's me, Rem.*

"Recognize me," she whispered.

"I do, Sara." His hand drew hers away from his body. "Aw, honey, I do."

She pulled back and found his eyes open and studying her. He stroked her cheeks and his fingers came away wet. She hadn't known she was crying.

Without volition, her head rested on his chest and she shivered. Even with his heat, she was frozen.

"Rem, love me. Please."

He saw something in her—her desperation—because he lifted her away from him and sat up. Strong hands wrapped around her arms and pushed her to the edge of the bed, where she sat bewildered.

"What are you doing?"

"Getting dressed." In one motion, he stood and pulled up his jeans, adjusting the bulge that made zipping them tricky.

He wanted her.

She took one step toward him, but he raised a staying hand. She shivered again. Her lips felt numb. So cold.

Warm tears melted down her cheeks, cooling by the time they reached her chin.

When he rounded the bed, Rem hauled off the sheet.

He brought a rocking chair out of the corner of the room and settled it in front of the window.

"You're freezing." He stepped toward her and wrapped her in the white sheet.

Before she could react, he lifted her and sat in the chair with her on his lap, leaving her legs to drape across the arm. He locked her in an embrace so tight she couldn't move.

She tried to wriggle her hands free.

"Don't," he ordered.

"Rem, I want to go to bed. Please do this for me. I want to touch you. I need you."

"I told you earlier. I can't rescue you anymore. You have to come to this yourself."

"Come to *what?*" But she knew. She had a terrible feeling that somewhere deep inside her psyche, she knew. It was time to look.

An unfocused image appeared in her mind, terrifying her.

No. She struggled against him, but he tightened his hold.

"Rem, I can't do this."

"You can."

"When did you get to be so wise?" Despite her sarcasm-laden tone, she was serious. When had Rem become so strong and sure?

"Ma's strokes forced me to grow up, Sara. To see things differently."

"Then help *me* see differently."

"I can't. I won't take responsibility for you any longer."

"What does that mean? I'm the one who takes responsibility for everyone else."

"I know, but you don't take care of yourself."

"What are you talking about?" She turned away from

another flash of memory. Light sparkling on silver. It terrified her.

"Let it come, sweets. I'm here to hold you if you fall, but you have to find your answers on your own. There can be an *us,* there can be *that,*" he gestured with his chin toward the bed "—but only if there's honesty between us."

"I—I want that, too." But… "Rem, I'm scared."

"Don't be. You're not alone."

She burrowed against him. "I'm not strong enough."

He brushed his lips across her forehead. "You're the strongest woman I know."

"What, *honestly,* are you talking about?"

"You'll figure it out. You know where to start."

"Timm's birthday," she said dully. Everything came back to that seminal moment when her childhood had ended.

"What am I supposed to be looking for?"

"Be quiet and think. Remember."

No. She couldn't remember—wouldn't—because whatever it was would tear her apart.

She saw *something*…looked like a can…in her hand… No!

"No, Rem."

He didn't respond. His hand cupped her head and held it against his chest. She felt that chin she loved rest on her hair so softly and she wanted to cry even more. *Why?*

For Rem, for Timm and her parents, for Davey who got too wild after his younger brother's burning and then died riding a bull. For Finn. For her.

"What's happening, Rem? What am I supposed to remember?"

"You'll get there."

"Where?"

"Remember," he whispered. "Go back to the moments before the accident."

The black cloud finally broke apart and there it was—the memory she'd been running from for twenty years.

Rem hadn't burned Timm.

She had.

CHAPTER THIRTEEN

THE HOWL THAT ERUPTED from Sara cut through Rem.

She'd remembered.

He resisted the urge to carry her to bed, resisted burying himself inside her to offer the forgetfulness, the mind-numbing sex she craved. That was nothing but a quick fix.

If he and Sara had any chance of survival, she needed to live through every part of this. There could be no shortcuts.

She shuddered in his arms as huge shivers wracked her body.

Involuntarily, his arms clamped around her to still her.

"Sara," he whispered against her hair. "Sara."

The moonlight played over the folds of the sheet, turning it and her pale skin to alabaster, as though she were a finely sculpted statue with a tortured face.

He would continue to take on her pain if he could, as he'd claimed it all as his own since Timm's birthday. But he couldn't do that any longer. All he could do was hold her, stay with her, let her know he wouldn't leave.

She tipped her head back. Her eyes begged him to help her to forget, but the truth had been hidden for too many years.

Their lives could no longer work that way. In order for them to come to a better place, something had to give, and it had to be the lie Rem had told to save his little buddy.

They'd reached a point of no return and his poor, sweet Sara had a lot of suffering ahead of her.

He could clarify, though. He could share the blame with her, but couldn't accept it *all* anymore.

"Sara, honey, I'm here."

"It was me," she wailed. "Not you."

"Not completely you. What do you remember?"

"The can. In my hand. I sprayed him, not you."

"No, you didn't. I did that, but you wanted to."

"What do you mean?"

"You bought the streamers with your allowance and brought the can into the dining room when your mom came in with the cake." He held her face still because she was shaking her head, but he needed to know that she understood. They had each played a role that day.

"You intended to spray Timm," he said, "but lost your nerve. You pushed the can at me and told me to do it. And I did."

"So it was still my fault. I made you spray him."

"Sara, you didn't *make* me do anything. I thought spraying Timm would be hilarious. We just picked the wrong time to do it. Besides, I was older than you. I should have known better."

"Is that why you were screwed up for so long, because you thought you should have known better?"

"Yes."

"Why didn't you tell me?" He felt her hands scrabbling to be free and eased his grip. She clutched his hair and brought his face closer. "Why did you let everyone blame you?"

"For you."

"But why?"

"You were my little buddy. I didn't want to see you hurt."

"But I was as guilty as you were. More so. I bought the stuff. I intended to use it and then pushed it on you. You should have hated me, not protected me."

"No, I could never hate you. You were a kid who made a mistake. A really simple, goofy mistake."

"Why didn't Mama punish me, too?"

"She didn't know. In the pandemonium, nobody saw who had the can. You were frozen. Terrified."

She shivered.

"After the paramedics took Timm away, I confessed to your father. When he talked to you, he realized that you remembered nothing. Later, he asked me if we could keep it that way and not traumatize you with the truth. He also decided it would be a good idea if I stayed away for a long time so you wouldn't remember. So I did."

"I missed you." She cupped his face. "I missed you so much. I lost Timm and I lost you. I lost my parents because they didn't have time for me. I lost my childhood."

Her eyes filled with tears again and he doubted she could see him anymore.

"I disappeared, became invisible. It was like I didn't exist anymore. It wasn't fair. I blamed you for all of that, but it was never your fault. It was always mine."

She grabbed handfuls of sheet and pulled it close to her chest. "Why didn't I remember? Why did I bury that for so long?"

"You went into shock almost immediately. I remember putting my arm around your shoulders and you were an icicle. The only way your family could get you to sleep that night was by drugging you."

"But still, why didn't I remember later?"

"You blocked it out. It was the only way for you to deal with it. You were just a kid when it happened."

"So were you, but you remembered. Why is it coming back now?"

"Finn, I guess. And me."

"You?"

"We've torn each other apart in the same old pattern. It couldn't last forever."

"But—"

"Maybe you want more now? A healthy, adult relationship with me?"

She covered her eyes. "I don't deserve you."

"That kind of talk pisses me off, Sara."

"But it's true."

He stood so quickly with Sara in his arms that the rocking chair shot across the floor. Damned if he was going to let her destroy herself in a new way.

He wanted his sweet friend back, not another form of the neurotic woman she'd grown into.

He stood Sara on the floor and hauled the quilt to the end of the bed. Then he began to unwrap the sheet from around her.

"The whole point of remembering, Sara, is to purge, not to beat yourself up. Lie down."

When she obeyed, he unraveled the sheet and spread it over her, letting it float onto her body with a whisper's kiss. He laid the quilt on top then climbed in beside her and held her.

Eventually, her shivers subsided and she fell into a sound sleep. Rem held her long into the early hours while the sun's rays tiptoed across the ceiling like a lover sneaking home.

SARA AWOKE AND STARED AT an unfamiliar ceiling, wondering where she was.

A split second later, realization dawned. Rem's bedroom.

Feeling hollowed out and dead, she rolled over. She was alone. Rem had left her. Surprise, surprise. After what she'd learned about herself, she wondered how he could have stood talking to her over the years.

She leaned down to pick up her nightgown from the floor and had to grab the mattress to stop the spinning in her head.

She had buried a vital detail, a defining moment in her life, for so long. How had her mind suppressed it? She'd blamed Rem, had been so harsh with him. And yet, he'd asked her to marry him anyway. Foolish, misguided man.

She pulled her nightgown over her head, then stepped out of the room.

At the same moment, Finn stepped out of his.

"Morning, sweetheart. How do you feel?" she asked. "How's your head?"

"Hurts bad again today. My neck, too. Maybe I had too much fun yesterday."

He frowned and looked behind her. She turned her head. He was staring at Rem's room...that she'd just walked out of.

"It's not what it looks like," she whispered.

"Yeah, right. I'm not stupid." He returned to his room and slammed the door.

"Finn—" She would have gone to him, but her stomach rebelled and she ran to the washroom. All that came up was liquid. She'd eaten so little yesterday.

She rinsed her mouth and rested her forehead on the cool edge of the sink.

Finn would think the worst of her now. Did it matter? She didn't deserve the great kid he'd been all these years. No wonder he'd been turning away from her lately. He'd seen the flaw in her character that she'd been suppressing for so long.

She'd burned her own brother.

She ran to the toilet again, but nothing came up.

Rem, forgive me. Timm, forgive me.

To soothe her gritty eyes, she splashed cold water on her face.

As she trudged down the hallway to her borrowed room, she listened for noises downstairs. She had no idea what time it was.

After she was dressed, she crossed the hall and knocked on Finn's door.

"Mom, go away."

"Finn, please let me in. There's something I have to tell you." Now that she knew the truth, she needed everyone to know.

"Go away."

She gave up and went downstairs, where she found Nell awake.

While Sara helped her get ready for the day, Nell watched her closely and Sara wondered what she saw on her face. The shell she'd developed over the years had become porous overnight. She couldn't stand here and let Nell see who she really was.

And who is that exactly?

Someone who isn't as good as she was yesterday.

"Sara?" Nell asked, but Sara smiled sadly, waved and stepped out of the room.

She went in search of Rem, starting in the stable.

Sure enough, that's where she found him, sitting on a bale of hay brushing Gracie.

Rem looked up and stared for a moment. "How are you?"

"Fine," she answered, but her voice was so flat she might as well have said *I'm dead.*

Concern etching his features, he stood and approached,

but she backed away. She didn't deserve his sympathy. After the responsibility he'd taken on for her, he shouldn't care. She'd caused him no end of grief for too long.

Her back hit Rusty's stall door and he nipped at her hair. She hadn't even combed it today, let alone pulled it into a bun or ponytail.

"You're not fine. Come here."

She said "no" but no sound came out. She felt so bad, had done such a bad thing, that she felt herself disappearing again, as she had after Timm's burn. This time, though, there were no drugs, no painkillers strong enough to block the pain.

Pandora's box had been opened and Sara didn't stand a hope in hell of squeezing everything back into it again.

She needed to get away.

The walk to the car took too long, her feet heavy and her legs weak.

She felt Rem shadowing her.

"Where are you going?" he asked.

She opened her car door, then leaned on it for support. He stopped in front of her.

"Tell me what I can do."

"Nothing." She tossed her purse onto the passenger seat. "I have to deal with this on my own. Call Alice and get her here to take care of Nell today."

"Already done. She should be here any minute."

"Keep Finn here with you. You would have made a great father all along, Rem. You *will* make a great father."

"Sara—"

"You were right. You shouldn't rescue me anymore. I can take care of myself." Even though she felt like an old woman. So, so tired.

"Sara—"

She cut him off again. She had things to say and a dwindling supply of energy.

"I have to leave for a while. Get another nurse from TLC to help Alice, to take my place."

"Where are you going?" Rem was starting to look panicked.

She shook her head. "Don't worry. I'm not going to hurt myself. I just need time."

Finn came out on the veranda.

"What's going on?" His jaw jutted forward stubbornly but she saw uncertainty in his eyes. Poor boy. His life was about to change so much.

She looked at Rem, at his gorgeous blue eyes swimming in his tanned face. Swimming? She touched her cheeks. Her hand came away wet. Crying yet again. Impossible. She wasn't a crier.

"Tell him, Rem. The whole truth."

"No."

"*Yes.* He needs to know who we really are."

"Are you sure?"

She nodded. "He deserves that. I messed up in so many ways."

"Mom?" Finn sounded desperately young.

"Take care of him for me. Tell him I'll be away for a while." She climbed into the car.

"Sara, don't go."

Starting the engine, she pulled away from the hand reaching toward the door. She swung around in the yard, just missing Rem who was still trying to stop her.

She was going to her house to spend time alone. A lot of time, a lot of alone. But first she had things to do.

Sara drove into Ordinary and parked on Main Street. Sunday morning. Everything was quiet.

The door of the newspaper office was unlocked and open, though, so Timm had to be here.

She walked around the counter and into the back, just as he stepped out of the washroom.

When he saw her his eyes lit up. "Great party yesterday. How's Finn this morning? Worn out?"

She nodded.

When Timm approached and saw her face, his expression changed to concern. "What happened?"

She stepped close. "Timm, you know I love you, right?"

"Of course."

"You know I would never do anything to hurt you?"

"You're scaring me, Sara. What's going on? Has something happened?"

Sara nodded again. "Last night, I remembered things, Timm. Things I wish I'd known all along. I'm not the person everyone thinks I am."

"Sara, what the *hell* are you talking about?"

Timm didn't swear often, so he clearly realized the depth of her pain and confusion.

"On the day of your party—" She swayed a little and Timm forced her to sit. He pulled another chair close and sat facing her. He took her hands in his.

"Talk," he ordered.

She felt the prickle of tears behind her eyes but refused to let them flow. She could fall apart again later. At the moment, she needed to be strong.

"Your getting burned wasn't just Rem's fault. It was also mine."

"What do you mean?"

"I bought the streamers. It was my idea. When the time came, though, I lost my nerve and threw the can to Rem. I pushed him to spray you.

"If it hadn't been for me, those streamers wouldn't have been at the party and you wouldn't have been burned."

"You've been carrying this secret all of these years?"

"I didn't know. I had suppressed it."

Timm frowned. "Why did Rem tell you?"

"He didn't. I remembered."

"You poor girl."

"Poor?" He didn't get it. She raised her voice. "Timm, what happened to you was *my* fault. All these years I blamed Rem and treated him badly when I should have been blaming myself."

"Stop using the word *blame*. I've accepted the reality of my life and I'm happy. Rem and I are friends. I don't *blame* anyone, least of all you."

"I blame myself."

"You would. Man, you can be a hard-ass, Sara." He gripped her hands. "Let it go. It's no longer an issue for me."

"It's an issue for me. It's huge." On the drive into town she'd remembered more. "I was mad at you, I don't remember why—I think you broke one of my toys or something—and wanted to get back at you by humiliating you in front of your friends. Instead, I set you on fire. I'm not the person I thought I was."

"Because you made a mistake when you were a kid? Because your big brother had probably been nasty to his pesky baby sister and you wanted to get even?"

"I thought I was so right about everything. Why did Rem still speak to me after I let him take the blame all those years?"

"If you didn't remember then you didn't *let* him. If he'd wanted you or the world to know, he would have opened his mouth and told the truth."

"Why didn't he?"

"If you haven't figured that out yet, you're blind. He loves you, Sara."

"Who, Timm? Who does he love? The little girl I used to be? Or the self-righteous prig I became? Who am I that anyone should love me?"

"You're a good person."

Sara jumped up out of the chair. "No, Timm. I'm not." She ran through the office, toward the front door that promised escape.

"Sara, you—"

"No. I have to leave for a while. You take care of that beautiful baby."

She heard him call her again but she was already outside running to her car.

She drove to her mother's house and packed a bag. Papa used to have camping equipment somewhere. She searched the attic until she found it wrapped in plastic and stuffed into big plastic containers. She helped herself to a sleeping bag.

From her bedroom, she took a quilt that she rolled around the sleeping bag and tied with string.

She loaded her car with food from Mama's cupboards and fridge then called the hospital to tell them she needed to take time off for health issues, starting immediately.

She drove out of Ordinary toward Haven.

Halfway there, she turned down her narrow road and drove for a mile until she came out into the clearing and parked in front of her house.

Her very own private cave, which is exactly what she needed right now, someplace to hide.

Only Finn knew about it at this point and she'd sworn him to secrecy until she'd finished decorating it in her own way.

She'd had grandiose plans to renovate and make the

house her own. In her bid for total independence, she'd been brutally frugal. When Papa died, she'd put her share of his insurance money into the bank until she was ready to buy.

She'd planned to set up house here with Finn and never need anyone else again.

Then she'd wanted to invite her family for a dinner to show off her pretty home. That wasn't going to happen now.

She got out of the car, but instead of unloading the supplies, she wandered to the creek, to the spot where she and Rem had spread a blanket one night and made Finn.

A Russian olive tree had taken root. There wasn't much of their spot left.

Despite Rem's rejection of her at their son's birth, she'd bought this place so she could own this moment in time when she'd let go of work and responsibility and had taken something she'd wanted for herself.

So pathetic to have bought it.

She took her key out of her pocket and stared at it in the palm of her hand. It had meant so much to her to be able to buy this place.

She entered the house and walked the empty rooms. This should be home, but it didn't feel like it. She didn't know where home was anymore, or whether she deserved one.

Back outside, Sara pulled everything she'd brought with her out of the car and carried it inside.

She unwrapped the quilt from around the sleeping bag and spread them out in the middle of the living room floor.

She sat cross-legged on the sleeping bag and stared at the wall. The inner well of darkness hadn't emptied after she'd remembered the truth. It had instead grown deeper.

Sunset found her still there, still wallowing in that darkness with no idea how to climb out.

She'd thought she'd felt bad after Timm's accident, that nothing else in her life would ever feel so bad again. She'd been wrong.

This pain, this darkness, unrivalled in her experience, cut a jagged hole through her. For the first time in her adult life, *über*capable Sara Franck didn't know what to do.

REM RAN INTO FINN IN THE kitchen, pouring himself a bowl of cereal for breakfast.

"Where did Mom go?" he asked.

"She didn't tell me. She just said she needed time alone."

"Is she okay?"

"I don't know."

Finn had stayed here for the past week, but this morning it felt real. Permanent. Sara was gone, who knew where or for how long.

Rem had wanted to be a father. Well, this was it.

"What do you want to do today?"

Finn looked up from pouring a glass of OJ. He had something on his mind.

"There's a party at the school for kids and their dads."

"Why?"

"It's Father's Day."

Father's Day. Rem hadn't thought about that in years.

"I want to go."

Rem nodded, uneasily aware of where this might be headed.

"I want you to come with me. I want to tell everyone the truth."

"That I'm your dad."

"Yeah." Finn stared at his bowl of cereal and held himself unnaturally still, as though holding his breath.

All right, Rem thought. It's time. With that decision, a weight he'd carried for too long lifted from his shoulders and a sense of rightness and peace took its place. "Okay," Rem said.

Finn's gaze shot to Rem. "Really?" A smile spread across his young face. "For sure?"

"For sure, buddy." Rem grinned and pulled his son into his arms for a quick hug.

They left for the one o'clock party at noon because Finn wanted to visit Melody first.

"She told me she doesn't have a dad, either. I mean, like I didn't used to." He sounded flustered. "I mean—"

"Relax. I know what you mean. What happened to Melody's father?"

"She wouldn't tell me. She just looked really sad. Maybe he died."

When they arrived at the hospital, they found a police presence and confusion in the foyer.

Rhonda was working the admission desk again.

"What's going on?" Rem asked her.

"You know that little girl you saved? Melody?"

Rem nodded.

"Some man came in, yelling and screaming that she was his daughter and that he was taking her home."

"What?"

"Yeah. He made a real scene. We had no father listed on the admitting form, so we didn't tell him where she was. Randy ran to tell Liz and the next thing I heard, they were all gone."

"Gone?" Finn asked. His voice squeaked, as though his body knew he'd turned twelve yesterday and it was time for puberty to set in.

"*All* of them?" Rem asked. "You mean Randy, too?"

Rhonda nodded and leaned close. "I could tell Randy really liked Liz."

"But— Where did they go?"

"Nobody knows. I have no idea how he did it, but the man found Melody's room. When he saw it was empty, he went ballistic. Started tearing up the place and running around the hospital looking for her. That's when we called security and the cops."

"Where is he now?" Rem asked.

"In jail."

Finn had gone as white as Rhonda's scrub top and Rem put his hand on the boy's shoulder.

"Come on." He led him out to the parking lot.

"I don't understand," Finn said. "Melody told me she didn't have a dad."

"It could be one of two things." They got into the Jeep. "Maybe Liz took Melody away from her dad without permission. It can happen when a divorce is bitter and there's a custody dispute."

Rem hesitated before mentioning the other possibility, but Finn had a right to know. "Or he might have been abusive and Liz and Melody had to run away from him." The guy certainly sounded like a nutcase.

"But how did he find them here? Haven isn't a big famous place."

Rem started the engine. "My guess? He's from somewhere in Montana and saw Timm's article about their car crash."

"That sucks." Finn crossed his arms and stared out the window.

Rem drove to Finn's school where boys, girls and men streamed from the parking lot and through the front doors.

"Let's go tell everyone you have a dad," Rem said. "Okay?"

Finn turned to Rem and his look of gratitude warmed Rem to his toes.

Rem walked into the school beside his son, damned proud to finally, *finally,* tell the world the truth—that he was the father of a truly great kid.

CHAPTER FOURTEEN

REM WAS WORRIED.

Sara had been gone for well over a week. He'd given her time to heal, but this was too long.

Adelle had checked Sara's bedroom. Her bed hadn't been used and several drawers were open, from which she had apparently pulled clothing. Her overnight bag was missing, as was food from the kitchen and a couple of pots.

Rem checked every motel, hotel and B and B within a fifty-mile radius.

Adelle found Sara's address book and he called everyone in it. No one had heard from her.

He called every hotel and motel in Bozeman in case she'd run back there. No Sara.

Rem couldn't sleep. He dropped things. Fumbled in his work.

She'd said she wouldn't hurt herself, but there were so many ways of hurting yourself without being the least bit physical.

Finn found Rem in the stable one evening with his head in his hands.

When he heard the boy come in, Rem looked up.

"Are you thinking about Mom?" Finn asked.

"Yeah, I'm worried." A thought struck him. "Why aren't you worrying more about her? Are you too mad at her to be scared?"

Finn looked anywhere but at him. "No," he mumbled. "I'm not as mad as I was."

"You know where she is, don't you?"

"Yeah, I can guess, but I'm not allowed to tell. It's supposed to be a secret."

"Tell me."

"No. Mom said not to."

Rem hadn't told Finn why Sara had gone away. He figured it was Sara's secret to share with the boy, not his. Rem was too worried, though, to honor that request anymore.

"Do you know why your mom ran away?" he asked.

"Is that what she did? She ran away? I thought she was taking time for herself."

"When was the last time your mom did *anything* for herself?" Finn didn't miss the sarcasm.

"When she bought the—" He looked guilty, suddenly, as though he'd been about to spill that secret he wasn't supposed to share.

"Tell me. If you won't, I'll ask Adelle."

"Oma doesn't know about it."

"She doesn't?"

"Why do you think Mom ran away?" Finn was starting to look worried. Good. As far as Rem was concerned, he should be. His mom was missing. Even if he was angry with her, he should still care that she'd been gone for a week.

Rem told Finn about Sara's memory coming back.

"Why didn't you ever tell her?" he asked.

"Because I wanted to protect her."

"It was such a kid's mistake. I can't believe she took it so hard."

"Your mom takes everything seriously."

"Yeah." Finn seemed to wage an internal battle. He chewed on his lower lip. "She's at the house."

"What house?"

"The one she bought. We went to clean it when we first got back to Ordinary. It's pretty old. I don't know why she wanted it, but she saved up for it for a long time. That's why we bought so much secondhand stuff."

"Where's the house?" Rem asked.

Finn described how they'd driven there the one time he'd gone. Rem was blown away. Sara had bought the abandoned Webber place, where they'd made love by the creek. A wild, crazy, sentimental impulse for a practical woman.

Sara, who are you really? He suspected there was more left of the young, carefree girl than she let others see—maybe more than she let herself admit.

He strode to the Jeep. He wouldn't rescue her, but he needed to know she was safe.

"Are you going there?" Finn asked.

"Yeah."

"Can I come?"

Rem stopped and turned to Finn. "I need to do this alone right now. I'll come right back and tell you how she is. Okay?"

"'Kay."

Twenty minutes later, he turned down the road onto the Webber property. Someone—Sara—had put up a new sign. Private Property. No Trespassing.

Another minute later, Rem parked behind her car.

The place looked run-down. Was she sleeping in this?

When he stepped up to the door, his boots rang on the veranda floor. He knocked but no one answered.

If she'd gone out for a walk, he shouldn't invade her space. He needed to see where she was living, though, needed to reassure himself that she was okay.

The unlocked door creaked when he opened it, but no other noises sounded in the house. She wasn't there.

He walked down the hall past the living room. Through the open doorway, he noticed nothing but a pile of quilts and an overnight bag.

The next room on the left was the kitchen. The smell hit him before the sight did. Empty tins of tuna, soup and beans littered the counter. Leftover food sat in an open plastic bag she was using for garbage. She wasn't eating much of what she opened, perhaps just a mouthful or two.

A pot sat in the sink, full of stale water. It looked like she'd started scrubbing it and then had given up.

She wasn't taking care of herself or anything else.

He ran to the back of the house where he assumed he would find the bedrooms. Both were empty. Nothing. Not a stick of furniture.

Where was she sleeping?

Something niggled at him and he rushed back along the hallway and entered the living room. Just inside the room, he stopped. That wasn't a pile of quilts in the middle of the floor. It was a sleeping bag underneath a quilt and there was someone in it.

He pulled back the cover. Sara lay sleeping.

Her face looked thin, gaunt. So tired.

He nudged her shoulder and whispered her name.

She opened her eyes slowly. It took her a moment to realize where she was and who was bending over her.

"Rem? What are you doing here?"

Her breath was foul. So was the sleeping bag. How many hours had she been sleeping every day? When was the last time she'd changed clothes?

Her overnight bag lay on the floor against the wall, zipped and undisturbed. Rem pulled back the top of the sleeping bag. Sara was wearing the same shirt she'd had on the day she'd left his ranch.

"When was the last time you had a shower?"

"Don't know. Tired. Want to go back to sleep."

"No. It's eleven. You should be up by now."

"Why?"

"Because."

He grabbed her under her armpits and hauled her out of the bag.

He turned his head away from her. "Seriously, you reek. When was the last time you bathed?"

"I already told you. I don't know. Leave me alone."

He let go of her and she landed with a thump on the floor.

Her bag must have toiletries. He scrounged through it until he found body wash, shampoo and conditioner. He also found a box of talcum powder that smelled like Sara usually did, light and fresh.

Picking up the sleeping bag, he carried it and the powder to the veranda where he threw the bag over the railing inside out and sprinkled talc on it.

She ran after him.

"Hey, that stuff's expensive."

"I'll buy you more. Get fresh clothes out of your bag," he ordered. "You're going to shower."

"You're not the boss of me!" she shouted.

Rem huffed out a laugh. "Mature, Sara."

He heard her run back into the house.

He walked back into the living room and pulled up short. Sara sat on the floor with her arms crossed and a mulish twist to her mouth that matched the one he'd seen on their son. *Their* son.

Renewed with a stronger determination than ever to get this woman into the shower and over her blue funk, he went over and picked her up. When he was sure she was steady on her feet, he let go and tugged a shirt, pants and clean underwear out of her bag.

"Do you have a washer and dryer here?"

"A wringer washer."

"Fine. Strip."

"What?"

"I said strip." He started to carry everything to the bathroom. "We're going to wash those clothes." He stopped and turned back to her. "Or do you want to burn them?"

"No, I don't want to burn them. And I don't want to shower, so get lost."

Beneath her anger, he saw what was really going on. Sara was hurting and was using her knee-jerk anger to cover it. She didn't think she deserved to be clean, to be cared for, to be loved.

"Sara, you're too good a person to waste yourself like this. Come on."

When she didn't follow, he threw her clothes over his shoulders. Then, before she guessed his intention, bent over and tossed her onto his shoulder, as well.

"Hey. Put me down."

"Nope. You're going to shower if I have to shower with you."

She grew still and flattened her palms on his back above the waist of his pants. Momentarily. Then, as if remembering that she didn't deserve whatever fantasy had just run through her mind, started to struggle again.

"I'll shower when I want to, buster, and not before."

In the bathroom, he dropped her onto the toilet and she yelped.

The room had an old claw-foot tub with a shower curtain. Maybe a bath wouldn't be as messy. He had a feeling that any way he did this, it would be sloppy.

He ran her a bath that was as hot as his elbow could stand, pouring in a generous amount of body wash to make bubbles. She needed a really good soak.

He hauled his shirt over his head and unbuckled his belt.

Sara's eyes widened. "What are you doing?"

"Getting you in that tub if I have to wrestle you in. I don't want my clothes to get wet."

"All right. Stop undressing. I'll get in by myself."

He turned away to hide his smile. She was tempted by him and knew she shouldn't be and maybe thought she couldn't resist him. That flicker of temptation was a good sign. Maybe he could coax her back from the brink.

He refastened his belt, but left his shirt off in case she reneged.

Placing the toiletries on a small shelf beside the tub, he turned his back and listened to the rustling of her clothes behind him. Good. She was getting undressed.

"You said you were through rescuing me," she said above the heavy pounding of the water. He turned around. She stood naked before him. Those sweet breasts. Those hips. Those legs.

He scrubbed a hand down his face. "Sara, get into the bath. Now."

She turned off the tap and stepped into the tub, sinking gingerly into the hot water. The suds covered a good portion of her, thank God.

He sat down on the closed toilet lid. "I was wrong. I need to rescue you. It's in my blood. I can't watch you let yourself go like this."

"I'm not letting myself go. I'm taking a vacation."

"When in your entire life have you ever smelled this bad, even on vacation?"

She didn't respond because they both knew the answer. Never.

Despite her resistance to the bath, she lathered her hair thoroughly. He reached for the showerhead and rinsed her hair for her.

"Use the conditioner and I'll rinse that, too."

She leaned her head back and he rinsed the conditioner out while she watched him hover above her. Her expression said so much that she couldn't put into words. *I hurt.*

Baby, I know. But he didn't know how to help her other than to do this, the physical stuff to keep her body together while her soul healed.

When she finished washing, she stood and reached for a towel that wasn't there. She hadn't brought any.

He handed her his T-shirt.

"I can use my dirty top."

"That stinker? No way. Use this."

She used it, then handed it back to him damp.

Once she was dressed, he noticed that her pants sat low on her hips. She'd lost weight in just a week.

"Pick up your dirty clothes," he said, and snagged the shampoo from the shelf. "Where's the laundry room?"

She led him to a small windowless room on the far side of the kitchen. They filled the tub of the wringer washer, he added a little shampoo and Sara dropped her clothes in.

Next, he took her hand and led her to the kitchen. He pushed her gently onto the floor against the wall. "Sit. I'm making lunch."

He found a couple of unopened tins of food and washed out the pot.

He boiled pasta, drained it and added a tin each of tuna and spaghetti sauce and heated it all through. Voilà. It was the best he could do.

As he cooked, Sara showed no interest in what he did or in her surroundings.

He filled a couple of bowls and left the room.

"Come on."

When she didn't obey, he turned back.

"Do I have to throw you over my shoulder again?"

"No." This time she followed.

He went outside and sat on the top step.

She sat beside him and he handed her a bowl. "Eat," he ordered.

She took a mouthful.

After a few moments, while Rem monitored her from the corner of his eye, he asked, "Why did you buy this place?"

She stopped eating and put her bowl on the veranda.

To his surprise, she rested her head on his shoulder.

"You know why," she whispered.

"Because Finn was conceived here?"

He felt her nod against his arm.

"I screwed up so badly with him," she said.

"We both did."

"I blamed you for too much. You weren't this big, messed-up guy, this genetic wild man who would hurt his son. You were messed up because you—*and I*—accidentally burned your friend."

"I know, but now I have this amazing son and life is good. He's a great person, Sara. You did a fine job raising him. We've been spending a lot of time together."

"How is he?"

"Good. His headaches are gone and I put him on a horse again. You should see him. Despite that fall, he's a natural."

She remained quiet for a moment. "I miss him."

She pulled back to look at him, her eyes bleak and the skin around them dry and tight. "Does he miss me?"

"Yeah. He was worried about you this morning after I explained why you ran away."

"He knows what I did?"

"Yeah. He still loves you. He says we were both so young we shouldn't feel guilty. It was an accident."

"A big one."

"Sara," he said, soft and low, because he really didn't want to be angry with her. "Stop thinking about it. Forgive me. Forgive yourself."

"I can't. I don't deserve to."

"That attitude pisses me off."

"I seem to be doing a lot of that lately."

"Yeah, you are. Stop feeling sorry for yourself."

"It's more than that."

He put his empty bowl aside and picked up hers.

"Here, eat."

She took another mouthful.

"I know it's more than self-pity. I know you're in pain, but there are people who love you and who are worried about you. You deserve all of us. You deserve life."

"Rem, can you leave now? I need to be alone."

It hurt that she asked him to go so quickly.

"I'll leave when you finish eating. When I'm sure you've had enough."

She ate slowly, as though her stomach had shrunk and had to learn how to stretch again.

He picked up her hand and studied it. She had small hands, fine-boned and beautiful. He kissed the smooth back.

"I love your hands."

"What are you doing, Rem?"

"I don't know. Telling the truth, I guess. Behaving honestly."

"These days, I don't like honesty."

"It will hurt for a while, but not always. You'll come to terms with it and get better."

"I don't think so, Rem."

"You will."

"How can something this big ever become manageable?"

She handed her bowl to Rem. "You gave me too much. Finish, please?"

She'd put a good dent in it so he did.

He took the bowls to the kitchen where he washed all of the dishes and gathered the garbage to take away with him. He left the dishes to drain because there was nothing to dry them with.

Checking the rest of the tins and boxes in the cupboard, he made note of what she needed.

Sara still sat where he'd left her. He didn't think she'd moved a muscle.

"I'm going now."

She nodded.

"I'll pick up groceries for you."

"No. Don't."

"Are you sure?"

"I'll get them."

"Promise?"

She nodded.

"Don't come back for a while," she said, and Rem felt a keen disappointment.

He turned his car around in the yard and drove away, while Sara stared across the creek and into the distance.

REM WAS RIGHT. SARA had to do something. She couldn't spend the rest of her life curled into a fetal ball inside a sleeping bag. Trouble was, she didn't know where to go from here.

Nothing in her experience had taught her how to deal with learning the truth about her role in Timm's burning.

A pheasant crept out from under the Russian olive tree that was threatening to choke the stately cottonwood under which Finn had been conceived. Russian olives were greedy. Sara didn't doubt that it would eventually kill off the native cottonwood.

She loved that tree.

She walked to the edge of the creek, or as close as she could get without being impaled by the olive's two-inch thorns. The pheasant flew back into the tree for cover.

Laying her palm flat on the deeply ridged bark of the cottonwood, she could almost imagine she felt a failing heartbeat.

Help me.

How could she resist the plea?

She could get rid of the Russian olive. By saving this tree, she would be doing something worthwhile.

Cocking her head, she studied it from every direction. Not an easy job, and she would need tools.

For the first time since running away from Rem's ranch, she left the property. At the highway, she drove to Haven.

She couldn't face her neighbors in Ordinary, her townspeople. She wasn't the great person they thought she was.

Two hours later, she returned with loppers, saws and more tinned food.

She started working right away, sawing off tree limbs bit by bit, beginning with the smallest and tossing them aside to get at the larger branches.

She'd bought thick gloves—those thorns could be lethal—and wore two flannel shirts despite the heat. Even so, by the end of the afternoon, her arms and back were scratched.

Her arms throbbed. Her spine ached.

She kept going anyway, her feelings flat, her motions robotic, but what the hell? She was outside and she was doing something.

At six o'clock, she opened a tin of baked beans and heated it on the stove. She ate her dinner straight from the pot, on the veranda so she could review her progress. She'd barely scratched the surface.

So much work and so little to show for it. What was the point?

She finished the beans and rinsed the pot. She thought of brushing her teeth, but again thought: *What was the point?*

She crawled into her sleeping bag.

ANOTHER WEEK PASSED.

Still, Rem worried.

Discreetly, he asked around town. She hadn't been in to buy groceries. She hadn't filled her car at the station. What was she living on?

Again he drove out and again found her curled into a ball in her sleeping bag.

They followed the same routine as the week before, but with one difference.

"What happened to you?" he asked when he got her naked for her bath.

"What do you mean?"

"How did you get these scratches?"

"Oh, the tree did that."

"What tree?"

"The Russian olive."

"What about it?"

"I'm cutting it down." She stepped into the tub and sat.

He went to the living room and rummaged through her bag until he found skin cream.

When she dried off, he rubbed the lotion on her back.

"Why are you cutting down the Russian olive?"

"It's killing the cottonwood."

"Yeah, they do that." The skin that hadn't been ravaged by thorns was more delicate than anything he'd ever felt. He smoothed cream onto it for the pure pleasure of touching her.

He slid his hand up her side and around to the front. Lord, her stomach was soft, so soft he didn't think there was a word that could describe it, at least one he knew.

He pulled her back against him and reached lower.

Her hand stopped his journey.

"Rem, no."

"Why not? I want to. You want to. At least, you did a couple of weeks ago."

She turned in his arms, her naked body still warm and damp from her bath. She smelled like lily of the valley. She felt like a willing woman. Her eyes, though, said something different.

"What's going through your head?" he whispered.

"I don't know. I'm not…ready. I don't know if I ever will be again."

"Why can't we ever be ready together, at the same time?"

"I don't know. I think it's hopeless."

He shook her, gently. "Don't talk like that." He handed her a bra. He couldn't hold her like this, bare and vulnerable in his arms, without wanting to make love to her.

He was only human and this was torture.

She stepped into her panties.

He held her shirt while she slipped her arms through. She buttoned it, then put on her pants, and Rem could breathe again.

Again, just like last week, he made lunch and they sat on the veranda.

Limbs and branches lay scattered on the ground beneath the olive tree. Sara was right. The cottonwood was choking.

He didn't know how long the job had taken her, but there was still a lot of tree to cut down.

"What are you doing here, Sara? What does that tree represent for you?" With his fork, he pointed toward the olive. "Is this some kind of penance?"

"I don't know."

"Is it a blaming process or a healing one?"

She struggled with her thoughts. "I don't know that, either."

He jumped up. "At this rate, it will take you forever. I'll see what I can get done before I leave."

"No!"

He stopped halfway to the tree. "Why not?"

"It's *my* job."

"But I can help you with it."

"Stop it. Don't rescue me."

Rem laughed, grudgingly. "You and Lady Serena."

Sara cocked her head. "Who?"

"Lady Serena. From Finn's comic book story. She rescues herself."

The ghost of a smile spread across Sara's face. "Yeah, I like that." She sobered. "Seriously, though, don't rescue me."

Chastened, he asked, "An hour ago, you sure looked like a woman who needed rescuing. Do you want me to stop coming around?"

"I like seeing you. I appreciate the things you've been doing for me, but that tree is *mine*. It's something I *have* to do."

"And you don't know why."

She shook her head. "I don't know why."

He hated seeing her like this, gaunt and lifeless. Despite his frustration, though, he knew she was right.

Maybe cutting down the tree would bring her a sense of achievement, of accomplishment. Maybe it would make her feel capable again.

AFTER REM DROVE AWAY, Sara wandered down to the tree and picked up a saw. Once again, she cut off limbs. Once again, the thorns tore her apart.

When she drove into Haven, she picked up fresh fruits and vegetables. She had to get healthy, to get her strength up for cutting down that tree.

She needed to get out of that sleeping bag every morning and stay out.

The following morning, she drew on the willpower that had got her through the lean years of raising Finn while attending school.

She dragged herself out of the sleeping bag, washed her face, brushed her teeth, ate a breakfast of fruit and milk.

Picking up branches and dragging them behind her, she piled them together in a clearing behind the house. She couldn't just leave them there, though. Russian olives were the hardiest trees in Montana. They could take root anywhere.

She searched her property for stones, large ones, and carried and rolled them back to the clearing, arranging them around the detritus of the massacred Russian olive.

Planting the rocks around the edges, she prepared for a bonfire. When she thought she had enough rocks to do it safely, she set the pile alight.

It took a while, but it finally flared and burned.

She stared at the glowing ashes long after darkness fell

and finally hauled herself off to bed when she knew the fire was out.

The following morning, she started again. The olive gave up its limbs reluctantly and Sara's arms and back throbbed, but she refused to stop.

That evening, she burned more, watched while the fire abated into ash, wondering why this solitude she'd craved for so long didn't satisfy her.

CHAPTER FIFTEEN

WHEN REM RETURNED FOUR DAYS later, he found Sara in bed again. This time when he tried to bathe her, she fought him.

"Why bother?" she screamed.

"Because you're alive and you stink."

"So what? No one cares anyway. *I* don't care."

"I do." He got into her space and picked her up. "You want to do this the hard way? Fine."

He shouldered the front door open and carried her down to the creek, trying not to worry about how light she'd become.

"What are you doing?" She struggled against him.

"You think your puny efforts will stop me, little lady?" He sneered like a villain in an old movie. "You could have had a hot bath, but, no, you chose this instead."

He carried her straight into the creek until he stood knee-deep in water. Her legs recoiled, but she didn't stand a chance. He dropped her in.

She hit bottom and gasped. "Cold. Get me out of here."

"Ready for your bath now?"

She glared up at him, crossing her arms like a sulky kid. He waited and gradually her tension eased.

"It's pretty here, isn't it?"

She was pretty here. Despite the bags under her eyes and her skinny frame, she'd relaxed without her responsibilities to weigh her down.

"You ready for your bath now?" he repeated.

She pulled her top off and sat with her breasts exposed to the sun. How much more was Rem supposed to take? He wanted her.

Sara stood and shimmied out of her wet sweatpants. "I'm going to have my bath here."

Rem ran to the house, slopping in water from his wet socks and pant legs. He retrieved her body wash, shampoo and conditioner and snagged a towel from the rack. She'd bought towels. Good. She was caring for herself a bit better.

When he reached the creek, Sara reached for the shampoo. Her wet nipple puckered in the cool morning air.

She lathered and rinsed, conditioned and rinsed, all while Rem stared because there was no way he couldn't. He undressed and walked into the creek to join her.

She came up from dunking her head, skimming hair away from her face, like a nymph. Water sluiced down her body and Rem took her in his arms.

Her eyes popped open. "Rem."

"I want you, Sara."

"I know." She relaxed in his arms and rested her head on his chest. "I want you, too."

Thank God. Rem ran his hands over her back and down to her behind, pulling her against his erection. She couldn't ignore his body language.

"Rem, I can't right now," she murmured against him. "I want to so badly, but I'm screwed up. I want to be myself when we make love."

"When? Not if?"

"Definitely when."

She stepped away from him, her message clear, but he captured her waist. It was too tiny. His fingers almost met around back. She remained unmoved.

He accepted the inevitable and let her go. He took her hand and helped her out of the creek.

She dried herself, then handed the towel to him.

He dried off and put on his boxers, all the while watching her walk to the house with her dirty clothes bunched against her chest, her behind tempting him.

Fine. There was more than one way to show love.

He hung his wet clothes on the porch railing to dry, then cooked her breakfast and carried it to where she sat on the steps combing her hair.

"Eat."

She took the plate. "Rem, I'm sorry. You know I want you."

He sighed. "I know your body does, but I want all of you. I want your love."

"When I'm ready to give that, you'll be the first to know."

He dressed and left her sitting there, staring at the lopsided tree.

At the rate Sara was going, any healing was going to take years, far too long for Rem's peace of mind. He wanted her whole now. He wanted her in his arms and loving him as much as he loved her.

When he drove away, he knew he couldn't leave her like this. Despite signs of improvement—work on the tree and better food in the refrigerator and pantry—she was still losing weight. Still despondent. Still depressed.

On his way back through Ordinary, he stopped at the newspaper office where he waited for Timm to finish with someone he was dealing with in his capacity as mayor.

"Rem, good to see you," Timm said when the person left.

"We have to do something."

Timm's expression flattened. "About what?"

"Sara."

Timm frowned. "What's wrong? Is she okay?"

"No." He explained where she was and what she looked like.

Timm swore. "I should have been on top of this."

He had bags under his eyes, compliments of the new baby. He published the paper twice a week and, as mayor, made himself available to townspeople at any time of day or night.

No wonder he'd lost track of his sister. Sara was, after all, a grown woman.

Rem outlined his plan. Timm agreed to help.

At the police station, he found Sheriff Kavenagh and extracted a promise for his help.

He called in favors from family and friends. Once they heard his idea, they all committed. No one turned him down.

He had two days to pull this thing together. With a little luck, there would be no sick animals in the county during that time.

At his last stop, his own ranch, he found Finn with Gracie and Rusty in the stable.

"Finn," he called. "Do you want to help me with something I'm doing for your mom?"

"Yeah." He looked despondent.

"What's wrong?"

Finn shrugged. "I miss her."

Rem wrapped one arm around his son's shoulders. "Me, too."

"I'm still mad at her, but not as much as before. I guess she had her reasons. I want to see her."

"You're in luck. We're going there on Sunday."

"You and me?"

"Yep. I'm getting as many friends and neighbors together

as I can. We're going to help your mom get started on fixing that house. You in?"

"Yeah, I'll come for sure." Finn smiled and it was the happiest Rem had seen him since Sara left. The boy loved his mom and that was good. Sara needed a lot of love these days.

"I need some advice. What kind of things would be a real treat for her?"

"I always wanted to buy her pretty stuff because she won't buy any for herself." He scrubbed Rusty's nose with his left hand. They'd had the cast taken off and Rem made sure Finn kept that wrist exercised. "I never had any money, though."

"Didn't your mom give you an allowance?"

"No. We never had the money when she was going to school, and when she was working, she was saving for the house."

"You start helping me with chores and I'll give you an allowance."

"Awesome! I like that idea. If I was rich, I'd take her to a spa, or buy her expensive stuff for her face."

"Expensive stuff, huh? Good thing I got paid this week when I took Lady back to her owners. We can pick up some great things for your mom."

"Can I help you choose them?"

"Sure. Do you want to go visit your grandmother today or tomorrow?" Finn lived here permanently now. Gradually, everything the kid owned had made its way to the ranch.

"No. Max Golden is there all the time now. They're like a couple of goofy lovebirds. Gross."

Rem laughed. Fine by him if Finn wanted to live here. Rem was happy to have him and would love this to be truly permanent once Sara decided what was going on in her life. It seemed that Sara needed that house, though.

That left him wondering, what about him? Where did he fit into Sara's life these days?

He wanted her to want him as much as he did her. He planned to make that happen on Sunday.

"I want to ask you something about your mom."

Rem's tone must have been ominous because Finn stopped petting Rusty to look at Rem. "Is she okay?"

"She's got some stuff to figure out, but, yeah, she's okay. I want her to marry me, though, and come live on the ranch. How would you feel about that?"

Finn grinned. "I want that to happen."

"Yeah?"

"Yeah. She should be happy. She never has fun."

"I agree. Here's what we're going to do."

He outlined his plan and Finn agreed with it right away.

They got into the Jeep and drove into town. They picked up Adelle and visited Angel above the newspaper offices.

After oohing and aahing over baby Karl, Rem got down to business.

"Do you two think you could pick out some nice colors for the rooms in Sara's house? Whatever you think she'd like."

"Her house?" they asked in unison.

After the first time Rem visited Sara at the house, he'd let Adelle know that her daughter was safe and that she just needed time away, but hadn't told her exactly where Sara was. Until now, he'd figured that was Sara's secret to share. He took it as a compliment that Adelle trusted his judgment.

He described what had been happening and exactly what he intended to do about it.

ON SUNDAY MORNING, REM LEFT early to go out to Sara's property. He wanted to get there before everyone else did.

Max said he'd pick up Finn and bring him out later.

Since Sara left, Adelle helped Rem take care of Ma on the weekends, but Rem had arranged for Alice Betts to stay all day today.

He drove up in one of his friend's, Hank Shelter's, pick-ups with the back full of the furniture he and Finn had chosen for Sara's bedroom. He wasn't sure whether he was doing the right thing, but he couldn't leave Sara out here to fade away. He wanted his girl back.

Sitting in the yard, in the clear light of early morning, he remembered telling her that their ship had sailed and was never coming back. He remembered how sure he'd been that Sara would never be part of his life.

Now, here he was trying to change all of that. One way or another, he was getting the girl. Maybe not today. Maybe not next week. Maybe not even next month. But Remington Caldwell was determined.

In the past, the timing had never been right for them. Today, he was making it right.

He entered the house and found Sara sleeping on the floor. He bent over her. She smelled clean. Maybe his concern was getting to her.

"Sara," he whispered, and she rolled over.

Her eyes were open and watchful. She touched his face.

"Hey, you," she said, and she seemed lighter, less withdrawn and dark. He felt lighter, too, as though he'd been holding his breath and had finally released it. He scooped her into his arms.

"You smell good."

"I had a bath before bed last night."

She looked better, not a lot, but she was getting there.

"You can put me down now."

"I don't want to."

She snuggled her head against his shoulder. Lord, he hoped he wasn't screwing up today.

At some point, life had to start working out for them, didn't it?

He'd spotted clothes drying over the veranda railing. He put Sara down and walked out to get them.

Hank Shelter drove up in another pickup and Rem waved.

He rejoined Sara in the living room and said, "You might want to get dressed. You've got company."

"What? Who?"

Handing her the clothes, he said, "Get dressed."

She pulled off the old T-shirt she'd been sleeping in and Rem's breath caught. She was naked, and he didn't know how many more times he could see her that way and still control his desire.

"Um, you might want to do that in the bathroom. Your company is already here."

She shrieked and ran to the washroom.

Rem rolled up the bag and put it in the corner with the quilt.

Hank and Amy Shelter entered with Reverend Wright and his wife, Gladys, Amy's mother.

A minute later, Max Golden and Adelle showed up with Finn.

"Finn," Rem said, "your mom's out back in the washroom. Go wait for her to come out. I know she'll want to see you before everyone else."

Finn looked apprehensive but complied.

FINN WAITED FOR HIS MOM outside the bathroom door. He could hear her brushing her teeth.

He hadn't seen her in almost a month, longer than ever

in his whole life. He was nervous. Maybe she wouldn't want to see him 'cause he'd been so mad at her.

The door opened and she stepped out, then stopped and stared at him. She was skinny and she looked tired. It scared him. He wanted his healthy mom back.

"Mom?" His voice broke.

"Finn," she whispered.

She pulled him into her arms and held him so tightly he couldn't breathe but didn't care.

He put his arms around her and squeezed back.

"Mom, I missed you so much."

"I missed you, too." She stepped away and stared at him. "You look good. What have you been doing?"

"I've been living at the ranch and helping Rem with stuff. He showed me how to take care of horses."

"You look healthy. You have a tan. You look strong." She brushed her fingers through his hair and said, "My beautiful boy." He thought she might start to cry.

"Mom, he takes me with him when he goes on his vet jobs now that school's over." Finn couldn't keep the wonder out of his voice, couldn't hide how good it made him feel to have a dad to hang out with and do awesome things with.

"So he's a good dad?"

"The best."

A breath whooshed out of her, like she'd been worried.

"Are you still angry?" his mom asked.

"Yeah, a little, but I think I'm starting to understand."

"Friends?"

"Yeah, Mom, we'll always be friends."

She seemed to finally notice all of the noise in the living room. "What's going on? Rem said I was going to have visitors. Who?"

"Lots of people from town. It was Rem's idea. He said if

he had to wait for you to finish this house to find out if he could marry you, he'd have to wait for a couple of years."

"Oh. Marry me."

She sounded real faint.

"How would you feel if that ever happened?" she asked him.

"I'd really like it, Mom."

She smiled and looked so pretty.

"Hey, look," he said, and pointed down to the skate-boarding shoes she'd given him for his birthday. "They fit. They're great. I never thanked you. I love 'em, Mom."

"Something else is new. Your cast is gone."

"Yep. Rem took me to get it off last week."

"How does your wrist feel?"

"Stiff sometimes, but almost good as new."

"Let's go see who's here." She stepped past him, but then stopped. "I'm so glad Rem's a good dad."

"He's awesome, Mom. Unbelievably sick."

She smiled quietly, as if she felt warm from the inside out.

He and his dad really needed to fatten her up, though. Finn didn't like her skinny.

SARA ENTERED THE LIVING ROOM, followed by her son, and stared at the people in her house—Hank and Amy Shelter, who ran the Sheltering Arms ranch for city kids recovering from cancer; the Reverend and Gladys Wright, Amy's mom; Angel's brother, Matt, and his wife, Jenny, who owned the candy store in town; Chester Ames and Missy Donovan. Sheriff Kavenagh—Cash.

Mama and Max Golden.

Mama was handing around donuts and cinnamon buns, while Max served coffee from thermoses.

Timm walked in with Angel and baby Karl. How old

was her nephew now? Five, six weeks? Sara didn't know. She'd lost track of time. She didn't even have a calendar here.

"Sorry we're late." Timm looked sleep deprived but happy.

Finn handed her a cinnamon bun and Mama doctored a coffee the way Sara liked it.

The noise level rose, but it was all good.

This empty old house hadn't known laughter in decades. It was time for that to change.

In the middle of the room Rem stood watching her and looking uncertain, as though he wasn't sure how she would react to his surprise.

She'd asked him not to rescue her, but somehow this felt different…like…like showing affection and caring and sharing. Why on earth Rem wanted her to have a party in an unfinished house was beyond her, though.

"What's going on?" Wide-eyed, Sara stared at everyone.

Timm stepped forward and hugged her so hard her feet came off the ground. "We're here to make this place livable for you."

Sara peeked over his shoulder. Everyone watched and smiled.

Timm said, "I love you, sis. Don't ever forget that. Do you know how important you were to me when I was recuperating? All of those hours you read to me and sat with me kept me sane. I knew how much you gave up and I've never forgotten it."

Adelle swooped in for a hug next, laughing and prying her daughter out of her son's arms. "You tried so hard to make Papa and me happy in those dark days. I never once said thank-you. Today, I will show you how much it meant to me, my beautiful daughter."

Angel hugged her, too, and whispered into Sara's ear, "Thanks for making me feel like part of the family and for bringing Adelle around."

Hank Shelter wrapped her in a big bear hug. "I've never forgotten all of those hours you spent with my cancer kids when you came home on holidays. You were so busy, but still came out to watch over them and give them the benefit of your nursing skills when needed."

"Hank," Sara said. "You do such amazing work. How could I not want to help out?"

He smiled and stepped away from her.

Rem approached.

"Was this your idea?" Sara asked.

He nodded.

"Why?"

"Thought I should show you how much you mean to everyone, and how much we care for you."

"Do they know what I did?"

"Some do."

Sara stepped around Rem. "Can I have everyone's attention, please?"

Rem took her arm. He guessed what she was about to say. "Sara, this isn't necessary."

When everyone was listening, she said, "I'm not sure any of you would want to be here if you knew the truth about me. All of the years since Timm's accident, I've blamed Rem for burning Timm. I didn't remember until a few weeks ago that I was equally responsible. I've behaved appallingly for years and I don't deserve his forgiveness— I don't deserve anyone's forgiveness. If you feel you want to leave now, I understand."

Timm said, "Sara, honey, you were a child."

"You've done a lot for the people of this town over the years," Hank Shelter said. "*That's* what we base our opinions on. I'm not sure why you would think this makes any difference."

There were murmurs of assent and more hugs. Sara had never felt so appreciated before. Over the years, she'd felt lifeless, gray and invisible, but she *hadn't* been. She'd been an active, giving member of the community and the town had noticed.

Angel held Karl in one arm and took Sara's hand in her other. She coaxed her outside to the veranda where lawn chairs were set up for them.

Lawn chairs? Sara hadn't bought any.

Finn followed and said, "Angel, can you make sure my mom eats?"

"No problem, Finn. I can be totally tough with her."

"But I want to hold Karl," Sara said.

"Later, Mom. Eat first." Finn stepped back into the house and Sara couldn't remember when she'd felt so cherished by him.

Through the open living room windows, she heard Rem and Timm discuss how things should be organized.

"Okay, everyone, listen up," Rem called. "All the supplies have been clearly marked to show which room they're for. As you unload supplies from the trucks, be especially careful that the paint goes into the correct rooms."

Rem started the line of men and women snaking out to the trucks.

So that's what everyone was doing here. This wasn't just an intervention. They were going to paint her house.

Her friends and family unloaded painting supplies and stepladders and traipsed back inside with their arms laden.

Sara saw Rem and Finn take several boxes out of a pickup truck and carry them around the house to the back door. There was something big in the bed of the truck, but it was covered with a tarp and Sara couldn't tell what it was.

Mama joined them on the veranda.

"Angel and I have so much to show you. We picked beautiful colors for your rooms."

Mama and Angel had gone shopping together? So much had happened in the weeks she'd been away.

The colors were gorgeous, exactly what she would have chosen but brighter. Deeper. More vibrant.

"Where's the paint chip for the bedroom?"

Angel and Adelle smiled at each other. "Rem picked that one. We don't know what color he chose."

Finn stepped out with a small plate of fruit. "Eat this, Mom. I don't want to see any leftovers."

He sounded so much like her she laughed.

CHAPTER SIXTEEN

REM GRABBED HOLD OF FINN as he came in through the front door.

"Let's get started on that bedroom." Once they were inside the room, he asked, "What do you think? Is she happy?"

"Big-time, Dad. I've never seen her this happy."

Yes. *Yes.* Sara deserved this and more.

"Come on. Let's get this painted so it can be dry enough for us to put the bed together later."

With so many busy hands in the house, the washing and painting went quickly. Only Finn and Rem worked on the bedroom.

At lunchtime, coolers came out of car trunks and food was spread on folding tables on the veranda.

People had been instructed to bring only non-alcoholic drinks for lunch. Rem needed everyone on the ball and the work moving quickly. He wanted this done in one day. He couldn't ask anyone to commit more time than that.

Rem sought out Sara and found her down beside the creek sitting on a towel she'd spread on the ground.

"Can I join you?"

"Of course."

He handed her a plate of food and sat next to her. "Finn says you have to eat all of this."

Sara laughed. "Rem, this is overwhelming but so good. How did you convince everyone to help you?"

"I didn't *convince* anyone. I asked and they agreed right away. You heard how much they appreciate you."

"But—"

"No buts about it, Sara. You've been part of this community your whole life, even when you weren't living here. You've helped every one of these people in some way over the years. You aren't the evil, worthless woman you think you are.

"You made one mistake a lifetime ago and it's over. Timm has a good life. His scars are a nonissue. You think his wife loves him any less because of them? Do you think Karl will?"

Sara shook her head.

"Right. So that's settled. No more guilt, for either one of us."

He pointed to the pile of ashes inside a circle of stones. "What's that?"

"I've been burning the branches from the olive tree, so it can't take root anywhere else."

"Smart girl."

He glanced at the bare trunk. "I can cut that trunk down for you."

Sara paused before answering. She needed to make sure Rem understood.

"Rem, what you've done here today is the best thing anyone has ever done for me. I'll never forget this day."

He stared at her as if he sensed the *but* that was coming.

"You've shown me how much people care for me, how much they respect me. You've convinced me that I really can move on from what I did. Thank you."

Still he waited.

"I need you to understand this, though." She pointed to the bare trunk of the Russian olive. "*That* is my job— my bane, my penance, my contrition, whatever you want to call it. In gathering everyone here today, you've helped me. You proved a valuable point that, trust me, I will never doubt again."

She brushed a lock of hair from her face. "If you cut that trunk down for me, you would be rescuing me. Do you see the difference?"

He watched her solemnly, his eyes vibrantly blue in the sunlight. "I think so."

"You don't have to rescue me anymore, Rem. You're already my hero."

"I never did it to *be* your hero."

"And yet, you are."

"I did it because I loved you. I still do. I always have and I always will."

Sara closed her eyes for a minute so she couldn't see the brilliance of the man she loved—the color and magnificence that was Rem. She loved him, too, but still didn't have herself figured out.

She opened her eyes. He watched her. She leaned forward, watched those blue eyes darken and kissed him, a gentle touch of her lips to his.

"Give me more time, Rem. We've waited this long. It's just a little longer."

"Okay."

He glanced around the grounds, spotted a pile of olive limbs that hadn't yet been burned and the tangle that was the front garden and said, "Love what you've done with the place."

Sara laughed and felt the last awkwardness between them disappear.

REM THOUGHT HE MIGHT BURST.

Fired up from his conversation with Sara, he returned to the bedroom and he and Finn finished it at about two in the afternoon. They left the windows wide open to air out the lingering paint smell.

Rem had picked up fast-drying paint for this room. He wanted Sara out of that sleeping bag and in a proper bed by tonight.

He wandered through the rest of the house and found a lot of work already done.

He stepped outside.

Adelle and Angel, with Karl in her arms, sat on a couple of chairs.

"Rem, will you please help that stubborn daughter of mine?" Adelle said, her frustration evident.

Rem looked where she pointed.

Sara, on her knees, sawed away at the olive trunk.

"She won't let me. Says this is something she has to do alone."

He was impressed with the progress Sara had made since lunchtime. Her arms had to be burning.

He paced the length of the veranda and watched. He listened to Adelle complain. It went against the grain to stand here and do nothing, but Sara needed this.

He walked down the steps to approach, but stopped on the bottom. At a footfall behind him, he turned.

"What's she doing?" Finn put his hand on Rem's shoulder and Rem was thrilled by the casual intimacy.

"Cutting down a Russian olive tree. She won't let me help, though."

"Maybe she would let me." He brushed past Rem and approached his mom.

Rem couldn't hear their exchange, but there was no mistaking Sara's stubborn, emphatic head shake.

Finn returned with a frown. "Her face is all red. Maybe she'll hurt herself, like have a stroke like Mrs. C."

"She'll be fine," Rem said. At the sound of the door

opening, he checked out the veranda behind him. More people stood watching. In fact, without counting to be sure, he was fairly certain everyone was here.

They murmured and mumbled, but no one interfered.

Finally, when it looked like Sara was within an inch of felling the beast, he ran over.

Sweat dripped from her forehead and stained her shirt. Finn was right. Her face was bright red.

"Stop sawing, Sara."

"No, Rem. I'm so close." She panted. "I can do this myself."

"Yes, you can." He rested his hands on both of hers, stopping her movements. "And you will. But you don't have to saw anymore. Stand up."

She stood and dropped the saw. He placed both of her hands on the trunk then let go. He held his palms away from her and his body, so she would know that this would be all her own effort. "Push."

She did and the tree moved. She pushed harder and it toppled. "I did it!" she screamed.

She flailed her arms and jumped up and down. "I did it."

A roar went up from the spectators on the veranda.

She squealed and jumped right into his arms.

He clasped her to his chest and swung behind the cottonwood and kissed the ever-loving daylights out of her.

"I'm so proud of you."

"Me, too." As she glowed in his arms, Rem knew there was no way he was going home tonight.

SARA HAULED THE TRUNK to the fire pit.

Rem called Hank down from the veranda.

"What's up?" Hank asked.

"You have anything in your truck we can use to pull that stump out?"

"You bet."

He retrieved chains and the two of them hooked them up to the stump and the pickup. Hank stepped on the gas. The stump resisted. Hank got out of the truck.

"Damn Russian olives. Those roots probably run clear under the creek." He banged his hat against his thigh.

Rem grunted. "I hate these bastards."

"Hold on," Matt called. He jumped into his pickup, turned it around and backed up beside Hank's.

Matt unlocked the toolbox in the bed of his truck and hauled out more chain, hooking his truck to the stump, as well.

Hank and Matt revved their engines together and the soil around the stump gave way, heaving out of the earth like some primordial fossil arising from the dead.

Cheers rang out from the veranda.

This was Sara's victory and Rem made sure she was absorbing how much these people appreciated her. She'd needed help with this part, but she'd taken that tree down on her own and he couldn't be prouder. And her friends couldn't be happier to do their part.

Roots stretched far into the earth and under the creek. Matt carried over a small chainsaw and cut them off. All three men carried the stump to Sara's pit.

In front of friends, family, God and the universe, Rem hauled her to him and kissed her.

Let her make of that whatever she wanted.

AT AROUND SIX, PEOPLE started cleaning the house and packing up their vehicles.

Rem got Timm and Finn to help him carry the bed frame and mattress in through the back door and put it together. Rem carried in the linens and dropped them onto the bare mattress.

"Thanks, guys, I can take it from here."

From the living room, Max called for Finn. "Oma and I are leaving now."

Finn gave his dad a quick hug and ran out of the house. Rem watched him go, still struck by how odd it was to be a father. A functioning, totally committed father.

About the only thing in his life that had ever felt better was that night with Sara under the cottonwood.

"Funny how we've both come to fatherhood at the same time," Timm said, reading his mind.

"Yeah, it's pretty amazing."

Rem made the bed with the linens he'd bought, including something called pillow shams, that looked pretty but were completely useless.

By the time Rem and Timm joined Angel and Sara on the veranda, everyone else had cleared out.

Angel bundled up Karl and they said goodbye, too, leaving Sara looking lost.

"You okay?" Rem asked.

"I think so." She'd been watching the car leave, but now turned to Rem. "Thank you for doing this. It was wonderful."

"Will it help you to move forward?"

"Yes."

"There's cold barbecued chicken in the fridge, and potato salad your mom left for you," he said. "I'll make up a couple of plates for us."

When he came back outside with the food, he found that Sara had walked down to the sizable hole in the ground where the tree had stood.

"You going to fill that?"

She turned to him and smiled. "Yes."

He handed the plates to Sara. "Wait here," he said and retrieved a tarp from the truck, which he spread on the ground.

They sat and ate quietly, without conversation, and Rem marveled at how civilized it was. For so many years, silences between them had seethed with unspoken resentments.

So much had changed in the weeks since she'd moved back home to Ordinary. So much had changed since they'd squared off in the hospital after Liz and Melody's accident. That day, he would have never thought that his son would end up living with him for the summer.

He took her empty plate from her, pleased that she'd eaten every bite.

He turned to look at the house. "It's a great little house."

She studied it, too. "It's perfect for me, isn't it? I worked a long time for this, Rem. Thank you for giving me back my enthusiasm for this house."

"What do you think of the colors?"

"I love them. Mama and Angel did a good job."

Rem brushed a strand of hair from her face.

"Why wouldn't you let me see the bedroom?" she asked.

He smiled, but didn't answer. He knew she was intrigued but wouldn't pester him.

They spent the evening cleaning the kitchen and sweeping floors.

Rem swept the bathroom floor and scrubbed the tub and sink. He pulled out the bag of toiletries Angel had picked up for him. Turning on the hot water, he dumped a bunch of bubble bath into the tub. Angel managed to find some that smelled like lily of the valley. Good. He didn't want to smell like anything highly perfumed. He wanted Sara to have a bath in her freshly painted bathroom, but he didn't plan on letting her take it alone.

CHAPTER SEVENTEEN

PUZZLED BY THE SOUND of running water, Sara walked to the bathroom. Rem had lit candles on the counter. Bubbles overflowed the tub.

"Do you think maybe you used too much bubble bath?"

"A tad." Rem grinned.

"Is this for me?"

"Yes."

"Thank you."

"And me."

She stopped breathing. "For both of us? Together?"

"Uh-huh."

"I don't know…"

Before she could finish that thought, whatever it was going to turn out to be, Rem placed his lips on hers.

He didn't move, didn't persuade, just waited for her to react. She kissed him back, because in truth she'd been missing human contact, missing civilization, and Finn and her mom. And Rem. She'd been missing Rem. So much.

While they kissed, he unbuttoned her shirt and pushed it from her shoulders, cupping her breasts. Her nipples rose to meet his touch.

She undressed him, too. She'd always loved his chest. She spread her hands on him.

When they were both naked, they stepped into the tub and lathered each other, got down and dirty to make sure they were clean.

The last time they'd made love, last summer after Rem had been stabbed, Sara had been terrified because she'd almost lost him, and still too full of raw and negative emotion.

Tonight she felt good. Clean. Accepting. Ready to touch and be touched. Ready for affection.

Rem stepped out of the tub and water and suds sluiced from his body. Sara loved looking at him almost as much as she enjoyed touching him. She'd never had enough chances to see him naked so now she looked her fill.

He dried off and tossed the towel over the rack. "Stay there for a minute. I'll be right back."

A couple of minutes later, he returned, took her hand in his, helped her out of the bath and dried her off, running the towel over her breasts, abrading her nipples.

"I feel like a pampered princess." She tried to take the towel from him, but he wouldn't let her. She felt shy.

"You deserve to be pampered." When she started to frown, he continued, "You've always been a hard worker."

"I've never pampered myself—"

Rem grinned. "I know."

"—let alone had a man do it for me."

He ran the towel down her back and over her bum. When he bent forward, he made sure to let his hair brush her breasts, toying with her, arousing her.

You beautiful man.

"It's about time you were pampered."

He picked her up and carried her into the bedroom.

Sara glanced around. Small glowing bags on the floor lined the walls and lit the room with a soft sheen.

The walls were a muted mauve-gray. "I love the color."

"It reminded me of your eyes."

Against the far wall, a luxurious brass bed, with reflections from the candles on the floor shimmering in the frame, sat covered with the prettiest bedclothes she'd ever seen.

A puffy duvet covered the bed, dark yellow with huge sprays of purple and mauve lilacs.

She'd never seen anything more feminine or more temptingly old-fashioned.

"This isn't me," she protested, but was charmed in spite of her protestation.

"Yeah, it is." Rem dropped her into the middle of the bed and she sank into the duvet. Oh, heaven. Her head landed on fluffy pillows with ruffled shams.

She craned her neck. "How many pillows did you buy?"

"Half a dozen."

"Six! I don't need six pillows."

"I do, and I'm staying here tonight."

Sara smiled. "I kind of figured that out." She turned onto her side so she could see the candles. Rem stretched out beside her and his hand caressed her hip.

"What are they, Rem? How did you make them?"

"They're paper bags—"

"Paper!"

"—filled with sand and tea lights. They're safe."

"I like them." Sara felt herself glow, felt warmth spread inward from the heat with which Rem watched her, and outward from a well of desire to change, to be more.

She turned over and took Rem in her arms. "I missed out on years of fun. I want to have fun. Let's make love."

"I thought you'd never ask."

She started with his mouth because he'd always been a great kisser. She nibbled, tasted, licked his lips.

He took over, tilting her head with his palm, and gave her his tongue. She needed to taste more of him and slid her lips over his neck and collarbone.

"Mmm. You smell like lily of the valley. Manly."

He laughed and she laughed with him, fun during love-play was a revelation.

She teased his nipples with her tongue, and hoped she pleased him.

He touched her hair, tried to reach for her, but no. She was taking what she wanted. She reared up and took his hands and wrapped his fingers around the brass rungs of the headboard.

"This is a great bed." She grinned and he groaned because he couldn't quite reach the nipple that came so close to his mouth.

"Stay put," she whispered, rubbing that nipple across his lips. "Don't move."

"I want to touch you." Poor man sounded like he was in pain.

"No." She breathed into his ear. "Tonight, you are my plaything. Tonight, I'm having fun."

"Hallelujah." His voice sounded strained. "Hurry. Please."

With the lightest touch, her fingers traced the line of hair to his stomach. When she used her nails to circle his navel, he sucked in a quick breath. Glorying in her power, she did it again.

Her fingers found him. Smooth and large, he filled her hand. She played with him while her lips traced the path her nails had taken. Her tongue dipped into his belly button.

Her cheek touched the tip of his erection and he gasped, but didn't let go of the brass rails.

She made love to him until he came close to climax. The luxury of having this time to play with Rem, to enjoy his body, to treasure him, moved her. She'd loved this man for so long.

She rose above him, straddling him, and then welcomed

him into her body. A sigh eased out of him; an answering joy echoed through her.

Remington Caldwell, I love you. Every part of you. Every inch of you.

She felt his heartbeat inside her and it beat in cadence with her own.

It had always been Rem.

"Perfect," he whispered, his hands moving over her body. Everywhere.

Pleasure climbed and Sara held on for dear life because she was losing control and she trembled, broke, spread over and around Rem and flew.

For a long time they were quiet then Sara whispered, "I love you."

"I love you, Sara Franck. I have my entire life."

Eventually, she disengaged from him and lay down beside him.

"I want more," she said, and Rem bolted up. He took her hand in his and led her out of the bedroom.

"What? Where—?"

"We need another bath."

"Another one?"

"I'm nowhere close to being finished. I've wanted you for too long to stop now."

Another bubble bath later, he followed her back into the softly lit bedroom.

Sara lay down on top of the beautiful duvet.

Rem stared at her. "Sara, you're so damn beautiful."

With the way he looked at her, reverently, she believed him and felt beautiful instead of an invisible gray wren.

"You bring color to my life, Rem."

He bent forward and whispered her name over her body, everywhere, and she shivered. Oh, glorious.

She awoke later cradled in Rem's arms. They lay on

their sides, spooning and he held her back against him. She realized what had awakened her——her body's response to his. He wanted her again and she wanted him.

They fell apart together and held each other while they floated back to earth.

Sara had never known such pleasure, so much love, so many sensations, such pure sinfulness. She reached over her shoulder to touch Rem's face.

Ah, Rem, my beautiful, wicked, bad boy, I love you.

CHAPTER EIGHTEEN

SOMETIME IN THE MIDDLE of the night, Rem asked her to come home with him.

"No, Rem. I need to stay here."

She'd frustrated him. He moved to rise. "Rem, you said you wanted honesty between us. Let me explain what's going on with me, okay?"

He nodded. "Please, I want to know."

"I don't know who I am right now. It sounds corny, but it's true. I'm not the superpractical Sara I thought I was. Her character was a reaction to what had happened in her life. I'm trying to find out who I am without outside influences. These days, I'm just trying to *be.*"

"So…" Rem fiddled with the ruffled edge of a pillow. "I'm an outside influence you'd rather not be exposed to?"

She ran her fingers through the hair on his chest. "I'm happy you're here tonight, but I have to do the rest by myself."

Rem opened his mouth to object, but Sara covered his lips with her fingers. She needed to make him understand.

"What you did yesterday was amazing. You've renewed my faith in myself. Those people wouldn't have come if they didn't love me and accept me, or at the very least, respect me."

"They do."

"I love that you did that for me. I don't want you to live here, though."

He looked crestfallen and she rushed on. "*When* I can be in your life permanently, you'll be the first to know. Right now, I need to be alone."

Rem rested his forehead on hers. "You said 'permanently.'"

"I did."

He clasped her to him so tightly she could barely breathe. Breathing was overrated. Being held by Rem was not.

WHEN REM AWOKE, SUNRISE painted the walls a warm hue, picking up on the hint of lilac in the gray.

Sara's skin glowed.

The candles had burned out and the bedclothes had fallen to the floor. Rem picked up the sheet and covered Sara with one graceful arc, thinking of the night she'd remembered her role in Timm's accident.

She'd looked like a statue that night, cold and dead.

Now, she was warm and alive, becoming whoever she was meant to be. He wished he could stay and help her on that journey, but she didn't want him.

Get your self-pitying head out of your arse. The woman wants you. She proved that last night.

She doesn't need me, though.

True. Not at the moment.

He respected her need to do this alone, but staying away would be hell.

He didn't hear from her for another two weeks. During that time, he talked to his ma, who told him not to go to Sara. He talked to Timm, who *ordered* him not to go.

Desperate, he talked to Adelle and Max, who both told him to leave her be.

Easy enough for them to say. They weren't torn apart worrying about her and wondering whether she had enough to eat or whether the nights in her tiny house alone were too cold.

Cold! He'd bought her a bed and a duvet. She owned a sleeping bag and quilt. Last thing she would be was cold.

Even so, he wanted to be in that bed with her, curled around her under the duvet.

He found solace in his work and in his son and in his mother's progress. But none of it was enough when Sara lived on the other side of Ordinary and he couldn't touch her.

SARA WORKED HARDER THAN SHE ever had in her life. She'd finally figured out what she had to do. She needed to make a home for herself here on this tiny plot of land, and to turn it into something she deserved. She'd finally come to believe that she deserved it.

She had her furniture in Bozeman taken out of storage and delivered.

She bought new kitchen appliances in Haven. She borrowed Mama's sewing machine and made curtains.

She rented a power washer and cleaned the white siding on the house until it sparkled.

She ordered unpainted gingerbread scrollwork over the internet, nailed it to her roof and painted it lilac.

She bought oversize wicker furniture for the veranda and painted it to match. She sewed puffy chintz pillows for the armchairs.

The railings were painted a deep purple.

And because her time away from Rem and her son was making her sick, Sara mailed them an invitation to tea on her front lawn on the coming Saturday.

She mowed the grass, cleared and replanted the flowerbeds with mums and asters in reds and yellows. To her joy, she also found small mauve Michaelmas daisies, which she planted in red pots to line her steps.

Through it all, she reflected...on life, responsibility and purpose, on isolation and solitude. Who was she and where did she belong?

Early on Saturday afternoon, the day of the tea party, she double-checked the food, then sat on the veranda in one of her new armchairs.

At the first rumble of a car engine, she jumped up and rushed to the steps, where she waited for the two most important men in her life to arrive.

When Finn climbed out of the Jeep, she ran to him and wrapped him in a rib-cracking hug.

Even though he sounded chagrined and moaned, "Mo-o-om," he hugged her back hard.

"You're getting so strong. Is Rem working you hard?"

"He makes me do chores, but then he gives me an allowance."

"You like living on the ranch?"

"Yeah, I do." He stepped away from her and scuffed the toe of his Vans in the dirt. "It would be cool if you were there, too, though."

"Go take a look at the house while I talk to Rem."

Finn rushed to the front of the house. "Wow, this place looks sick."

Sara stared at Rem, devouring him with her eyes. He looked good.

She approached slowly. "You're getting more tanned. Are you spending a lot of time outdoors?"

"I've got two more horses to tame. Finn's helping me."

Funny how a month and a half ago that statement would have terrified her. Now, she liked that Rem was teaching her son to do it properly.

"He must love that."

"He does. I swear he's going to be a vet."

"Like his father."

"Yeah, like his dad."

They stared at each other and Rem's warm regard spread through Sara. She hoped he could feel hers in return.

It had been two very long weeks since their night together.

Rem wore a dark denim shirt that made the gorgeous blue of his eyes pop. As he drank in the sight of her, they darkened with desire.

She rushed into his arms, inhaling him, hugging him as if she were trying to climb inside him.

When she could finally let him go, she grasped his face. "I missed you," she whispered fiercely.

"You, too." Rem's voice carried a matching thread of desperation.

"Come look at my house," she said, and wrapped her arm around his waist. He ran his hand across her shoulders. His gaze darkened again, but this time not with desire.

Her need for this house still troubled him.

As they walked to the house, she stared into his eyes willing him to have patience.

"Where are you guys going?" Finn called.

Sara glanced up and realized she and Rem were so focused on each other they had nearly walked into the garden.

They laughed and changed direction.

They all stepped into the house and Sara held her breath, nervous. Would they like her house?

Finn said, "Wow, what a makeover."

Some of the furniture she'd had when they'd lived in Bozeman had been secondhand, and hadn't looked good enough when she put it into this little dollhouse. She'd sold it and bought new stuff—a chintz sofa and matching arm-chair.

She'd installed molding on all the cheap doors to spruce them up, then had painted them ivory and installed new brass doorknobs.

"I haven't worked on the bathroom yet. I'll be starting on it tomorrow."

Sara ran ahead of them to the kitchen. She wanted to be able to watch their faces when they saw it.

Rem stepped in first and his eyes widened. "This is awesome, Sara."

Finn entered next, with exactly the same reaction. "Sick, Mom. Totally sick. You should go on a design show and do makeovers."

Angel and Mama had chosen a pretty pale yellow for the kitchen walls. Sara had kept the paint chip and had bought matching paint for the cupboards so the kitchen looked seamless.

She'd added molding to the cupboard doors and painted it a darker yellow. Her idea had been so weird she hadn't known whether it would work, but, wow, it sure had.

She'd bought an oak table and chairs and had sewn yellow placemats to match the moldings.

The only modern touch—stainless steel appliances—looked fabulous.

"Smells awesome in here," Finn said. "What is it?"

"Gingerbread in the oven."

"When's lunch?" Finn asked, rubbing his belly. Sara laughed, so happy to see her beautiful boy.

They sat on a blanket on the lawn and ate egg salad sandwiches and giggled when blobs of filling dripped onto their plates.

After dessert, they played universal badminton, their

aim only to keep the birdie off the ground for as long as possible.

Finn ran off to look for frogs in the creek.

Sara lay on the blanket and sighed. "I haven't laughed that hard in a long, long time."

Rem stretched out beside her and chewed on a long blade of grass. "It's good to see you happy. This house does that for you, doesn't it?"

"Yes." She rolled onto her stomach and studied it. "It's like a dollhouse to me. I've never lived in anything so pretty. It gives me great pride to know that it's mine and that I fixed up so much of it myself."

"I like the gingerbread and the colors you chose for the outside."

"It might not be what other people would choose to live in, but it resonates with me. It's sweet and it's frivolous. I've never allowed myself to be frivolous."

Rem tickled her nose with the blade of grass. "Frivolity looks good on you."

Sara leaned forward and kissed him, then rested her head on his chest.

"I could stay here forever. With you. Like this."

His fingers combed her hair with a gentle touch. "Me, too, but real life beckons. I have work to do and a house, land and a mother to care for."

"Yes. I'll have to go back to the hospital soon." She stiffened suddenly. "I never thought about it, but if Finn's living with you, I should be paying support."

"None of that talk. The boy's fine with me. Bite your tongue."

She leaned close. "I'd rather you did that for me."

He pulled her head to his and they kissed, their tongues dueling.

He bit her tongue and she yelped. She heard Finn run back from the creek and pulled away from Rem.

"Guys," Finn said, "are you going to start being gross all the time?"

Sara smiled. "Maybe."

Finn groaned, but it sounded fake.

Sara sat up. "Tell me about everyone. How are Mama and Max? Is it working out?"

"Boy, is it ever," Finn said. "They're getting married and Oma's going to move to Max's house and then Uncle Timm and Angel are moving into Oma's house."

Sara clapped her hands. "I love it. I'm so happy for Mama." She should have been there to hear Mama's news in person. She stared at the house. Soon she would be ready to step out into the world again.

"What about Karl? Is he growing? Is he cute?"

"Yeah, I guess. He's a baby."

"How is Melody? How are her injuries? Is she healing?"

Finn turned glum. "I don't know," he mumbled.

Sara looked at Rem with a question in her eyes. He told her what had happened at the hospital with the man who the police had determined was Melody's real father. Liz's husband.

"We haven't seen her since," Finn said. "She hasn't called or anything." He sat with his arms resting on his updrawn knees and stared into the distance. Was Melody his first love?

He turned to his mom. "When are you gonna come home with us?"

"Not today, Finn."

"Then when are we ever gonna be a family? I miss you, Mom."

Those words were magic to her.

"There isn't a single day that passes that I don't think of you and miss you, too, but I'm not ready yet."

Finn ran to the Jeep.

Sara twined her arm through Rem's and walked him to the driver's door. As he got inside, she stared at her house pensively.

On impulse, she said, "Rem?"

"Yeah, honey?"

"Invite me to supper at the ranch next Sunday."

"Sara, will you join us next Sunday for supper?"

"Yes. I'll see you at four." She ran around the Jeep and reached in through the open passenger window. "Finn, I'll see you at the ranch next Sunday. Okay?"

"Okay, Mom. Love you."

"Love you, too."

She waved them off and watched the road long after the Jeep had disappeared.

THAT WEEK, SHE PUSHED herself on the bathroom.

She bought a new toilet and sink and paid a plumber to teach her how to hook them up. When she was finished, he checked her work and gave his stamp of approval.

Planning to leave that lovely claw-foot tub as is, she painted the cabinet and added a new mirror.

On Friday, she drove into Haven to buy new clothes. She'd prettified the house and now spent the day prettifying herself, including getting a new haircut and a mani-pedi.

On Sunday afternoon, she roamed the rooms of the house, cataloging her changes. She loved this cozy little space. It suited her to a T. She'd given herself a wonderful gift, one that she now understood she deserved.

What didn't suit her was living alone. She'd dreamed of her own place for so long. She had achieved the independence she'd craved, that had been her goal since the moment her son had been born. But...

She needed people now, and she needed to love.

She picked up the bag she'd packed and carried it out to the car.

Turning around, she studied this little gem of a house.

She stepped up onto the veranda, locked the door and tried not to be sad, to accept that she was making the right choice for all the right reasons.

She drove down the long laneway and pulled over before turning onto the highway. She parked and took the sign she'd made up earlier out of her trunk along with a rubber mallet.

At the corner of her fence, she removed the sign that read Private Property/No Trespassing. In its place, she hammered in the for-sale sign, pounding the stake with a sense of satisfaction.

Yes, this was the right choice. She had no more points left to prove, to herself or to anyone else.

Someone else could enjoy the retreat she'd made. She was on her way to join her family.

REM WATCHED FOR SARA.

As Sunday afternoon wore on, tension built in his shoulders.

Finally, after four, when he still hadn't heard her car pull into the yard, he could stand his own company no longer and left the house.

Ma, Adelle, Max and Finn were probably happy about that. Ecstatic. Rem wanted his woman here with him and would be miserable until he had her in his arms.

The scent of the stew he'd put in the slow cooker this morning followed him out the door.

Where was she?

Once on the veranda, he spotted Sara's car parked at the end of his driveway. Why wasn't she coming in? Did she have cold feet?

Lord, he hoped not. He was ready to explode with anticipation. He wanted her living with him on his ranch, but if she had to live in her own house, he'd get used to it, as long as she was committed to him and to expanding their family. Yeah, he wanted more children and suspected she did, too.

He wanted to marry her. If she needed it to be some kind of new type of marriage, one in which they lived in separate residences, okay, fine. As long as they loved each other.

He'd do whatever it took. He'd move into that dollhouse with her and commute to the ranch every day. The thought of making love to her every night in that brass bed appealed. If she asked, he'd give up the ranch entirely, would devote himself to his veterinary practice. They'd bring Ma over, too, if they had to. One way or another, they'd work it out.

He ached.

From this distance, he couldn't tell whether Sara was sitting in the driver's seat.

He ran back into the house for his binoculars. The car was empty. He scanned the road. No Sara. Where was she?

He caught a glimpse of yellow in the oak tree, in the leaf-covered branches on the side that hadn't been burned by Liz's car fire.

That flash of yellow was Sara, sitting on the lowest branch on the field side, away from the road.

Rem grinned, left the binoculars on a chair and jumped off the veranda, his eyes never leaving that yellow.

He walked down his driveway and realized, as he got closer, that she could see him through the leaves.

Something seemed different about her, but the breeze kicked up and leaves obscured her for a minute. When they fell back into place, he realized what had changed. She'd cut her hair.

A cute cap of brown, feathered and layered, framed her face and brought out her eyes. She'd added some kind of blond highlights, too.

He stood under the tree and looked up.

"Hi," he said, because he was tongue-tied and didn't know what to ask first. Are you here to stay? Will you marry me? How are we going to work out our life together, in some kind of New Age pattern? *Are* we going to work out a life together? Please?

He decided to go with what was uppermost in his mind. "I love you."

She looked down on him and smiled.

She wore a mauve top with tiny mauve ribbons for straps. She had pretty shoulders. She'd gained some of her weight back, too. A warm breeze blew her soft, flowing yellow skirt around her knees. Strappy, sexy little sandals showcased her legs. The thin straps curled around her slim ankles. She sat with her back against the trunk, and the sandal on her lower foot had come undone and hung below her heel. Only the barest uplifting of her toes kept that sandal on her foot.

He reached up and ran his finger along her arch and she shivered. She was a sensuous creature and didn't even know it. He had discovered it that night under the cottonwood tree by the creek.

Grasping the ends of the strap, he wrapped them around her ankle and tied it for her. Slowly, he feathered his fingers along her foot.

"Come on down, honey." He ran both hands up her calves as far as he could reach. "There are things I want to do with you."

Her smile radiated peace and warmth.

"Do you need help getting down?"

"No. I'm good."

She turned and placed her hands on the strong branch of the tree and lifted herself off. She fell down, but hung on. Her camisole hiked up and bared a patch of skin above her waist.

Oh, the things he wanted to do.

She let go to drop to the ground and he caught her. Her top hiked up higher as he snagged her around the waist.

With his hands on her soft skin, he spun her around in his arms so she faced him.

Her eyes were once again the eyes of the happy young girl he used to know. Gone were the anger, the fear and the soul-destroying baggage she'd carried.

"Hey, you," he whispered. I see *you.* I see young, beautiful, carefree Sara Franck. *Welcome back.*

"Hey, you," she whispered in return, and he realized that she saw the same peace reflected in him.

"We walked through fire and survived, Rem."

"We did, didn't we?"

"We deserve each other."

Finally. "The time is right, isn't it?"

"It's perfect," she said.

He swung her into his arms and twirled her around, then carried her to the car and set her down on the hood, where he stood between her legs.

"I know how to charm women and how to seduce them, but I don't know how to be romantic. So I'm just going to blurt this out. Marry me."

"Yes. Kiss me, Rem."

He did.

IT WAS ALL FINALLY HAPPENING.

This man who thought he wasn't romantic was so wrong.

He was the most romantic man Sara had ever met. He'd helped her to reclaim the part of herself she'd thought was dead. He'd bought her a brass bed with ruffled shams and had seduced her by candlelight, for goodness sake.

She ended the kiss before they both became too heated.

Rem rested his forehead on hers and said, "It's finally going to happen, isn't it?"

"Yes," she whispered. "Let's go tell the family."

She hopped down from the car and they walked up the driveway hand-in-hand.

"Rem?"

"Yes, Sara?"

"I'm putting the house on the market."

He stopped and took both of her hands in his.

"I'm going to come here to live with you, Nell and Finn. Can I ask for one change to the ranch, though?"

"Of course. Anything. What?"

"Can we get rid of your old bed and move my new brass bed into your room?"

"You mean into *our* room? You bet." He grinned and they continued toward the house.

Finn appeared on the veranda.

"Mom," he yelled, and came running. He wrapped her in a hug.

"You're taller than me!" she yelped. "How did that happen in only two months? How did that happen since last weekend?"

He grinned. "Grandma and me are writing a comic together. She's providing the story. I'm doing the illustrations."

"It's a family affair," Sara said with a smile. Finn deserved a family after so long without.

Families came in so many shapes and sizes, and exhibited a million different manifestations of love.

Finn ran back inside and yelled, "Mom's home."

A moment later, Nell came out leaning on a cane on one side and on Mama's arm on the other. Max stood in the doorway beside Finn to watch the reunion.

"Nell, look at you," Sara breathed.

Nell smiled with both sides of her mouth and Sara's vision misted. She climbed the steps and took her into her arms.

With her right hand, Nell patted Sara's back.

"Nell, you've done so well."

"Yes, I worked hard."

Adelle reached for Sara next and pulled her close. "You look so good," she said. "I'm so happy."

Sara left her mother's hug and reached for Rem's hand. "Finn, Mama, Nell, Max," she said, "we're getting married."

Amid the screaming, Rem's cell phone rang. He answered it, with his finger closing off his other ear so he could hear.

"Yeah," Sara heard him say. "She's here and she said yes."

Sara heard hooting on the other end of the line. Rem was getting it in stereo. He hung up.

"Timm, Angel and Karl will be here in half an hour." He threaded his arm through Sara's and guided her inside behind Nell and Adelle. "What do you think of Sara's hair?"

"Love it," Nell said.

"Beautiful," Adelle added.

"She looks younger," Finn called from the living room.

Sara followed Nell and Mama into the room.

"Where are your car keys?" Rem stood beside her with his hand out. "I'll bring it into the yard."

She gave him the keys and he said, "Finn, let's go drive your mom's car up to the house. She left it at the road."

Five minutes later, Sara wandered out to the veranda.

The car moved down the lane but by fits and starts, first too fast and then too slow.

What was wrong with Rem?

When the car got close enough, Sara realized the problem. Finn was in the driver's seat and Rem was giving him instructions from the passenger seat.

Sara dropped into a chair behind her and pressed her hand against her heart.

What on *earth* had she got herself into?

Finn got out of the car and punched the air. "Yeah!"

Rem hauled her bag out of the backseat, grinned and called, "Honey, we're home."

CHAPTER NINETEEN

ON A BALMY NIGHT in September, a week after Rem and Sara's wedding, Rem stood in the moonlight, tossing stones into the creek. There'd been no sense in waiting. Neither had wanted a big affair. Reverend Wright had married them at the ranch, and family and friends had partied long into the night. Rem was happy and at peace. At last.

He and Sara had come out to the dollhouse on a date. Twenty minutes ago they'd finished eating and Sara had offered to do the dishes since he'd cooked.

The house hadn't sold yet so they came here often for privacy.

He heard rustling behind him and Sara walked down the lawn wrapped in a quilt with a bottle of champagne in one hand and a pair of flutes in the other.

"Can you open this and pour?"

"Sure." He unwrapped the cork and twisted off the wire.

"Can you take the glasses from me?" Sara handed him the flutes.

"Drop the quilt, honey, and you can hold them while I pour."

"Okay," she said, smiled and let the quilt fall to the ground. Rem nearly swallowed his tongue. She didn't have on a stitch of clothing. Her curves had come back and she was the most perfect creature on this earth.

Rem poured champagne into the flutes, tucked the bottle into the cool water of the creek and wrapped one arm around his wife's waist, bringing her flush against him so he could kiss her silly.

When he finished, pulling away slowly, they toasted.

"To our future." Rem clinked his glass against Sara's.

"To our family," Sara said and took a sip.

Rem handed her his flute and spread the quilt on the grass. She sat and waited patiently for him to join her.

He undressed then, stretching out under the stars beside her. She put the glasses aside and lay willingly in his arms. They stared at the stars together.

In time, under the twinkling stars and the magical winking on and off of fireflies, they made love.

They also made a baby sister for Finn.

* * * * *

HEART & HOME

Heartwarming romances where love can
happen right when you least expect it.

REQUEST YOUR FREE BOOKS!
2 FREE NOVELS PLUS 2 FREE GIFTS!

Harlequin®

Super Romance®

Exciting, emotional, unexpected!

YES! Please send me 2 FREE Harlequin® Superromance® novels and my 2 FREE gifts (gifts are worth about $10). After receiving them, if I don't wish to receive any more books, I can return the shipping statement marked "cancel." If I don't cancel, I will receive 6 brand-new novels every month and be billed just $4.69 per book in the U.S. or $5.24 per book in Canada. That's a saving of at least 15% off the cover price! It's quite a bargain! Shipping and handling is just 50¢ per book in the U.S. and 75¢ per book in Canada.* I understand that accepting the 2 free books and gifts places me under no obligation to buy anything. I can always return a shipment and cancel at any time. Even if I never buy another book, the two free books and gifts are mine to keep forever.

135/336 HDN FC6T

Name _____

(PLEASE PRINT)

Address _____ Apt. #

City _____ State/Prov. _____ Zip/Postal Code

Signature (if under 18, a parent or guardian must sign)

Mail to the Reader Service:
IN U.S.A.: P.O. Box 1867, Buffalo, NY 14240-1867
IN CANADA: P.O. Box 609, Fort Erie, Ontario L2A 5X3

Not valid for current subscribers to Harlequin Superromance books.
**Are you a current subscriber to Harlequin Superromance books
and want to receive the larger-print edition?
Call 1-800-873-8635 or visit www.ReaderService.com.**

* Terms and prices subject to change without notice. Prices do not include applicable taxes. Sales tax applicable in N.Y. Canadian residents will be charged applicable taxes. Offer not valid in Quebec. This offer is limited to one order per household. All orders subject to credit approval. Credit or debit balances in a customer's account(s) may be offset by any other outstanding balance owed by or to the customer. Please allow 4 to 6 weeks for delivery. Offer available while quantities last.

Your Privacy—The Reader Service is committed to protecting your privacy. Our Privacy Policy is available online at www.ReaderService.com or upon request from the Reader Service.

We make a portion of our mailing list available to reputable third parties that offer products we believe may interest you. If you prefer that we not exchange your name with third parties, or if you wish to clarify or modify your communication preferences, please visit us at www.ReaderService.com/consumerchoice or write to us at Reader Service Preference Service, P.O. Box 9062, Buffalo, NY 14269. Include your complete name and address.

Lucy Flemming and Ross Mitchell shared a magical,
sexy Christmas weekend together six years ago.
This Christmas, history may repeat itself when they find
themselves stranded in a major snowstorm…
and alone at last.

Read on for a sneak peek from
IT HAPPENED ONE CHRISTMAS
by Leslie Kelly.

Available December 2011, only from Harlequin® Blaze™.

EYEING THE GRAY, THICK SKY through the expansive wall of windows, Lucy began to pack up her photography gear. The Christmas party was winding down, only a dozen or so people remaining on this floor, which had been transformed from cubicles and meeting rooms to a holiday funland. She smiled at those nearest to her, then, seeing the glances at her silly elf hat, she reached up to tug it off her head.

Before she could do it, however, she heard a voice. A deep, male voice—smooth and sexy, and so not Santa's.

"I appreciate you filling in on such short notice. I've heard you do a terrific job."

Lucy didn't turn around, letting her brain process what she was hearing. Her whole body had stiffened, the hairs on the back of her neck standing up, her skin tightening into tiny goose bumps. Because that voice sounded so familiar. *Impossibly* familiar.

It can't be.

"It sounds like the kids had a great time."

Unable to stop herself, Lucy began to turn around, wondering if her ears—and all her other senses—were deceiving her. After all, six years was a long time, the mind could play tricks. What were the odds that she'd bump into *him,* here? And today of all days. December 23.

Six years exactly. Was that really possible?

One look—and the accompanying frantic thudding of her heart—and she knew her ears and brain were working just fine. Because it was *him.*

"Oh, my God," he whispered, shocked, frozen, staring as thoroughly as she was. "Lucy?"

She nodded slowly, not taking her eyes off him, wondering why the years had made him even more attractive than ever. It didn't seem fair. Not when she'd spent the past six years thinking he must have started losing that thick, golden-brown hair, or added a spare tire to that trim, muscular form.

No.

The man was gorgeous. Truly, without-a-doubt, mouthwateringly handsome, every bit as hot as he'd been the first time she'd laid eyes on him. She'd been twenty-two, he one year older.

They'd shared an amazing holiday season.

And had never seen one another again.

Until now.

Find out what happens in
IT HAPPENED ONE CHRISTMAS
by Leslie Kelly.
Available December 2011, only from Harlequin® Blaze™

American ★ Romance

LAURA MARIE ALTOM
brings you
another touching tale from

When family tragedy forces Wyatt Buckhorn to pair up
with his longtime secret crush, Natalie Poole, and care
for the Buckhorn clan's seven children, Wyatt worries
he's in over his head. Fearing his shameful secret will
be exposed, Wyatt tries to fight his growing attraction
to Natalie. As Natalie begins to open up to Wyatt,
he starts yearning for a family of his own—a family
with Natalie. But can Wyatt trust his heart enough
to reveal his secret?

A Baby in His Stocking

Available December
wherever books are sold!